WHERE THE WATER FLOWS

Romola Farr

For Rowena & Chris who met on January 6, 1967
...and fell in love.

CHAPTER ONE
Saturday, 4th September

Cadence Clearwater garnered attention wherever she went. If people knew the truth, they would shudder and recoil from her *svelte beauty*, a compliment she refused to accept no matter how often her Aunt Angela would repeat it.

Through the carriage window the verdant, rugged countryside gave her pleasure and she looked forward to stretching her long legs after church on Sundays. Getting away, or *running away* as categorised by her aunt, had flicked a psychological switch and it was a feeling she liked. The train's WiFi wasn't great, but she had WhatsApp and Snapchat and was grateful for the almost constant contact with her best friend, Diana, back home in Southern California.

Damn. The boy across the aisle had caught her eye. She looked down at her phone's screen. Her thumbs hovered. Waited. She cast a quick look back. He caught her eye again, this time with a smile. Determined to break the connection, she stared out of the window and focused on a high, jagged ridge that cut through many shades of rolling green and gold.

It didn't work. She could feel the heat from his eyes like a hair-curling wand burning her neck. There was only one solution. She grabbed her shoulder bag and hurried down the aisle, knowing he was staring at her retreating back.

Joel Redmond removed his Bluetooth earbuds and returned them to their box. He glanced at the Longines watch he'd inherited from his late father and wondered whether his acting career would have such an illustrious start. Unlike many young actors whose parents disapproved of their child's risky career choice, his mother gave him all her support. She was sort of in showbusiness herself in that she represented writers who wrote for film and TV. She understood why he had such a drive that wouldn't be deflected by rational concerns such as high competition and low income. But, deep down, he knew she gave him her support because she nearly lost him to leukaemia.

A voice over the train's tannoy snatched Joel back from his reverie. 'We will shortly be arriving in Hawksmead. Please take all your possessions with you, including anything you may have placed in the rack above your head, especially if it's an umbrella – we have way too many in lost property – and where you're going it rains cats and dogs, and sheep and goats – and that's on the fair-weather days.'

'You are sure it's Hawksmead and not Undermere?' the elderly man enquired from the front passenger seat.

Audrey Cadwallader glanced at her husband as she negotiated the humpback bridge over the River Hawk. 'Eleanor clearly said Hawksmead.' She looked at the dashboard clock before swerving through the S-bend at the top of the High Street. 'The camera didn't flash, did it?' she asked, anxiety in her voice.

'I think it's been vandalised.'

'Good.'

'Good?'

She slowed as they drove past the Olde Tea Shoppe. 'I hope Eleanor's all right. She seemed very low when we spoke. Really sick.'

Malcolm looked at his wife. They'd only known each other for six years but he could not imagine life without her. It was such a relief they'd both come through the pandemic without a sniffle. Lucky as they were, their hearts went out to all the people who had suffered and were still suffering both in their health and financially. And now their friend Eleanor was ill with some new, hideous variant.

The long train eased to a perfect stop. As soon as the door light came on, Joel pressed the open button, removed his mask and took his first breath of dank moorland air. He lifted his rucksack and grabbed his suitcase on wheels. This was it. This was the start of his dream. The beginning of...

'Are you getting off?'

It was a young woman's American voice, slightly muffled. He turned and looked at the girl who'd been sitting across the aisle. The lower part of her face was obscured by a black face mask emblazoned in white with the words, *Back off*.

'Yes, sorry.' He stepped down from the train and carried his heavy suitcase away from the doorway before extending its handle. The statuesque beauty hauled the first of two matching aluminium suitcases onto the platform. The imagery emblazoned on the side was that of a lioness... teeth bared, and claws extended as she pounced on a white hunter with a rifle.

'Can I help you with your other case?' Joel asked.

'I got it, thanks.'

'You're American?'

'And you're English.' She placed the second case on the platform and extended the handle. At the far end, a uniformed guard put a whistle to his lips and blew a shrill blast. Warning beeps were followed by the sound of compressed air as the door slid back into place. There was another shrill blast and the long train eased out of the station.

Joel walked behind the young woman who was wearing a powder pink sweater, pale blue denim jacket, white jeans, and black converse trainers. Slung over her shoulder was a brown leather bag, with a bright chrome buckle and chrome studs spelling the words, *Suffragette Sister.*

Joel took the bag to be an invitation. 'I like your purse.'

She ignored his comment.

He persevered. 'Isn't that what you call handbags in the States?' Even though he hadn't seen her face unmasked he could tell by the way her hair bounced on her shoulders, the way she swung her legs from her hips, her perfect posture, and by the few words she'd spoken, that she was a knock-out ...and he was captivated. For the first time in quite a while, his nineteen-year-old mind was focused on something other than his beloved theatre.

'Joel Redmond?' spoke a refined voice.

He turned and looked at a tall, slim man with a good head of greying hair, slightly stooped, clean shaven, wearing a tweed jacket, blue shirt, brown corduroy trousers with belt, and brown brogue shoes. Except, all Joel saw was an old man standing beside a woman, who looked slightly less old. 'Yes?'

'Joel Redmond?' the woman asked, her voice equally refined.

He was acutely aware that the gorgeous American was getting away and snuck a glance at her retreating back before forcing himself to answer the lady's question. 'Yes. Do I know you?' He saw them both smile.

4

'My name is Audrey Cadwallader, and this is my husband, Malcolm. We're friends of Eleanor Houghton, your godmother. Unfortunately, she's tested positive for the new variant going around.'

'So,' the old man said. 'If it's all right with you, we'd like to welcome you to our home.'

'Until Eleanor is out of the woods,' Audrey added.

Joel was stumped. 'That's really kind.' *Was he being kidnapped? Was he being lured into some sort of trap? Or had he been watching too many TV dramas?* 'Do you mind if I give Aunt Ellie a call? Just to double-check.' He pulled his phone out of his jeans pocket and saw two missed calls, and several unopened messages. That was the price he paid for his mother booking him a seat in a *quiet carriage*. Why hadn't he put his phone on vibrate?

'Take your time,' the man said. 'Our cottage lies between here and Undermere. There's a bus that runs every hour to your drama school, or we can drop you off.'

'You must be very excited about going to USDA, so prestigious,' Audrey added, with a big congratulatory smile.

Joel put his phone back in his pocket. 'I'll give Aunt Ellie a call a bit later.'

'The car's just out front,' Malcolm said. 'I hope you're hungry. We have homemade scones and damson jam, and shop bought clotted cream. Or, if you prefer, crumpets, and a freshly baked Victoria sponge.'

The elderly couple guided Joel through the ticket hall and out into a small car park. Audrey pressed a key fob and the indicator lights blinked on a silver Honda Jazz. *An old man's car.*

'You sit up front with Audrey,' Malcolm said, 'and I'll

put your bag and rucksack in the boot.'

'It's really heavy,' Joel responded. 'I'd better do it.'

'How dare you?' Malcolm said, his voice laced with fake indignation. 'I've never been so insulted in my life!'

'Oh, really, really sorry. I didn't mean...'

Audrey laughed. 'He's joking.'

Joel looked at her. 'Are you sure?'

'Come and sit in the front beside me,' she said. 'The old man can go in the back.'

'Will he fit?'

Audrey giggled. 'He can still bend at the knees.'

Joel put on a mask, covering his nose and mouth, and got into the Honda; Audrey sat beside him, without putting on a mask. He heard the boot lid slam shut and Malcolm folded himself in behind Audrey where there was more leg room. She started the engine and pushed the gear shift into Drive. They pulled out of the station forecourt and headed up Hawksmead High Street.

Cadence Clearwater was hot. Dragging her two heavy suitcases, even though they had wheels, was hard work and she felt in desperate need of a shower. She had travelled from Orange County, California, and was more tired, more jet-lagged than she thought possible. Despite her face mask with the words *Back off*, she had received unwanted attention from two men in the departure lounge, and an elegant woman seated next to her on the plane.

'First flight to England?'

Cadence was immediately attracted by her British accent and clear diction. 'Yes. First flight, ever.'

'Oh, my darling. A virgin.'

For a moment Cadence thought her fellow

passenger was talking about something else entirely, and she would've been right.

'Pace yourself, don't rush to grab free drinks, or food, or search for a movie,' continued her new friend. 'Take off your mask and relax. Use the time to take the pace out of life. Contemplate. Meditate. I tell that to all my actors.'

'Actors?' One simple word and Cadence was fully focused. She took off her mask.

'I'm an agent,' her neighbour said. 'Zoom meetings are all well and good but, every now and then, I have to fly out to Hollywood to show, cold, hard steel when negotiating for a client; or to cuddle.'

'Cuddle?'

'*Hashtag MeToo* only impacts men on women or men on men. We women have a free pass to do what it takes to get what we want.'

Cadence felt the woman's fingertips rest on the back of her hand, and it was a gesture she knew all too well. Women, seemingly happily married women, would reach out to Cadence even when she was a young teen working part-time in her mother's beauty salon. They would tell her their most intimate desires backed by subtle touches on her hand, or arm, or face.

'I hope to get an agent when I finish my course.'

The woman snapped her fingers. 'I knew it! You are simply too gorgeous to be anything but on the big screen.' She picked up her bag from the floor and opened the flap. From an inner pocket she removed an embossed card. 'Here's my private number. Call me when you're settled in London.'

'I'm not staying in London. I'm studying at USDA, Undermere School of Dramatic Art.'

'I know what USDA is my sweet.' She sat back in her

seat, disappointment clearly evident.

'You don't rate USDA?' Cadence asked a little tentatively.

'It's the best place to study theatre and film in the country. It's just not London.'

The plane rolled over the bumpy taxiway as it headed towards the end of the runway.

Cadence was puzzled by the agent's response. 'Is it really important to study drama in London?'

'It's much more convenient for busy agents to see showcases, but USDA is renowned for churning out graduates who go on to become names. It's certainly the hardest drama school to get into, so well done my girl.'

'My dream is to work for the Royal Shakespeare Company, or on the West End stage, or Broadway. I don't want to work in Hollywood. It seems so toxic.'

'Not if you're represented by an agent of my calibre.'

This time the agent's hand rested on her denim covered thigh. She sighed, inwardly. It was going to be a long flight. Not that her travelling companion was unappealing – far from it – but Cadence felt ill-equipped to handle the situation. She was thrilled to have the opportunity to make such an important contact, but what was expected of her in return? Good acting or something else? She looked at the embossed card. If the agent knew the truth, she wouldn't want to go near her.

'Coming up on the right,' the old man said from the rear seat of the Honda, 'is The Falcon. An excellent alehouse.'

Joel didn't bother to look.

'And there's the girl from the station,' Malcolm added, 'sans masque.'

Joel snapped his head, in time to see the full face of his long-legged dream as she hauled her two large cases through the pub's swing doors.

'Very pretty,' Malcolm concluded.

'She's American,' Joel said.

'You know her?' Audrey sounded surprised.

'We exchanged a few words as we got off the train.'

'If you like,' Malcolm said. 'I'll make a few enquiries and find out her name.'

'Malcolm!' Audrey admonished from behind the wheel. 'I don't think that's a good idea.'

Joel slackened his seatbelt and turned to Malcolm. 'If you could find out her name and number, and anything else you can, that would be great.'

'Sounds like stalking to me,' Audrey muttered.

'And almost next door,' Malcolm added, 'is where you'll be staying once Eleanor is well again.'

'It's a tea shop,' Joel responded.

'Yes,' Malcolm said, 'with scones and cakes to challenge mine.'

Audrey turned to Joel. 'The old man loves to bake.'

'And on your left, dear boy,' Malcolm said, 'is my favourite place in all the world.'

Joel read a hanging sign. 'Merlin's Hardware Store. A wizard way to work.'

'He likes to restore antique furniture,' Audrey said as she stifled a yawn.

Joel looked back at Malcolm. 'Was Merlin a wizard like Harry Potter?'

Malcolm laughed. 'He was a wizard in King Arthur's Court, long before young Potter was a twinkle in Miss Rowling's eye.'

'Welcome, my dear.'

In the gloom of the pub, Cadence saw a great bear of

a man with a chest the size of a barrel. 'Hi.' She pulled her bags through the double doors and wondered whether she would be able to fight him off should he decide to come on to her. What was she thinking? Paranoia had really set in thanks to the long plane flight, trapped by a woman who'd got more and more frisky.

'I presume you are Cadence Clearwater Revival.' He laughed at his own wit.

'I'm sorry, I don't understand. Revival?'

'It's his silly joke.'

Cadence was relieved to see a little blonde woman coming out from behind the bar counter.

'I'm Heather,' she said, 'and this is Ted.'

'Hi. Cadence Clearwater.'

'Let me explain,' Ted said. 'When I was about your age...'

Were you ever my age? thought Cadence.

Ted continued, '...there was this famous rock band called Creedence Clearwater Revival. They were rather good.'

'Thank you, I'll check them out.'

'Save your energy,' Heather said as she approached her. 'They were around even before my time.'

'Right,' Ted said. 'Heather will show you to your room and I'll bring your bags.'

'Do you have WiFi?' Cadence asked.

'Top of the range,' Ted replied. 'Password is Cyrano de Bergerac... all for one, and one for all.' He laughed again.

'That was the Three Musketeers not Cyrano de Bergerac,' Heather said, her expression, long-suffering. 'Ted was once an actor,' she explained, almost confidentially. 'He still thinks he is.'

Cadence smiled. 'In a way, we're all actors.' She looked at Ted. 'I can see this is your theatre. The bar your stage.'

'Please,' Heather said. 'Don't encourage him.'

Cadence smiled. 'Ted, I have an admission.'

'An admission?' he asked.

'All my life,' she said, 'people have joked about my name and that damned rock band. It's a bit of a sore point. After fifty years, you'd think they'd be forgotten.'

'Who could forget *Have you ever seen the rain*?' Ted said.

'Certainly not this autumn,' Heather chipped in. 'Right. Let's get you settled in. I'm sure you want to let your parents know you've arrived, safely.'

'Thank you.'

'Leave your cases here. Ted'll bring them up.'

Carrying her shoulder bag, Cadence followed the little blonde lady through the large bar area, with its dark wood panelling. Fixed to one wall were faded black and white framed photos from a bygone era. She paused a moment to look at happy families having picnics in front of an imposing building; summer fêtes on a green with a large church behind; photos of school plays, one of which she recognised by the nose, was taken from a production of Cyrano de Bergerac.

'Did your husband play Cyrano?' Cadence asked Heather.

'In his dreams. He was Christian. Handsome but dense.' Heather pushed open a door and held it for Cadence.

'The girl who played Roxane was very beautiful,' Cadence said.

'Shall we go up?' Heather prompted.

Cadence smiled. 'Yes, of course.' She followed Heather up dark, worn, wooden stairs which led through a heavy fire door to a landing area.

'This is our room,' Heather gestured to a closed door, 'in case you need anything in an emergency. Your room is just down here. You'll notice we have two smoke alarms, which are tested, regularly.' She pushed open a panelled door on the far side of the landing and Cadence followed Heather into a spacious room, which looked recently remodelled, and was in stark contrast to the worn, beer-soaked bar below. There was a double bed with an oak bedhead. A small desk and chair. A large, freestanding wardrobe in dark burnished wood. A wall-mounted TV, an armchair, and a suitcase stand for unpacking. Across the room were two pairs of sash windows, draped with full-height lined curtains, which matched the green leaves and native birds printed on the wallpaper. Varnished wooden floorboards were partly obscured by a large rug, woven with yarn in symmetrical patterns, now wearing thin, its once rich colours, faded.

'This is real nice,' Cadence said as she placed her shoulder bag on the rug. 'Better than the photos on Airbnb.'

'Ted was in charge of the renovation, and he never serves up half measures.'

'He has good taste.'

'He does, under my guidance of course, but I'll pass on your observation.'

Cadence smiled and nodded.

Heather gestured to the television. 'TV is on the BT network and includes Freeview and Netflix. There's a WiFi router to ensure a good connection. Tea and coffee facilities, and...' she walked over to a doorway.

'And here is your en-suite loo, shower and bath.'

Cadence peered through the open door. 'I was warned to expect bathroom facilities to be real old fashioned, but everything looks new.'

'You're our first guest.'

'I'm honoured.'

'Downstairs, there's a utility room with washing machine and dryer, and you can use our personal kitchen whenever it suits. Best to steer clear of the pub kitchen as it can get a bit hectic.'

The door burst open, and the big, florid barman dragged in her two heavy suitcases.

'Heather, my dear,' Ted panted. 'I think we should consider installing a dumb waiter to haul up the luggage.'

'I'll resist making a joke!' Heather laughed.

'Could you recommend a local church?' Cadence asked.

Both Heather and Ted looked momentarily flummoxed.

Heather was the first to speak. 'Before we opened on Sundays, I used to go to the Methodist Church at the north end of the High Street. I can't say I enjoyed it, especially in winter. The floor has vents allegedly for heating, but fingers of icy air would shoot up my legs.'

Ted interjected. 'You could always try St. Michael's across the street. At communion, the blood of Christ is usually a very fine Rioja.'

Cadence smiled. 'British humour, I love it, it's so infectious.'

'Don't worry,' Heather said. 'I'm sure they'll find a vaccine for it soon!'

'Well,' Ted said. 'We'll leave you to get settled in.'

Cadence waited for the door to close before peeling

off her clothes and heading for the bathroom. The tiled floor was a bit chill underfoot, but the chrome showerhead looked promising. She turned a big brass tap and tested the water. It was cold and little better than a dribble. But, she was desperate to wash so braved it. Suddenly, it was too hot. She danced clear and twisted the tap as she tried to balance hot water with cold.

Disappointed, she dried off using a towel supplied by the Airbnb and retrieved a large comb from her toilet bag. A small sign stuck to the wall below a ceiling-mounted switch with a red LED light and pull cord attracted her attention. *Shower pump. Pull on before showering. Pull off after showering.*

'Now you tell me.' She smiled, sure that this was the start of many quaint differences she would delight in discovering between England and the United States.

Joel looked at the pretty front garden as he followed Audrey up to the middle of three cottages that looked straight out of Midsomer Murders, the TV detective series his mum used to watch. On his left were well-tended beds with rose bushes in various stages of bloom, graced by hollyhocks, wisteria, delphiniums, petunias... not that Joel could name any of them apart from the roses, which he did recognise.

Audrey used a single key attached to the car fob to turn all three locks. As soon as the door opened there was a strident beeping. She hurried through the narrow hallway and pulled open a door to an understairs cupboard. She pressed a button and Joel saw a keypad light up. The strident beeping seemed to get louder.

'Oh no,' Audrey said.

Malcolm appeared over Joel's shoulder. 'Press the

button with the green padlock, enter the code then press tick.'

'I've done that, but it won't turn off.'

'Are you sure you're entering the right code and not your bank pin?'

'Stupid!' Audrey shouted to herself, just before Joel was deafened by an alarm bell. Fortunately, it went off after about three seconds. Audrey closed the understairs cupboard door, red faced and with a sheen across her forehead. 'Sorry about that,' she said to Joel, then looked past him to Malcolm. 'Perhaps the alarm pin should be the same as my bank pin?'

'In other words, you're happy for our cleaner to know your bank pin?' Malcolm asked.

'Good point.' She smiled at Joel. 'Malcolm is the one who usually turns off the alarm. I'll have to do it more often.'

'By the way,' Malcolm said. 'What is your bank pin?'

'It's the month and year of our marriage.'

'How long have you been married?' Joel asked.

'If I tell you that,' Audrey said wagging her forefinger, 'you'll be halfway to working out my pin.'

'My mum used to take me to see Derren Brown. I tried to learn his techniques for reading people's minds.'

Malcolm closed the cottage door and placed Joel's rucksack on the floor. 'If you'd like to take that, young man, I'll carry your suitcase up to your room.'

'What about my shoes?' Joel asked. 'I always take them off at home.'

'We do, too,' Audrey said. 'You can add them to our row of footwear below the coat hooks.'

Joel removed his shoes and looked at Malcolm. 'No offence, but I think I should carry the suitcase upstairs.'

'If you insist, young man.' Malcolm grabbed the rucksack. 'Now if you'd care to follow me.' His voice sounded strange, wobbly. 'I'll take you to your tomb – I mean room!'

Joel looked at Audrey, perplexed.

'It's another of his silly jokes,' Audrey said. 'He's pretending to be the old servant in a Christopher Lee, Dracula film.'

'Christopher Lee?'

Malcolm turned on the stairs. 'Very tall.'

'Was he Saruman in Lord of the Rings?'

'Absolutely,' Malcolm said.

'That was before you were born,' Audrey added.

'I have all the films on Blu-ray.'

'Right,' Audrey said. 'Whilst Dracula shows you to your room, I'll make us a pot of tea. I'm sure you're gasping.'

'Thank you.' Joel lifted his heavy case, took a deep breath, and followed Malcolm up the steep stairs. When he got to the landing, he saw a spacious, old-fashioned bathroom on his right with a decent-sized bath, which he liked. On his left, Malcolm had entered a room with twin beds, a rounded bay with chintz curtains, and a dressing table and stool. But the focus of Joel's attention was an old-style desk with little drawers, decorative filigree, and a pull-out tabletop with leather inlay. 'Wow, that looks antique,' he said.

Malcolm placed his rucksack on the carpet. 'It's called an escritoire. French. Circa 1870. Oak.'

'It must be worth a fortune.'

'Fifteen hundred... although I'll take a thousand. Where would you like it delivered?'

Joel looked at Malcolm and realised the old man was

joking. 'You're funny.'

'I try to be, although Audrey informs me it can be very annoying.'

'Thank you for inviting me to stay. I'll call my mum and she'll do a bank transfer. Or do you prefer PayPal?'

'Young man. Do call your mother, but under no circumstances is she to pay a bean. Audrey and I are perfectly comfortable. It is a pleasure to have you as our guest.' Malcolm fished in the back pocket of his trousers and pulled out a slim, shiny, leather wallet and removed a cream visitor's card. 'Mobile and landline numbers, and our full postal address for you to give to your mother. Come down for cake when you're ready.'

'You're very kind.' Joel took the card and watched Malcolm leave and shut the door behind him. He sat on the bed nearest the window and looked at the card: *Malcolm & Audrey Cadwallader, Mint Cottage, Bradbourne Vale, Undermere*. With his thumb he scrolled down his phone's contacts.

'Hello sweetheart,' said a familiar voice.

Six short weeks later, as Cadence walked up to the Methodist Church at the top end of the little town, she counted Joel as one of her best new friends. Of course, he wanted more than friendship, they always did, but friendship was all she could offer.

The red-brick, nineteenth century church was busy on that autumnal morning. Heavy rain carried on a warm breeze over the last week had encouraged the grass to grow in the church's graveyard, separated from Hawksmead's Memorial Garden by a high wall. She knew the garden well thanks to one glorious afternoon she'd spent with her new friends. The centrepiece was a rough-hewn memorial stone carved with the names of five schoolboys. Two, she'd been told, had drowned in the River Hawk. The riptides in the Pacific Ocean had taught Cadence to be a strong swimmer, at least she was until the incident. She'd not swum since.

'Good morning, Cadence.' She had first met The Reverend Longden within a week of her arrival in the little mill town and although they were separated by more than seventy years, she'd liked him on sight. He was remarkably tall for a man of his great age, albeit a little stooped. He had a great dome of a bald head above a hooked-nose, and strangely curled ring and pinkie fingers on each hand. 'It's called Dupuytren's contracture,' the Reverend explained. 'I can grip the Lord's Book, but I wouldn't recommend standing close to me when I'm chopping firewood!'

She smiled at the memory as she made her way into the cavernous building with its vaulted ceiling, tall windows with clear leaded lights, and whitewashed walls leading up to an overspill gallery. It was furnished with carved oak pews, worn and burnished by countless posteriors, with a rear shelf for prayer and hymn books. Under her soles was an unyielding flagstone floor with metal grilles.

She sat near the entrance to the plain church and looked at the first hymn number displayed on a wooden board to one side of the high pulpit, and quietly sang the first verse, visualising the British spelling of *plow*. '*We plough the fields and scatter, the good seed on the land. But it is fed and watered by God's Almighty hand. He sends the snow in winter, the warmth to swell the grain, the breezes and the sunshine, and soft refreshing rain.*' Too much rain she thought. At least for the moment, and for the marriage of two people at the end of the Thanksgiving part of the service, it was mercifully dry.

She was surprised to see quite so many worshippers filling the Methodist Church, some escorting young children who carried a big apple or a giant potato in their little hands. They brought a smile to her face as Cadence reached for a woven kneepad hanging from a brass hook and knelt to pray, to give thanks for all the kindness shown to her since her arrival in Hawksmead. She asked the Good Lord to protect her Aunt Angela, back home in southern California, who had done so much to help her recover since the terrible day that cost the life of her mother. She whispered a prayer for her best friend Diana who had seen her through her darkest days. She also asked the Almighty to give her the strength to be a better, kinder, and more open person, although she knew in her heart that she could never be entirely open, entirely honest, entirely the person God and her late mother had meant her to be.

The River Hawk was in full flood, almost splashing the top of the stone arches below the ancient humpback bridge, the northern gateway to the former textile town. Downstream was an eighteenth-century cotton mill with a vast wooden waterwheel, now redundant. Upstream, the river snaked through boggy moorland, with its many contributory brooks and bourns feeding the swollen serpent.

A lightning strike at the end of summer had cleaved a mighty oak, which hung precariously above the fast-flowing river. Battered by days of wind and rain, the immense trunk finally cracked under its own weight, emitting a sound more commonly heard on a grouse moor. A section of the enormous tree crashed into the river causing a vast swell to wash over its banks. The severed trunk was pushed and cajoled downstream by the force of water, its branches scraping the riverbed until torn limb from limb.

A Ford Galaxy was almost halfway across the humpback bridge when the broken tree slammed into the supporting arches, cracking the thin strip of asphalt. A wall of water smashed into the side of the vehicle, propelling it over the stone parapet and into the churning river.

The tree trunk jammed fast against the ancient stone structure and swiftly created an almost solid dam. The rushing river sought release and breached its southern bank, carving a path through scrubland towards Hawksmead's Memorial Garden.

Cadence closed her hymn book as the organ music swelled then fell to an echoing silence. She smiled as the children were led out of the church by their parents.

There was a light rustling as the congregation looked at an order of service pamphlet printed on cream vellum. The rear doors to the vestibule opened to the delicate notes of Nocturne in E Flat Major by Frédéric François Chopin. A beautiful, melodic piece by the Polish composer that brought tears to many eyes as the bride and her Matron of Honour entered the church. At the front, stood the groom and his father, both using fingertips to wipe away their tears.

More branches, more organic flotsam added to the logjam, forcing the river to entirely alter its course. Rushing water felled shrubs and saplings as it poured into the walled Memorial Garden. Plants and bushes were ripped from the soil and wooden benches and picnic tables were tossed and spun in the growing mass of swirling water. The rapidly expanding lake was contained by the garden's horseshoe-shaped brick wall, built in the early years of Queen Victoria's reign.

Reverend Longden, tall, stooped, aged and so wise, hitched up his long black robe as he climbed the wooden steps to the carved pulpit and looked down at the congregation. Cadence felt almost overwhelming affection for this grandfather figure who opened his arms in welcome and beamed at the upturned faces of the couple who were to be married. But before he could utter a word, the air was filled with a cacophonous roar as windows to one side of the church imploded and vast plumes of solid water shot above heads. Within seconds, the interior of the church was a heaving, freezing lake, with waves bouncing back and forth between the high walls.

CHAPTER TWO
Sunday, 29th August

Seven weeks before the great flood and six days before her godson Joel was due to arrive in Hawksmead, the chiming bell in St Michael's Church at the southern end of the little town told Eleanor Houghton it was ten o'clock as she stepped out onto the pavement. She strode along the High Street, smiling at the occasional person she recognised without breaking step, and carried on past the beauty salon, Wax Polish; the offices of the local newspaper, Hawksmead Chronicle; and on towards the River Hawk and its narrow humpback bridge. She smiled as she passed the Victorian Methodist Church, so plain, so austere, and yet so welcoming thanks to Reverend Longden. Formerly the reserve organist, from tomorrow she would be the only person in Hawksmead who knew how to play the pipe organ with its numerous pedals, three rows of manual keyboards, and multifarious ivory stops that determined which pipes were to receive pumped air.

'I'm a pianist,' she'd told the dear Reverend when he'd first asked her to play. 'I will not be able to do your wonderful organ justice.'

'All you have to do is simply pull out all the stops and the choir will do the rest.'

'Choir? I didn't know we had a choir?'

'A choir of one led by Hawksmead's renowned opera singer.'

A wry smile crossed her face. 'Reverend, even my voice will not carry above the wind in the pipes.'

'We have invested in a microphone.'

'But, Reverend, playing and singing is a tall order.'

'Elton John managed it.'

Since then, she had played every other Sunday and at weddings and had grown to love the pipe organ. But dear old Mr Turnbull was retiring and moving to Eastbourne, so Eleanor was about to become the only musician in Hawksmead who could multitask her way around the greatest of all musical instruments. Through the closed church doors, she heard the strains of one of her favourite hymns - Praise to the Lord, the Almighty, the King of Creation and she couldn't help but join in, her pure voice carried on the fresh morning air.

Beyond the church's graveyard, behind the high brick wall, lay the Memorial Garden where Eleanor and many local people liked to reflect, to contemplate, to restore their equilibrium - a tranquil oasis, so vital during the long days of the global pandemic. Eleanor loved the garden with its vivid flora and secret hideaways, created by two of her special friends but, this morning, she was determined to stretch her legs and go all the way to the burnt-out shell of a former boarding school isolated on the moor.

At the end of the High Street, she glanced at a speed camera that had caught so many unwary drivers who put their foot down after crossing the narrow, stone bridge. It didn't bother Eleanor as an overdue cataract operation had forced her to give up driving. She decided it wasn't worth the risk of knocking-over a cyclist approaching at an angle, so used local taxis instead. The money she'd made from selling her beloved Mini Cooper had kept her afloat.

As she approached the bridge, she was momentarily

startled by a lone figure, wrapped up in a hat and raincoat. There was something about the intensity of the man staring down at the river that stopped her in her tracks. Before she could debate with herself what to do, he turned and looked straight at her. Even though they were at least twenty metres apart, she could not avoid his penetrating stare. She waved and walked with as much confidence as she could muster onto the bridge.

He raised his trilby. 'Good morning.' His voice had a rough edge, possibly east or south London. She forced a smile and continued on, almost scraping the opposite parapet wall. 'I didn't mean to startle you.' His words, spoken gently, and her old-fashioned upbringing, broke her step and she acknowledged his comment.

'Good morning,' she replied. 'Unseasonably chilly for September.'

'Ron Smith.' He held out his hand, protected from the elements by a brown leather glove.

She ignored his offering, checked there were no cars coming, and crossed the bridge to his side. They both looked down at the fast-flowing water.

'Ferocious.' He spoke loudly above the noise of the river rushing through the arches.

'More than enough force to power the looms.'

'The looms?'

'Hawksmead was expanded by Richard Arkwright towards the end of the eighteenth century. He built the cotton mill.' She gestured with her head to a substantial red-brick edifice, downstream. 'The river was redirected from its natural path to serve the giant water wheel. That's why the river is above the town and not below it. He also built numerous cottages to house the workers.'

'A man of vision. Industrious. I admire that.'

'The cottages are now prime real estate and the old mill, luxury flats.'

'And everything's made in China.'

Eleanor took a deep breath. 'Well, I best be going.'

'Would you care to join me for a cup of coffee? Breakfast? Early lunch? On my way from the station, I saw a tea shop. It was closed,' he glanced at his wristwatch, 'but it may now be open.'

'I was going to walk up to the old school out on the moor.'

'Really? I heard it burnt down.'

'It's being redeveloped. Or, at least, it will be.'

'Isn't it quite a walk?'

She looked at the man. Not handsome, but a good, lean face for his sixty or so years. Something about the pain she saw in his eyes struck a chord deep within. 'I think I will join you for a coffee.'

'Excellent.' He offered Eleanor his arm, but she kept a gap between them as they headed back to the High Street.

'What brought you to our little town?' she asked, as he matched her stride for stride.

He took a moment or two before replying. 'A pilgrimage of sorts. Not a happy one.'

'I'm sorry to hear that.'

'And you? You live here?'

'Yes. I grew up in Hawksmead but spent most of my working life in London.'

'Doing what, exactly? Sorry, a bit forward.'

'Singing. I am or rather was a professional singer.'

'What's your name? I've probably 'eard of you.'

'I don't think so. I did musicals. Occasionally, opera.'

They continued on down the High Street, past the Old Forge restaurant on the right and Merlin's hardware store. 'I love a good musical,' the stranger said. 'Phantom's me favourite.'

'You have great taste. I once toured in that show.'

He stopped and reached for her arm, but she shrank back. 'You played Christine in Phantom of the Opera? With all them high notes?'

Eleanor laughed. 'I couldn't get to them, now.'

'I would love to hear you sing.'

'I've hung-up my vocal cords.'

'I'm sure I heard the voice of an angel singing Praise to the Lord a short while ago.'

She smiled. 'Guilty.'

'Do you have a recording of your Phantom?'

'Somewhere, but I would rather listen to Sierra Boggess.'

'Never heard of 'er.' He shielded his eyes as he looked through one of the panes in the tea shop's bow window. 'It's still closed. All the chairs are upside down on the tables. And it don't look as though it's going to open anytime soon.'

Eleanor removed a heavy set of keys from her coat pocket. 'You're right. It's not open, but we can still have coffee and cake.' She used a different key for each of the three locks and opened the door.

'I'd better put on me mask.'

'I presume you're vaccinated?'

'Oh yeah. You bet. The full works.'

'Then, after you, Ron.'

She followed him into the old-style tearoom with its round oak tables and wooden chairs stacked seat down on top. 'Welcome to ye Olde Tea Shoppe.'

'Well, you're a dark horse.'

She laughed. 'Why don't you select a table and I'll make us some breakfast.'

'Should I turn on the lights?'

'Better not, otherwise everyone will want coffee and cake.'

He laughed.

'Cheese on toast?' she asked. 'A poached egg on top? Welsh rarebit with a bit of Worcestershire sauce?'

'Now I'm salivating.'

The force of water drove air up the organ's pipes adding a hideous, discordant scream to the tumultuous roar that continued to pour through the church's shattered windows.

CHAPTER THREE

On that same Sunday, six days before Cadence Clearwater and Joel Redmond arrived in Hawksmead, a beast swooped from the sky, its chop-chop sending rabbits scuttling back into their burrows. Graham Ashton, helicopter pilot, circled the charred ruins of the old boarding school, once a Victorian workhouse for unfortunates.

'You're okay with this?' his passenger in the rear seat asked.

'Excuse me, sir?' replied the pilot glancing over his shoulder at a well-defined, handsome face sporting headphones above a thick head of hair.

'Thank you, Graham, I was addressing Lady Cornfield.'

The pilot laughed. 'My apologies, sir.'

'Honestly Graham,' Lady Cornfield said, who was also wearing headphones. 'When are you going to stop eavesdropping on other people's conversations?'

Graham loved listening to the delightful tone and northern lilt of the kindest person he had ever met in all his years of being a professional helicopter pilot. The fact that she was also a natural beauty played a part, he had to admit, in his overall admiration. 'The thing is, Lady Cornfield, listening in on your conversations is one of the perks of the job. Almost better than a pay rise.'

'I'll bear that in mind at your next salary review,' Lord Cornfield responded.

'Thank you, Graham,' Lady Cornfield said. 'It's good

to know that my pearls are of such high value.'

'Usual touchdown, sir?' Graham asked.

'Wherever suits. The whole area looks pretty boggy.'

Graham manoeuvred the helicopter until it came to rest on a large, gravelled apron in front of the former school. Recent rain had encouraged weeds, thistles, and wildflowers to grow in abundance through many cracks in the hardcore. 'You may wish to sit tight, sir,' Graham said. 'A brief shower. Should pass in a few minutes.'

Lord Cornfield turned to his wife. 'You okay?'

'I'm okay,' she said.

'You're sure?'

Her hand caressed her baby mound. 'We're absolutely sure.'

Eleanor pushed open the swing door from her kitchen and for a microsecond, she expected to see a room full of chatting people pouring tea into bone-china cups, pushing sandwich triangles into cheerfully gossiping mouths, and choux pastries stacked high on tiered cake stands. Instead, she saw a sad-looking, lonely man, sitting in the bow window, lost in thought.

'Welsh rarebit,' she said as she placed in front of him a plate adorned with melted Cheddar cheese on home-baked bread, crowned with a perfectly poached egg. In her other hand was cutlery wrapped in a paper napkin which she put beside the plate.

'What a feast!' Ron said and looked up at Eleanor. 'I hope you've catered for yourself.'

'Back in a tick.' She hurried to the kitchen and kicked open the swing door. Moments later, she sashayed back through the tables and placed a tray with a pot of coffee, a jug of milk, a Victoria jam and cream sponge cake, two silver cake forks, and two fine porcelain plates decorated with wild berries in front of Ron. 'Do start,' she said as she pulled out a chair and sat down.

'Thank you.' He picked up his knife and fork. 'I am a complete stranger, but you're treating me in a way that would put the Good Samaritan to shame.' He cut the ladened slice of toast with great dexterity and transferred a forkful of dripping egg and melted cheese into his mouth, whilst Eleanor poured the coffee.

'Milk?' she asked.

'And two sugars, thanks.'

She slid a sugar bowl in matching porcelain, with a recessed lid to accommodate its small spoon, beside his saucer. 'Demerara, I hope you don't mind.'

Ron swallowed and scooped into his cup two great mounds of brown crystals. 'Eleanor, I dreaded coming here. I really did. But you've lifted me spirits, for which I am immensely grateful.'

'I'll put some music on.' She pushed herself up from the table.

'Would you sing a little for me now?' His hand rested gently on hers.

She smiled. 'As long as you play the role of Phantom.'

He chuckled. 'No problem. I do have a white mask in me pocket.'

A white VW Golf negotiated the cracks and potholes of the mile-long drive leading from the Old Military Road up to the former boarding school. Sitting on the clawed-leather backseat was a bullmastiff. He had an enormous head covered by scarred pelt, and a long tongue lolling out of immense jaws. As the Golf approached the helicopter, the dog barked with excitement at such a volume, the driver almost swerved off the gravelled apron onto the rain-soaked moorland.

'Steady Hector.'

The hound ignored his master's entreaty and continued to bark, swinging long, viscous, saliva trails.

Gary, thirty, slim, fit, turned to his dog and clicked a heavy leather lead onto his collar. He climbed out and pulled open the rear passenger door. The weight of the dog jumping to the ground knocked him onto his back. Leather lead trailing, Hector galloped towards the helicopter, with its slowly rotating blades.

Gary scrambled to his feet and ran after the dog, now barking and leaping with great enthusiasm. The passenger door to the helicopter opened and a willowy figure with leather boots, blue smock, and a thick windcheater stepped with care onto the ground. The dog lurched for the young woman and would have flattened her if Gary had not grabbed the lead and hauled the hound back.

'Hector, it's lovely to see you,' Christina said, keeping out of slavering range. 'And looking so well fed.'

Gary watched the woman's companion step to the ground behind her.

'I'm not confident he remembers me,' Lord Cornfield commented.

'Have you brought steak?' Gary laughed the question.

Lord Cornfield reached into the helicopter and removed a Marks & Spencer's cool bag. He unzipped the top and peeled on a blue butcher's glove. He dipped into the bag and retrieved a large hunk of dark red meat. It took all of Gary's strength to hold the mastiff back.

'Off you go, boy.' Lord Cornfield flung the meat onto soft moss. Gary released his grip on the lead and Hector bounded for the treat, then stopped and turned. He trotted over to Lord Cornfield.

'Hello boy...' Cornfield gently rubbed the dog's enormous, scarred head and ears. 'It's good to see you.' He smiled at Gary. 'He does remember me.'

Gary turned to the young woman whose beautiful blonde hair was neatly contained in a single plait and who he knew he still loved. How he wished she were carrying his baby. 'Christina, aren't you going to give Hector a hug?' he asked.

She smiled. 'I'm happy to wait my turn. I know where I stand in Hector's order of ranking.' She looked at the dog, so fearsome, so battered, so wonderful. 'Hector?' He turned his head towards her and barked making both Christina and her husband jump. 'Have you got a hug for mummy?' She opened her arms and Hector would've knocked her over if Gary had not grabbed his collar. She bent down and his long tongue slathered her face. 'Thank you, Hector. Go get your dinner.' She stepped back and pointed at the hunk of meat. The dog barked excitedly.

Gary released his grip on the collar, and they all watched as Hector galloped off.

Lord Cornfield removed the blue glove and tossed it onto the floor of the helicopter. He zipped up the cool bag and handed it to Gary. 'There are a few more dinners for Hector in there. Looking after him isn't cheap.'

Gary took the bag. 'You must see his new home. He has a solar-powered kennel with all mod cons where he can come and go as he pleases. As much as we all love him, he's not really a house pet.'

'Let me know the cost,' Lord Cornfield responded.

'Abel, you didn't let me go during the pandemic, despite my doing no work on the project. So, take it from me, you're quids in.'

Abel nodded and looked past Gary to the charred remnants of the once mighty and forbidding structure, propped up by scaffolding and bearing large danger signs warning ramblers not to enter. 'I would like to get things moving.'

'Me too,' Gary replied.

Christina glanced at her watch. 'Is Harry expecting us?'

'Yes. What about your pilot?' Gary asked. 'Hector makes it a bit of a squeeze.'

'Graham won't leave the chopper unattended,' Abel said. 'He's got coffee and sandwiches, a movie on his iPad and, as he once told me, a whole moor to piss on.'

Gary laughed as Christina reached into the helicopter for a coral red bucket bag. She loosened the leather drawstring and took out a small pack of wipes. 'How's the car?' she said as she cleaned her face and hands.

'Hector keeps it pristine,' Gary replied. 'I'll sit with him in the back. You drive. I'm sure you're itching to get behind the wheel after being chauffeured everywhere.'

'Believe it or not,' Abel said. 'We have both enjoyed the top deck of a London bus.'

'Now that I have to see.'

Abel spoke to the pilot through the open rear door. 'We'll be a few hours, Graham. Would you like us to leave you with the dog?'

'He's a lovely, cuddly pooch,' Graham said, his vowels perfectly rounded. 'But he doesn't really know me. So, if you're happy to take him, I would be more than happy to be on my own ...and more than a bit relieved!'

Abel laughed, closed the door, and followed Gary and Christina to the car. Gary put the cool bag in the boot as Christina peered at the rear seat. 'Oh my God!'

'What is it?' Gary slammed the lid.

'Have you seen the state of this leather?'

He came up beside her. 'I've spoken to Hector about that. I'd hoped you wouldn't notice.'

'Huh!'

'The key's in the ignition.'

Christina slipped behind the wheel and eased the seat forward. Abel walked around the nose and sat beside her.

'Hector!' Gary called. The dog gulped down a last morsel and barged him out of the way as he leapt onto the rear seat. Gary pushed him over and sat beside the oversized hound.

'I hope he's not going to dribble down my neck,' Abel said, sliding his seat forward so that his knees were bunched up.

'He only dribbles down people he likes,' Gary laughed. 'And it's so much better than the alternative!'

'I've dined in Michelin-starred restaurants,' Ron said as he sipped a second cup of coffee in the Olde Tea Shoppe. 'I've hired top chefs; I've demanded only the best for my palate, but your Welsh rarebit and Victoria sponge trump the lot. You're a woman of great talent, Eleanor.'

'Thank you, Ron.' She felt a glow spread through her body. Probably the menopause, she thought. 'It's a joy to serve a meal to someone other than myself.'

'What about your customers?'

'I have a confession.'

'An old friend in the police once told me ...never confess.'

She took a deep breath. 'I haven't reopened the teashop since the resurgence of the virus.'

'Why's that?'

She paused. 'I'm too frightened.'

'Of Covid?'

She nodded.

'But you've been inoculated? Had the vaccine?'

She took another deep breath. 'I suffer from an extreme fear of needles. Just the thought of an injection brings on a panic attack. When I was a child, a doctor would come to my school to inoculate the children for diphtheria, tetanus et cetera. My mother told me to try and get to the front of the queue so the needle would still be sharp.'

'I remember,' Ron said. 'They used to wipe the needle with disinfected cotton wool between jabs. Unbelievable.'

'I got shoved to the back of the queue and by the time it was my turn, the doctor had to push hard to get the needle in. And it broke.' She put her head in her hands and fought the growing sickness in her gut.

'Let's walk on the moor,' Ron said. 'Take a look at that old school.'

She smiled at him through swimming eyes. 'That would be lovely. Thank you.'

'It's funny,' he said. 'I thought you were going to tell me you've not had the vaccine 'cause it carries a microchip, which tracks your every waking thought.'

'Doesn't it?' She held his gaze... then burst out

laughing.

Christina accelerated along the Old Military Road up a winding hill and marvelled as she always did at the moorland landscape with its sharp-edged ridges, deep gullies, waterfalls, peaks fringed with clumps of trees, and mile after mile of enticing, rolling wilderness crisscrossed with dry-stone walls and crystal-clear streams.

'All we need is the Irishman,' Gary said, 'and the whole team is back together.'

There was a heavy pause.

'Any news of him?' Abel asked.

'Not that I've heard.'

'I hope he's okay,' Christina said, almost to herself.

Abel nodded. 'If he were in trouble, I would help him.'

After a few moments, Gary responded. 'I'm not sure I would.'

Another silence followed by the squeal of tyres as Christina swung into the car park of the Rorty Crankle, a former coaching inn.

'What about Hector?' Abel asked. 'Is he joining us for luncheon?'

'His table manners are not all that... I'll tie him up away from the entrance and leave him with a bowl of water and perhaps another hunk of prime steak.'

A few miles from the Rorty Crankle as the crow flies, Malcolm Cadwallader said, 'I've just had a brilliant idea.'

Audrey looked at her husband. 'I'm at a rather exciting part of my book, so I trust you're not exaggerating the quality of your idea.'

Malcolm chuckled. The elderly couple were sitting

in the front room of their terraced cottage; Malcolm in a worn Ercol armchair with an old leather-bound volume on his lap; and Audrey on a two-seater sofa with her stockinged feet supported by a worn pouffe, reading a novel on her tablet.

'I've been giving serious thought,' Malcolm continued, 'as to what we can do to regenerate Hawksmead. To lift spirits. To shake off the malaise of the last few years. To enthuse, to enrich, to reboot.'

Audrey looked at her eighty-one-year-old husband sitting across from her and marvelled at his lean frame and extraordinary wisdom. 'And your brilliant idea is?'

'A tea party in the Memorial Garden before summer's finally over. We could have music, sandwiches, cake, soft drinks, and whatever anyone wants to bring. There could be magicians, face painters, jugglers. Pony rides for children. Perhaps even a carousel.'

'And who is going to pay for it all?'

'I am. I expect others will chip in, but I want it to be a celebration, free for all.'

'Not a free-for-all, I hope!'

He laughed. 'I'll talk to Andy at The Chronicle. Perhaps pay for an advertorial. See if we can raise an army of volunteers.'

'We'd better coordinate diaries as I'm thinking of going south to visit my boys and their families, and a couple of old friends in Sevenoaks.'

'What about your dear papa?'

Audrey missed seeing her father but knew how lucky she was at the age of seventy-one to still have a parent. 'He's happy with a phone call. Doesn't want to take any risks. This latest upsurge has him worried.'

'As long as they're okay, that's all that matters.' Malcolm put his book down on a side table. 'Right, my nose is telling me lunch isn't far off.' He pushed himself to his feet. 'Don't move. I've still to make the gravy.'

Audrey placed her tablet on the sofa. 'I'll do it. I watched my mother make gravy and I've never tasted better.'

'As you have told me many times,' Malcolm muttered as he headed for the kitchen.

Icy water sent her spinning, just as a breaking wave had once swept her up as a child and she'd spun until all air was squeezed out of her.

'Lady Cornfield, welcome to my humble hostelry.' As big as he was effusive, Harry Willoughby almost swallowed Christina in his embrace. Abel and Gary looked on, having witnessed many times the *Christina-effect.*

'I think the boys would like a hug, too,' Christina said as she patted Harry's rotund girth.

Abel stepped forward, offering his elbow. 'We've met before, Harry. It's good to see you again.'

Gary opened his arms. 'I'm up for a hug.'

'That's more like it,' Harry roared.

Gary grinned. 'Not with you, dear man. I'm up for a hug with your good lady wife! Where is she?'

Harry called over his shoulder. 'Chef! My sweet, my chickadee, a policeman's here and he wants to arrest you.'

A door marked *Kitchen* swung open and a tall, slim woman in her fifties emerged wearing a blue and white striped apron.

On the same patch of cracked, worn tarmac where the

VW Golf had so recently driven, Eleanor and her new acquaintance ambled. She had thoroughly enjoyed catering for Ron and had partaken to such a degree herself that a walk up the mile-long meandering drive to the old boarding school was essential. The conversation, inevitably, had turned to her past life and try as she might to hold on to her happy mood, it evaporated in the early afternoon sun.

'I married my second husband because he was kind. But he was too kind. Too keen to help out his fellow man.'

Ron smiled. 'Not an attractive quality.'

'Good will poured out, often into places it was neither needed nor desired. It drove me bonkers'

'Sounds like a pretty decent bloke to me.'

'You should try living with such virtue.'

'My late wife was definitely my better 'arf.'

'The real problem was, he set his career sights too high.'

'It's always good to aim beyond your reach.'

She turned to Ron and almost gripped his arm. 'You can have no idea how hard it was to live with his frustrations. Why could he just not be happy with what he'd achieved, with what we had? It was still so much more than many others.'

'It's the pyramid of life, ain't it? We always look at those that 'ave more, not at the many with less.'

Eleanor stopped and stared unseeingly at the patchwork shades of green and gold that stretched for many miles. 'When Philip died, he was at his lowest ebb; the global financial crisis had hit us hard. We struggled to make ends meet. There was a time when writing scripts would augment his income as a copywriter but not having a literary agent severely stunted his writing career. No matter how good the script, how creative the story, the answer from every sodding agent was always the same.' She mimicked quotation marks. *We're not taking on anymore clients at this current time but thank you for your interest.*

Ron stood next to her. 'Writing is not an easy profession, that's for sure.'

She nodded. 'Especially since the internet. Before e-mail, film producers were receptive to direct contact from British writers, but when the internet enabled the world to flood their inboxes, they bolted the doors to everyone who didn't have an agent.'

'Surely a man with his gift could've got an agent?'

She laughed. 'Oh yes. He'd had two – one fired him for taking a job for a fee she considered too low – he had a final tax demand to pay - his second quit the business and moved to Australia. At the time Philip was busy making low budget films, until the banking crisis pulled the plug. Years of work finding backers went down the plughole.' She laughed. 'Apologies for the mixed metaphors.'

'I love a mixed metaphor,' Ron said. 'Sharpens the image.'

Eleanor nodded and took a deep breath. 'Anyway, he was on his beam ends and really needed an agent. But it was too late. Broadband was in full throttle and their doors were shut.'

'Timing,' Ron said, at little more than a mumble, 'is everything in life.'

She turned to him. 'Yes, timing and colossal misjudgement on Philip's part. He tried every angle to get agents to consider him. One even blocked him on twitter for spamming. But he wasn't a troll. He just needed help to get his work to the right people.'

'Aren't good writers an agent's lifeblood?'

She half laughed. 'They'll have you believe that. In reality, they want to represent the easy sell, preferably a TV celebrity with a book, who can get free publicity courtesy of the BBC.'

Ron nodded. 'It's a world I know nuthin' about. Where is your 'usband, now?'

She took a few moments to respond. 'It was a Friday afternoon,' she said, 'punctured by another stab-in-the-heart rejection email. To cheer himself up he turned to Facebook, as was his wont, and soon he was happily rattling off opinions to his online friends when he saw a post about a young boy needing a bone marrow transplant. It was the boy's only hope of surviving leukaemia. My husband already gave blood, so when he read the article, he saw an opportunity to do something even more extraordinary and volunteered to have a test.'

'I can guess the next bit.'

She nodded. 'About a week later, the hospital asked him to return for more tests.'

'And he was a perfect match?'

She nodded again. 'For the first time in a very long while Philip felt wanted - without him the boy had little hope but with the help of my husband's stem cells at least he had a chance. Philip knew the boy's name from the Facebook article but when he saw the boy's mother's name on the release form, it struck a chord.'

'I think I can see what's comin'.'

'Yep,' Eleanor said. 'She was a literary agent. When he got home, he checked through old emails, and I watched as his blood pressure rose with every re-read rejection message from the boy's mother. *Your work is of an extremely high calibre. However, we have come to the difficult decision that we will not be able to help you with representation, at this time.* The usual agent claptrap.' She turned her back to Ron and wiped a tear.

'I can see how much it wounds,' he said, 'even after all this time.'

'There were four rejection emails from the boy's mother. In her most recent message, she gave him a few tips on how to improve his writing skills: *You should try to avoid writing on the nose – be more obtuse. Perhaps, hardest of all, you must develop the discipline to kill all your little darlings – those bits of writing that you love too much. I wish you luck in finding a literary agent more suited to your skill.*'

'I'd rather be punched in the gob,' Ron said, 'than be patronised like that. What did he do?'

'He went to the hospital and, having Googled a photo of the boy's mother, managed to track her down in a corridor outside the children's wing. Once he explained who he was, she almost fell on him with gratitude. Over the next few days, they met several times for coffee and eventually he screwed up the courage to ask her to read some of his work. He told me her expression changed from almost total devotion to frosty aloofness. She agreed to read his material but would make no promises. He opened his bag and gave her a manuscript for a TV series he was developing. In my biased opinion, it was a brilliant concept. The agent, on the other hand, looked at the bound pages as though they were his dirty laundry, but she did eventually take them.'

'That was big of 'er.'

'The next time she and my husband met was when his stem cells were due to be harvested. They went for coffee, and he asked her what she thought of his script. She admitted to only skim reading the pages but said he was clearly a writer of merit, but she hoped he understood why, at this time, she could not offer representation.'

'He should've walked away. That would've focused her attention.'

'Trouble was, she knew he'd never let her son die. But he did walk away. He went out to get some air.' Her voice softened. 'I can imagine how she watched him go; his shoulders hunched but his bone marrow ripe for the taking. A good man, a good writer, but not good enough for her precious client list.' Eleanor searched her pockets for a tissue.

Ron gently rested his hand on her arm and offered her a pristine handkerchief.

She took the gift and blew her nose. 'Sorry to burden you.'

'You're not. You're sharing. We don't do enough of it.'

She dabbed her eyes and looked down at a few surviving wildflowers growing out of the roadside verge. 'He felt broken,' she said. 'Useless, not good enough, an utter failure. He wandered the streets paying no attention to where he was going. I know this because he rang me and told me what had happened and how he felt that his value to the world was no more than the sum of his spare parts. As his wife of many years, I knew how much he wanted to succeed as a writer; I knew how hard he worked to get good at his craft; yet, despite his big heart, his generosity...' Tears flooded her eyes as she fought to go on. '...the cold-hearted agent wouldn't give him a chance.' She sobbed into Ron's hankie. He put his arm around her shoulder. Haltingly, she continued. 'His phone call ended abruptly, and I assumed he went back to the hospital. But, later, I had a visit from two police officers who told me that he was in Intensive Care after being knocked down by a bus. A witness saw him talking on his mobile when he stepped off the pavement without looking.' She cleared her throat and stared unseeingly at the lush landscape. 'At the hospital, I stood at the foot of his bed and it did not take any medical qualifications for me to know that my darling husband would never recover. They'd found his organ donor card and I agreed that they could harvest all the organs they needed. Two people would share his liver, two would get his kidneys, one would get his heart and lungs; another, his small bowel; and another, his pancreas. I knew my lovely man would want to help as many people as possible.'

'And the boy?' Ron asked. 'What happened to the boy?'

'You mean the agent's little darling?' She turned her head away. 'It took two days for the boy's mother to locate my husband. We met for the first time in Intensive Care, and I could see the terror in her eyes and then the relief when she saw Philip was still alive, albeit on life support. I told her about the planned organ donations. She asked me to arrange for him to be moved to the same hospital as her son, as he had to take priority. But I'd read her rejection emails so I told her, *'Thanks to you spurning my husband, the lives of seven people will be saved'*. Of course, she begged me to help her son. She screamed. She wept. She pleaded. *'I will do anything you ask. I will sell all your husband's scripts. I will make him famous. I will make him the writer he always wanted to be, the writer he deserves to be.'* I listened, I made her wait, I led her to believe there was a chance I would change my mind. I made her watch as I kissed my beloved goodbye and then I delivered the crushing blow. *'I hope you can appreciate why, on this occasion, I must concentrate on my husband's existing recipients of his organs and reject your application for his bone marrow. I wish you luck in finding another donor.'*

They stood in silence. A crow squawked from a high branch in a lone tree.

Eleanor turned to Ron. 'Are you shocked?' She saw his disappointed expression.

'What 'appened to the boy, her son?' His voice caught in his throat.

'You mean, her little darling?' Eleanor paused. 'I was determined the literary agent would share my pain.'

Ron stepped away. 'I'd better be going. Thank you for breakfast.' He walked off, heading back the way they'd just come.

Eleanor called after him. 'The not so little boy is now nineteen years old. He's doing well. My husband's bone marrow saved his life.'

Ron stopped and turned. 'He's alive?'

She smiled. 'Joel has regular checks, but all looks good. His mother keeps me updated.'

Ron shook out a maroon handkerchief and blew his nose. 'I've gone soft in me old age.'

'I'm his godmother. His auntie. He's coming to live with me whilst attending drama school in Undermere.'

CHAPTER FOUR

A few doors from the Olde Tea Shoppe, Magdalena Jablonski was facing a brutal truth. Despite all her hard work since arriving from Poland, life's little white ball had skipped and rattled around fate's spinning roulette wheel, promising great good fortune but had landed on zero. And that's what she had. Zero. Nothing. It had all looked so encouraging when she spent every last penny creating a most desirable beauty salon; a place where women could go to be pampered, where their nails could be perfectly shaped, varnished or extended; and where unwanted hair was plucked, threaded or waxed. She even had the perfect name – *Wax Polish*. Her customers laughed when she first told them, but insisted she keep it. Why did they find it so funny? After all, she was Polish, albeit now a British citizen, and she offered wax treatments. But that was all in the past. The virulent cloud that had encompassed the world had poisoned her dream.

A problem shared is a problem halved. She had heard that expression many times but didn't believe it. The only way her problem could be halved was if someone gave her a lot of money. But who? She was no longer married and received no alimony. Worse than that; the prospects of marrying wealth were diminishing with every new day. She was thirty-seven, big-boned, athletic, rounded in all the right places and, people told her, beautiful. But, when she looked in the mirror, she didn't see a confident, striking woman... all she saw was fear. Yes, she was still a head-turner. Men found her luscious looks desirable, very desirable. She liked their company, had slept with a few, but her deep passion was forbidden fruit.

There was a knock on her door. It turned to loud thumps. It was Sunday. Who could it be? Had the bailiffs arrived to cart her business away? She could see the shape of a single man through the door's mottled panes. Bailiffs normally came in pairs, didn't they? Heart pounding, she turned the key in the lock and slid back the top and bottom bolts.

In the gastro pub out on the moor, Harry collected up the dirty plates.

'Would you care to see the Rorty Crankle pudding menu?' he asked. 'We also have a selection of British cheeses including Stilton, Stinking Bishop, Cornish Blue and, owing to public demand, a few smelly French such as Roquefort, Camembert and the most pungent of the lot, Vieux-Boulogne.'

All three of Harry's customers shrunk back at such a shocking suggestion. Abel was the first to speak. 'That was a sensational meal, Harry, but I fear Les Fromages Français will have to wait.'

'And the Stinking Bishop?' Harry asked.

'To be defrocked on another occasion. As for your chef, once the old school is developed into a country club, I may have to poach her.'

'Darling, that's a terrible suggestion,' Christina stated with some force. 'Harry needs Cathy, here.'

With plates balanced on one arm, Harry raised his free hand. 'Now wait a minute, Tina my dear. Let's not be too hasty.'

Gary laughed. 'Sweetheart, err Christina, Lady Cornfield, I'm not sure you fully appreciate the level of financial deficit incurred by hospitality during the long pandemic years.'

Christina looked contrite. 'My apologies, Harry, I must come across as a very spoiled brat.'

'After what you've been through, Tina my love, you deserve all the spoiling that life and Abel can give you. If you would excuse me.' He hurried away, kicking open the swing door to the kitchen.

The three sat in silence for a few moments.

Abel picked up his glass of red wine. 'I would like to propose a toast.'

Christina and Gary, who were both drinking sparkling water, raised their glasses.

'I would like to propose a toast to the United Kingdom.'

'To the whole UK?' Christina queried.

'If our great enterprise is going to succeed, the whole country has to be doing well,' Abel said.

'You're right,' Gary chipped in. 'To the UK and all of us who live here.' They sipped their drinks. 'And now the thorny bit,' he continued. 'The bill.'

'It's okay,' Abel said as he reached for his pocket. 'I'm buying lunch.'

Christina and Gary both burst out laughing.

'Of course, you're right, Gary,' Abel continued. 'We know what we want to achieve; it's time we put out to tender. Get a feel for how much the first stage of development is going to cost.'

'It won't be pretty,' Gary said.

'No, but with you managing the project, I am confident that waste will be kept to a minimum.'

Christina reached across the table and squeezed Gary's hand. 'Abel has great faith in you, we both do.'

Gary turned away to give a little cough.

The door swung open from the kitchen and Cathy marched up to the table followed by Harry. She looked at Abel. 'I accept. When would you like me to start?'

Abel smiled. 'In about two years.'

They all saw her face fall.

'But,' Abel continued, 'I do have a suggestion that may help oil the cogs.' He paused. 'I would like to buy a half share in this pub.'

'You mean,' Harry interjected. 'Instead of paying the mortgage company we pay you?'

'Instead of paying the mortgage, you pay yourselves,' Abel said.

'Deal.' Cathy offered her elbow.

'Not so quick with the funny bone,' Harry said. 'We've yet to hear Abel's offer.'

Standing some way from the parked helicopter, Eleanor and Ron stared at the charred remains of what was once a vast Victorian edifice. 'The extent of the damage is quite shocking,' she said.

'I'm surprised the fire destroyed so much,' he responded.

'My friend Audrey was here that night. She told me, despite standing at a safe distance, the heat from the flames was incredibly intense. Thankfully, no one died although one man was badly burned, I believe.'

'What's to 'appen to it?' Ron asked.

'Something new and exciting is to emerge from the ashes. If it hadn't been for the pandemic, work would've already started.'

Ron pointed to a stone ruin to the far side of the burned-out shell. 'What's that over there?'

'That is the old abbey. The Order fell-foul of Henry the Eighth when he was breaking England away from Rome. There are still some rooms underground where food was once stored.'

'Shall we take a look?' He turned and smiled at her.

'Thank you. I'll wait here. I hear it's haunted by some old codger in a hood.'

Ron laughed.

The sound of a car racing up the long drive attracted their attention. 'That'll be the owner of the helicopter,' Eleanor said.

Ron fished in his pocket, pulled out a mask and stretched the elastic over his ears. 'Can't be too careful, even outside. There's a new variant going around.'

They watched the white VW Golf spit gravel as it swung in a half circle and parked some way from the helicopter. After a few moments, the horn tooted.

'Best keep your distance,' Ron said, his voice slightly muffled by his mask.

She ignored his advice and hurried over to the car as the doors opened. Christina hauled herself out. 'Eleanor! How lovely to see you.'

'Can we hug?'

Christina opened her arms and she and Eleanor embraced.

'What's this I see?' Eleanor asked as she pulled away and looked at Christina's big bump.

Gary emerged from the rear of the car, keeping a firm grip on Hector's lead. 'Ellie, how are you?'

'Surviving, Gary. And you?'

'We're fine. Hector and I are still living in Woodland Rise with Tina's brother and his husband.'

'It's ages since I last saw you,' Eleanor said.

'Hector is a little antisocial. When are you going to reopen the tea shop?'

'Just as soon as I know it's a hundred per cent safe.'

'It'll never be completely safe.' He looked past

Eleanor to Ron standing some way off. 'Ah, now I understand why you've not been baking. Who's your friend?'

Eleanor turned and gestured for Ron to join them. He waved back but didn't move. 'We met this morning. He's a bit nervous about mixing with people.'

Abel came up behind Christina and put his arm around her shoulder. 'Hello Eleanor. You look well.'

'Thank you. And you both look wonderfully happy.'

Abel squeezed Christina's shoulder. 'I can't speak for the lady, but I've never been happier.'

Christina gave her husband a kiss.

'Eleanor,' Abel continued. 'Have you seen our pilot?'

She looked over his shoulder to the helicopter's empty cockpit. 'Silly question, but have you tried his mobile?'

'Not so silly,' Abel responded, as he thumbed his phone's screen. Within seconds, they heard a ringing in the helicopter.

'Where would he go without his phone?' Christina asked.

'He may have been taken by force,' Gary suggested.

'That's the policeman in you,' Eleanor said.

Hector barked, making them all jump.

'He's heard something.' Gary squatted down and rubbed Hector's ears. 'What is it boy?'

The dog barked again and dragged Gary off towards the abbey ruins with Abel following.

Christina turned to Eleanor. 'I'd better waddle after the boys. Make sure they don't get into trouble.'

Gary gripped Hector's lead with both hands as they weaved through the old stones that made up the remaining walls of the abbey. Beyond, he saw Graham sitting on a boulder by a rapidly flowing brook, water splashing over the grassy bank.

Hector barked and the pilot turned his head. 'Keep away!'

Gary hauled on Hector's lead and rubbed his head. 'That's all right, boy. Friend.'

Abel, followed by a panting Christina, caught up and they all looked at Graham who coughed... and coughed again.

'I have developed a temperature,' Graham wheezed. 'I came here to cool down. Then the cough came out of nowhere. I've had every vaccination going but it could be some new strain.'

'Or it could be regular flu,' Abel added. 'Do you have any other symptoms?'

'I have a skull-cracking headache, my muscles are stiff, and my throat's beyond sore. I feel bloody ill. Sorry sir, whatever it is, I cannot fly you back to Battersea. We need to isolate until we get tested.'

'We can go to Rise House, isolate there,' Gary said.

Abel looked at Christina. She took a deep breath and he put his arms around her. 'I'll call the estate agent where you used to work and see if there's an empty property we can rent.'

She shook her head. 'No, I'll be fine at Rise House.'

'I'll let your brother know,' Gary said. 'He and Luke will have to stay in a hotel in Undermere until we get the all-clear.'

'Make sure you tell him I'll pick up the bill,' Abel added.

'I'd better break the news to Eleanor,' Christina said.

'Eleanor?' Both Abel and Gary queried.

'We hugged,' Christina responded.

'And Harry up at the Rorty Crankle,' Gary said. 'Everyone who was in the pub with us should take a test.'

'Let's go,' Ron said, still wearing a mask.

'There they are.' Eleanor gestured to the old abbey as Christina, accompanied by the three men and the dog, came into view. 'They've found the pilot, that's good.'

'He's coughing.'

They watched as Christina broke away from the group and walked over to them. Ron held up his hand. 'Not too close, please.'

She stopped about ten feet short. 'Our pilot's not well, so we're all isolating at my family home until we can get tested.'

'Let me know if there's anything I can do,' Eleanor said.

'I think you should isolate, too.'

'Me?'

'You and I hugged. Perhaps take a test in a day or so.' Christina looked at Ron. 'You, too, Mr Smith.'

'Since you arrived, I've been wearing a mask. I'm definitely in the clear.'

Eleanor spoke to Christina. 'You have my number. Let me know as soon as you hear anything.'

'Of course. We'd give you a lift back, but I don't think you want to travel with us in the car.'

'It's lovely to see you, Tina,' Eleanor said.

'It's lovely to see you, too.' She turned to Ron. 'It was a pleasure to meet you Mr Smith.'

Ron nodded and they stood in silence as Christina headed back to the men who were standing by the car.

'A bit of a risk leaving the helicopter unattended,' Ron said.

'I think that's the least of their worries.' Eleanor pulled a mask out of her coat pocket and looped the elastic over her ears. 'Are you happy to accompany me home?'

'You bet.'

Gary observed Eleanor and Ron as they headed off across the gravelled apron. 'What do you think of her friend?'

No response.

He turned to Christina who was tapping her phone's screen with her thumbs. 'One minute, Gaz, I'm just messaging my brother.'

Gary looked at Abel who had wandered away from the car, talking on his phone.

As for the pilot, he was using the Golf to support himself while he coughed and vomited.

Abel finished his call and approached Gary. 'I've got another chopper coming up with two pilots.'

'Is Graham going to isolate with us?'

'Either with us...' Abel looked at the pilot, 'or in hospital.'

'I'll drive Graham and Hector to Rise House. You and Tina had better walk.'

Abel looked at his wife who had just finished texting. 'Are you okay walking?'

She nodded. 'As long as you're happy with waddle speed. But shouldn't we wait for the pilots to arrive?'

Abel glanced at the chopper. 'They'll be here within a couple of hours. I don't think we should wait.'

Gary fished in his pocket for a blue mask and looped the elastic over his ears. 'Mr Ashton...'

Graham turned to Gary and coughed again.

'I suggest you sit in the back with Hector.'

Graham nodded.

'You get in first and then Hector will sit beside you.'

The pilot looked as apprehensive as he looked ill. He

coughed and then eased himself into the Golf.

Gary knelt in front of Hector and put his face near the mighty, drooling jaws. 'Graham is our friend. He's our good friend.' Gary opened the nearside rear door and Hector leapt in. He almost smothered Graham before sitting on his haunches beside him.

Gary slipped into the driver's seat and slid it back. He looked through the open door at Abel and Christina. 'We'll see you at the house. I'll keep Graham isolated until we know for sure.' He closed the car door and started the engine.

Lord and Lady Cornfield watched the white car speed off across the gravelled apron with its innumerable weeds. 'I hope he avoids Eleanor and her friend,' Abel commented.

'When he was with the police, he qualified as a hot pursuit driver. It's how we met.'

'I hear he gave you a speeding ticket.'

Christina laughed. 'No. The cameras got me. But he did book me for a date.'

Abel nodded then looked at the helicopter. Christina rested her hand on his arm. 'Graham will be all right. We'll make sure of that.'

'I'm more worried about you.'

'Me?'

'Your lungs suffered in the fire. It's anyone's guess which bit of the nervous system the new variant will attack. We can't be too careful.'

'It certainly has put a spanner in the works.' She turned and looked at the burnt-out shell supported by scaffolding. 'I know how keen you are to get this thing going.'

'It can wait. My sole concern is you. How do you feel?'

She drew in a long breath through her nostrils. 'I can still smell the wonderfully damp moorland air.'

'And the baby?'

'All good.'

He offered her his arm.

Eleanor and Ron heard the high-pitched scream of the approaching VW Golf and stood by the edge of the roadside ditch. Ron, who had taken off his mask, hastily looped the elastic over his ears. The car slowed and Gary called out to them through the driver's window. 'I'll keep you informed, Ellie. Hopefully, we'll all get negative results.'

She blew him a kiss through her mask, and they watched the car speed off. 'It's easy to forget he was once a policeman,' she commented to Ron.

'Really? What's he doing now?'

'He works for Abel, Lord Cornfield. His job, when it starts, is to project manage the development of a luxury hotel, gourmet restaurants and leisure facilities. What's weird about the project, is that he was once held prisoner up at the old school by a criminal gang growing marijuana. If I were him, I wouldn't want to go near the place.'

'Quite some story.'

'At the time, Gary was married to Tina.'

'So, she dumped him for the Lord.'

'Two years forced separation took its toll and, well, let's just say that Tina and Gary will always be the best of friends.'

'I'm amazed he can work for the man who took his woman.'

'Nobody owns Tina, and there's more to it than that.'

'What? Like cheatin' on his wife with another man's

daughter?'

Eleanor took a moment before responding. 'Anyway, it's all water under the bridge.'

'Yeah.' Ron cogitated for a few moments. 'Sometimes, you just have to let go.'

'I don't know about you,' Eleanor said. 'But I'm getting chilled standing here.'

Ron looked up at the sky. 'Yep. We've had the best of the day.'

They walked on in silence, both seemingly lost in their own thoughts, neither able to appreciate the beautiful scents and damp aromas, or notice the happy, chirping, migrating birds feasting on bright red hawthorn berries before their long flight south.

Gary approached Sam, his ex-wife's older brother, who was standing by a couple of bulging suitcases in the porch to Rise House.

'We've packed what we could in the time,' Sam said. 'Just how long is it we're to be exiled from our home?'

The front door opened and Luke, Sam's husband, emerged, his expression equally sullen.

'We have to be careful, Sam,' Gary said, adjusting his mask. 'Graham, Abel's helicopter pilot, won't get out of the car until you're both in the clear. He's convinced he's got something pretty bad, and now I've probably got it too.'

'We've booked into the White Hart in Undermere,' Luke said. 'Bloody expensive.'

'Tell them Lord Cornfield's paying the bill.'

'We can afford to pay our own bills,' Luke stated, as he picked up a case.

'I know you can,' Gary said. 'But Abel feels responsible, and the cost is loose change to him, so let him do it.'

'Thank Abel for us,' Sam said.

'Will do.' Gary watched as Sam and Luke lugged their bags up the footpath to a recently arrived taxi. He heard Sam greet the driver.

'Hello Sean. It's good to see you.'

Gary smiled. Could the day get anymore weird? The taxi driver was once Tina's boyfriend, before Gary chased her in his police car, married her and, much to his considerable regret, cheated on her, and lost her to the noble Lord. He headed back to the VW and opened the rear door as the taxi sped off. Hector leapt out and barged past him.

'Wait boy,' he shouted as he tried to grab the long, trailing lead. The dog reached a side gate and scratched at the heavily scarred oak panel. Gary rummaged for his set of house keys and slid one in the lock. He unclipped Hector's lead from his collar, turned the key and the gate banged open. Hector galloped down the side passage and disappeared into the rear garden. Gary closed and locked the gate and headed back to the car, coiling the lead as he walked.

'Graham, you can come in now.'

He checked that his mask was in place and peered into the car. 'Graham?' The pilot was either asleep or unconscious. Gary walked around the car and opened the rear offside door. Graham toppled out and it was as much as Gary could do to stop him falling onto the tarmac. Using all his strength, he pushed Graham back into the car and closed the door. He took out his phone, swiped the screen, and dialled 999.

About half a mile away in her little flat above Wax Polish, Magdalena picked up dirty lunch plates and placed them in the sink. She turned to her guest whom she had known for several years, from when she owned an end-of-tenancy cleaning company, and he was the owner of a successful independent estate agency. 'Dessert from M&S, or just coffee?'

Trevor Harper appeared to ponder the question. 'Why don't you and I get married? We're really good together.'

Magdalena looked at the man and considered his dark, wavy hair now flecked with grey, his straight nose and softening jaw line. His eyes, a light brown, looked tired, almost beaten. 'And the joke is?'

'No joke. We've both been through hell and being alone is not much fun.'

'Cheesecake or coffee?'

'Coffee. Instant's fine.'

'I have Nespresso machine. Small or large?'

'Large, no milk or sugar.'

Magdalena busied herself with the coffee and ran through Trevor's words. Marriage? It would be her second and not the kind of relationship she wanted ... deep down. She made two cups of espresso and placed them on the table. 'More wine?' she asked.

Trevor reached for her hand. 'I meant what I said. Will you marry me?'

She sat down and poured Malbec into their wine glasses. 'Last time I look, you still married to Olivia.'

Trevor drew in a deep breath. 'Not anymore. Divorced, absolutely. I accepted the blame, signed over our forever-home, and she decides when and where I see my children. My once thriving business is on life-support; and I'm holed up in a damp, mouldy, mouse-infested flat instead of the wonderful house Olivia enjoys.'

'Why you let her go?'

'I made a stupid investment that lost much of her

inheritance.'

'I would kill for that, but I am not talking about wife, I talk about Tina, Christina, Lady Cornfield. Hiring her was best decision you make.' She paused. 'Why she not partner?'

Trevor lifted the tiny espresso cup. 'I wanted her to be, but she was, she is, too beautiful. It was a difficult sell.'

Magdalena nodded. 'Your wife. She think you want Tina to be partner in business ...and bed.'

'If I'd made Tina a co-director of Harper Dennis when she was barely out of her teens, it would've confirmed to Olivia her worst fears.'

'That you were in love.'

'Every client who met Tina fell in love with her, but I did all I could to keep my feelings under wraps.' He sighed. 'She was too young for me, anyway.'

'And now she married to man your age. Irony, yes?'

'I'm happy for her. She deserves the lifestyle he brings. From all accounts, he's a good man. Rich, handsome... England's answer to Bradley Cooper.' He chuckled and sipped his coffee.

'It's thanks to you she met her Bradley Cooper.'

Trevor returned the little espresso cup to its saucer. 'I've been the catalyst for much that's happened in Hawksmead.'

'Yes, you have.'

He looked at Magdalena. 'So, who's my competition?'

She smiled. 'Relax, your way is clear. She's married.'

A frown crossed his face. 'But, weren't you married, once? To a man?'

'Yes. Not dream match.'

Trevor finished his coffee. 'Thank you for being

honest.' He got up from the table. 'And thank you for lunch.'

'You not want answer?'

'Answer?'

'*Yes*, is answer.'

'To what question?' And then his face brightened. 'You will?'

'We make go of it. Good team. But,' she continued, 'one condition.'

Trevor let out his breath. 'No sex. I understand.'

'That's not condition.'

His face brightened. 'It's not?'

'No.'

He sat back down and took Magdalena's strong hand in his. 'I want to marry you. I'll accept whatever condition you make.'

'Okay. Follow me.' She stood and headed for the stairs that led down to her salon.

'I didn't think you'd want to be in your parents' bedroom,' Gary said to Christina. 'Your brother and Luke are in the largest spare room. So, you have a choice. Your old bedroom with your dolls and cuddly toys, or the boxroom, where I've been sleeping.'

Christina looked at Abel. 'Do you mind sharing with Jessica, Ashley, Sarah, Samantha, Brittany, and Emma, Victoria, Geri, Mel C and Mel B? I promise they'll keep quiet.'

'I'll tell you what I want,' Abel said. 'What I really, really want.'

Christina took his face in her hands and kissed his lips. 'Who knew you were a Spice Girls fan?'

'I'm a big fan, especially since Ginger married Red Bull Racing.'

'I think she married the man not the team.'

Abel laughed. 'You're right. Christian Horner's a lucky chap.' Slim, manicured fingers gave him a gentle jab in the ribs. 'And so am I,' he added, laughing.

She kissed him again. 'Let's go to our room and unpack. Wait a minute, we have no bags to unpack.'

'I'll call Eva and see if she can pop over to Mayfair and put together a few essentials. Sebastian can drive the bags up in the morning.'

'And I'll call the hospital and check on Graham,' Christina said, 'although it's a bit soon. I'll also try and arrange for some test kits to be delivered.'

Trevor lay back on a padded table and hoped that the pleasure to come was worth the pain. Pungent vapour permeated his nostrils as Magdalena heated up bright blue wax in an electrical warmer.

'I trust you've done his before?' he asked.

'Many times, but no chests. It's going to be new experience.'

'For me too!'

She picked up a wooden spatula. 'Close eyes and think of England.'

A dollop of hot wax was deposited on his chest which Magdalena spread around with her spatula.

'Deep breath,' she said, and she ripped off the hardening wax.

He gasped as a clump of chest hair went with it. 'Good grief!'

Another dollop was spread around. 'Now you know what it's like for woman,' Magdalena said, 'when she has leg wax.'

'I have the upmost respect.'

'And some husbands insist they remove every scrap of hair from bun,' she informed him as a clump of chest hair disappeared.

'OW!! I don't know how they do it,' he gasped. 'Nearly done?'

'Be brave. It'll be worth it, I promise.' Magdalena spread some more wax and whipped his hair away. And again. And again. 'All done. Don't move.' She picked up a tub of cream. 'You'll like this.' It was cool and soothing as she massaged it into his pink, hairless chest.

'Mmm… that feels good. Very good.'

She took his hand and pulled him up to a sitting position. 'Have you ever kissed Polish woman?'

'I don't think so.'

'If you had, you remember.' She pressed her full lips against his and a great surge of blood pulsed through his entire body. 'You buy ring,' she whispered.

'Ring?'

'Engagement ring.' She raised her right hand.

'Of course. Now that Olivia and I are divorced, I'll ask her for the rings back.'

'You want more waxing? Perhaps Full Monty?'

'No, no… we'll go to Undermere and buy a ring.' He kissed her again and it was full of great promise. He could be happy with this woman.

'Well Ron,' Eleanor said, standing outside the Olde Tea Shoppe, a few doors away from Wax Polish. 'It's been an absolute pleasure. A delightful surprise.' Her natural instinct was to give him a kiss, but she held back.

'It has.' He looked up and down the almost deserted High Street.

She rested her hand on his arm. 'Under the circumstances, until we know, I suppose we should stay outside and keep socially distanced.'

'Very boring.'

63

'I would like to see you again,' she said.

He peered at her over his mask. 'I would like to see you again, too.'

'Where are you staying?' she asked.

It was the briefest of hesitations. 'I'm in an Airbnb in Undermere. It's safe. If I have the dreaded lurgy, I'm isolated.'

Eleanor took her phone out of her pocket. 'Give me your number and I'll call you.'

'I don't have a phone.' He pulled off his mask.

She looked at him, startled. 'You don't have a phone?'

'No need for one. I live abroad and the only person I cared about, until I met you, has moved on.'

'But isn't it grossly inconvenient?'

'Maybe to others, not to me.'

'How can I contact you?'

'I'll buy a pay-as-you-go. Are you in the phone book?'

'If you Google, Olde Tea Shoppe, Hawksmead, my website will come up with all my details.'

'Perfect.' He looked to his left and then to his right.

'Fingers crossed we're okay,' she said.

Ron cleared his throat. 'I would be honoured to take you to dinner, before I leave.'

'That would be lovely.'

'Right, well, I'll be going.' He looped his mask over his ears and replaced his trilby. 'It's been an honour and a joy.'

'It has that. Goodbye Ron.'

He nodded, clearly reluctant to be on his way. 'I'll be off.'

She watched him stride down the High Street towards the railway station and could've sworn she heard him singing *Past the point of no return* from The Phantom of the Opera.

Trevor stared into Magdalena's sort of green, sort of hazel eyes and saw deep into her soul. He was thrilled when she led him to her bed, but now she seemed more interested in talking than making his day.

'I can't promise,' she whispered, her chestnut locks spreading out across the white pillow. 'But I want give it go.'

He sat up and leant back against the padded bedhead. 'When Harper Dennis was thriving, and my marriage was good, I thought I was cock of the walk. And then...'

'...and then Tina sold old school boarding house to Audrey.'

He half laughed. 'Yeah. Tina hated that building but I made her measure it up. If Audrey hadn't bought it. If Tina hadn't helped save Audrey's life, she would never have met Gary, and she would not have left the job she loved.' He turned away and planted his feet on the carpet. 'Perhaps this isn't a good idea.' He stood and pulled on his boxer shorts.

'You will never be happy, Trevor,' Magdalena said, 'until you let go of regrets. Until you do, you flounder. Flounder? Is that right word?'

He smiled down at her. 'It sounds about right.'

She sat up on her elbow. 'Tina showed us how, when Gary was missing and she lost parents, it is possible to break through dark shadow and find hope.'

'Yes, she did. She certainly did.'

'You know, Mister Trevor. During the time when all was closed and we couldn't mix, and I couldn't travel home to Poland, I felt truly alone. But you, my friend, reached out to me when I was deep low.'

He smiled. 'I reached out across the great divide of Hawksmead High Street.'

'Don't make fun.'

He sighed. 'If I joke it's because of how I feel about you.'

'You love me?'

He looked down at her beautiful, majestic face so full of ripe passion. 'Yes, I do. Isn't it obvious?'

'Perhaps what you feel is need, not love.'

He took a deep breath. 'It may not be teenage love with all those white-heat emotions. But, for me, anyway, it is the right kind of love. A good love.' There was a brief silence and then Trevor grinned. 'And, of course, I fancy you rotten. I would be the proudest man in the world to have you on my arm.'

She threw back the duvet and he marvelled at her relaxed attitude to her own nakedness; her big-boned frame, her plumpness without a hint of flab, her fulsome breasts, her rounded buttocks, and her soft almost iridescently white skin. She promised heaven and had given Trevor the key. But for how long? He had so little to offer by way of money, or income, but with her he felt empowered, energised to fight on. He would rise from the ashes of his own making.

She smiled and her teeth almost sparkled. 'You are kind man Trevor Harper of Harper Dennis Estate Agents. You have courage. You make mistake with money. Lose wife. But you will be success again. I am here for you. I can be your woman, but I am also Magdalena, lesbian.'

Blood coursed through his arteries. The way she mouthed the word *lesbian* was a massive turn-on. Why was he such a typical male?

She continued. 'I read your dirty brain. You want

exotic threesome with buxom beauty. No!' She wagged her forefinger. 'It is not about sex. Yes! It is about sex, but it is different emotion to be with woman. I don't have words even in Polski to express.'

'Do I know her?'

Magdalena's laugh was deep, throaty and genuine. 'Of course! It's Tina.'

'Tina? Christina? Lady Cornfield? Abel's wife?'

She gave Trevor a piercing look. 'Can you live with that kind of threesome?'

'You and Tina are lovers?'

The volume of her laugh jolted him. 'Of course not. She is straight. She is woman for man, only. But I will love her till day I die.'

Trevor was almost panting. The thought of Magdalena and Tina making love blew his mind.

'Now you know everything,' she continued. 'Can you cope?'

'Surely the question is, can you?'

She shrugged her bare shoulders. 'Have I choice?' Her expression remained serious. 'But you do.'

He took a deep breath. 'I'll be happy to take whatever leftover feelings you have for me.'

'You sure?'

'Absolutely. One hundred per cent.'

She grinned. 'Good. It is clear. Now I take care of erection!'

Christina stood at her old bedroom window in her family home and saw the man she loved, her Lord, his hands deep in his pockets, his head bowed as he paced aimlessly at the bottom of the overgrown garden. By the doghouse, Gary was topping up Hector's water reservoir. As for the dog, he was gambolling around, sniffing unimaginable scents; a frightening beast to anyone Hector considered a foe. Battle-scarred from when he was brutalised by a criminal gang that had held Gary prisoner for two years, the dog had been Gary's saviour. And a saviour again when Gary, Abel and Christina, plus Gary's jailer had been caught in the devastating fire that destroyed the old school. Abel's last throw of the dice was to fix the watch he'd given Christina to Hector's collar and trust the dog to find a way out through the dense, acrid smoke. It worked and they were rescued by firefighters. But the man, Gary's nemesis, who'd carried her unconscious through the blaze had paid a heavy price. His once handsome face had been badly burned by falling embers. Yes, he was a crook but, when all appeared lost, he had been her noble hero and she still thought about him. She also still thought about her marriage to Gary, her first love. Abel was different. Despite an age gap of more than twenty years, she felt a kinship that came from deep within her soul. He appealed to her on so many levels and every day she felt her love for him reach new heights. And now he was in pain, fearful for his friend. Why the virus was so devastating to Graham who was incredibly fit, she couldn't fathom. She, Abel and Gary still suffered the effects of smoke inhalation from the fire, but they and the helicopter pilot had been vaccinated and had assumed they were protected from serious illness... until now.

Magdalena slipped out of bed and left Trevor, who was lightly snoring. She hurried to her bathroom and sat on the loo, surprised by the glow of contentment she felt and by the speed she had twice peaked. *Twice!* That had never happened before. In fact, a single orgasm had been a blue-moon event during her marriage.

She stepped into the tap end of the bath and lifted the showerhead off its rest before turning on the water, which always took a few seconds to get warm. What were her true feelings for Trevor? Should they marry? She liked him and it was safe to say she found him physically desirable, but was that enough? They weren't *in love* but perhaps a slow burn was preferable to white-heat passion that could swiftly fade as it had in her first marriage.

She dabbed herself dry and brushed her teeth, her thoughts far removed from flossing. Why hadn't she dated women? Was she simply too scared, too ashamed, too Roman Catholic to come out? In her salon, Wax Polish, she had been up close and personal with many beautiful women but only once felt an overwhelming desire to touch, inappropriately.

Tap. Tap. She had been so lost in her thoughts as she massaged ESPA body lotion into her legs she had all but forgotten about Trevor.

'Are you okay?' he asked through the door.

'One minute.' She stared at her glowing naked form in the mirror above the basin. She looked good and, thanks to Trevor's persistence, felt good too.

Raging water smashed into her, wrenched her from Trevor's arms, and spun her over and over in its heartless embrace.

CHAPTER FIVE

Monday, 30th August

An iPhone vibrated across a bedside table. Christina opened her eyes and looked at a jagged shrinkage crack on her childhood bedroom ceiling as she waited for Abel to answer his phone. He rolled away from her and coughed.

Her hand felt the baby move and she smiled, then wrinkled her nose. 'What's that smell?' she asked, not recognising her own croaking voice.

'I think it's us.' Abel picked up his phone and looked to see who called.

She sniffed. 'Are you sure? I don't think I've ever smelt this bad.'

He put the phone back on the table. 'All I can smell are the drains.' He turned to face her. 'I think the virus has affected our senses. How do you feel?'

'Fine apart from the terrible stink.'

'It's not real. Unfortunately, the virus is. We must isolate up here, assuming Gary hasn't caught it.'

'That means he'll have to wait on us. Cook meals, bring us food. It's not really his skillset.' She squeezed his hand. 'It feels strange being back in my old bedroom. Did you sleep okay?'

'Not really. And your dolls were no help – they kept staring at me.'

She moved her bulk closer to him. 'Graham will be all right. He's not obese, he doesn't smoke, and as he's your pilot we can be sure he has no underlying health conditions.'

'That's why I married you.' He gave her a tight smile.

'Every day, you make me feel better.'

She ran her fingertips over her husband's bristly cheek. 'I think we need a few supplies. Knickers worn twice are not quite nice!'

'At least we can shower. Sebastian will be here sometime this afternoon with our things.'

'But today's a Bank Holiday. He might've made other plans.'

'He didn't mention any.'

'As if he would.'

'You're right. I should've been more considerate.' He flung back the duvet, and she watched him amble to the window wearing boxer shorts. He pushed it open. 'It really does stink of raw sewage.' He turned to her. 'Are you sure there's nothing wrong with the drains?'

She got out of bed and straightened her brother's T-shirt so it covered her large mound. As she approached the open window, cold slivers of air made her shiver. 'What a stink.' She turned to her husband. 'Do you have any other symptoms?'

'My throat feels as though it's been scraped out by sandpaper. Hopefully, the vaccine will keep the worst of the symptoms at bay.'

Hector barked and they both snapped their heads to look down into the garden. A fox was trapped by the dog's large kennel.

'Hector,' Christina called, and she rapped her knuckles on a windowpane. The massive hound turned to see the source of the sound and the fox scampered away across the lawn.

Below the bedroom window, Gary stepped onto the paved terrace. They watched from above as he doubled over and vomited into a trough with dead plants.

'Bugger!' Abel said.

71

Gary looked up at the bedroom window as he wiped his mouth on a sleeve. 'It's not the virus. I ate some smoked salmon pâté I found at the back of the fridge. Big mistake.'

Malcolm Cadwallader heard his taxi speed off as he headed up the path to a detached house, built in the 1960s. The name Cobwood was carved into a piece of weathered timber, fixed to the left of the porch. As he reached for the plastic bellpush, childhood memories of peeling away green husks, cracking brown shells and chomping on the delicious variation of the hazelnut, flooded his mind. A few minutes later he was sipping coffee with one of his oldest friends as they looked out of a picture window into the rear garden, with its small orchard of cob trees at the far end.

'Aren't garden fêtes usually in May or June?' Andy Blake asked.

Malcolm looked at the younger man who had poured vast sums into keeping the local newspaper alive. 'Don't you know, we're living in a post-pandemic era. Nothing is as it was.'

'Ne'er a truer word spoken. Still thanks to the virus I have saved money.'

'Explain.'

'We used to print the paper; now, we're one hundred per cent online.'

'Ah,' Malcolm said with a wry smile. 'You could save even more money by not publishing at all.'

'My very words,' came a voice from the kitchen. 'Malcolm, can I tempt you to a biscuit?'

'What are you offering?' Malcolm called back. 'I have a refined palate.'

'I'll bring in the biscuit barrel. There's a potpourri of

chocolate chip cookies, Jammie Dodgers, Hobnobs and Bourbons.'

'Thank you, I'll have a Rich Tea.'

'That's what I thought. I'll be through in a minute.'

Andy chuckled. 'Maggie's always on at me to pack it all in and retire, but where would I find my fun? You see, thanks to my boy Tony focusing on our website, our subscriber list has expanded and now The Hawksmead Chronicle has readers throughout the world. And, to cap it all, we're almost breaking even.'

'You'll be going on Dragons' Den to seek investment.'

Andy raised his brows. 'That's actually not a bad idea. I don't need their money but a bit of free publicity for The Chronicle wouldn't come amiss.' He smiled. 'You could come in with me. We could present together.'

Malcolm rocked back on his heels as if he'd taken a body blow. 'You think they would invest in an octogenarian?'

'Not a chance, but we would have a lot of fun.'

Malcolm paused for a few moments. 'I'll give it some thought. In the meantime, I need to buy some free publicity for our garden fête.'

'Buy free publicity - a brilliant oxymoron. You'd be *perfect* for Dragons' Den'.

'This is crazy,' Abel said, carefully carrying a tray with lunch into the bedroom. 'It's everywhere.'

'The virus?' Christina asked.

'Dog hair.'

'At least he's happy,' she replied, looking out of the window into the rear garden.

'I don't think waiting on us morning, noon and

night is Gary's version of happy.'

She laughed. 'Come and see.' Abel joined her at the window, and they watched Hector gambolling around the large rear garden playing with Gary.

'I must take a closer look at the kennel,' Abel said. They both peered down at the miniature double-fronted wooden house with solar panels on its sloped roof.

'My dad used to keep the garden all neat and tidy,' Christina said, 'but I think the wild-look suits Hector more.'

Abel laughed. 'I'm sure it does, although I doubt the neighbours are quite so happy.' He looked at his watch. 'I feel so helpless being stuck here whilst Graham is fighting for his life.'

She touched his arm. 'We know he's in good hands.'

Abel took a breath, turned away and coughed. 'God, it's a bugger. I thought we'd come out the other side ages ago, that it was over, and then this happens.'

'Call the hospital. Use your title. It'll get you through, quicker.'

He looked at her. 'I'll get my P.A. to call.'

'It's a Bank Holiday,' she said. 'I'll do it.'

'Thank you.' He sat on the unmade double bed. 'Graham's been with me a long time. I know his wife, his daughter. I can't let them down.'

The Intensive Care Unit at Undermere General Hospital, where critically ill patients were referred with all manner of complications, was where Clinical Director, Professor Massimo Bisterzo, spent most of his working day and, often, working night. He could, if he chose, piggyback his NHS role as a Critical Care Consultant with lucrative private work, but would rather spend what free time he had playing golf or tennis, and following Formula One motor racing.

'I am becoming so British,' he once told a friend. 'My support for Ferrari is not absolute.' It was a confession that shocked him.

Another shock was the rapid decline in the condition of the sedated patient lying before him, whose breathing was controlled by a ventilator carrying oxygen-enriched air via a clear plastic tube through his mouth, down his trachea and into his lungs. Graham Ashton was a helicopter pilot who was going to die unless Massimo did something pretty fast. Ashton had tested positive for the latest and most deadly variant of Coronavirus, although Massimo didn't need a test result to know that the man lying before him was in the grip of a virulent disease. He had hoped, synthetic neutralising antibodies would crack the viral nut, but the pilot was still going down. He also hoped that his Personal Protection Equipment including a special mask, Perspex visor, long-sleeved gown, latex gloves, and full quota of vaccinations would protect him. But he hated putting it on, loved taking it off, and loathed putting it on again. The whole process took so long he often needed a pee by the time he was ready to face another highly infectious patient. He had given up drinking tea and coffee – their diuretic-effect only made the problem worse. He sipped enough water to avoid a dehydrating headache but not so much he couldn't last a whole six hours without having to undress and dress again.

Massimo drew a deep filtered breath and spoke to Doctor Manson. 'Any thoughts?'

'His wife and daughter are on their way,' she responded.

'How long?'

'They're coming from Sussex.'

They both looked at their unconscious patient.

'This is worrying,' Massimo said. 'I will notify the Department of Health.'

'I think he should have an X-ray.'

Massimo looked at the young woman who had a remarkable intellect and more than a caustic turn of phrase. 'Interesting. Your reasoning?'

'This virus targets people with pre-existing conditions.'

'Mr Ashton is a pilot,' Massimo responded. 'The Civil Aviation Authority requires an annual medical. He's slim, a non-smoker, low cholesterol... we know he's been vaccinated.'

'Exactly.'

Massimo and his registrar locked eyes over their masks and through Perspex visors.

'What are you thinking?' he asked.

'Adenocarcinoma.'

'It would have been detected when he had his medical. Unless...' He picked up the patient's chart, examined the handwritten notes, then hung it back on the end of the bed. 'Adenocarcinoma is a typical carcinoma in the lungs of a smoker and would stand out like a black marble in a bag of white marbles. But, with our friend here, it's a few grains of black sand in a bag of white marbles. Much more diffuse and much harder to spot.'

'Blood test?'

'Probably undetectable.'

'But the virus...' She looked at the patient. 'The virus discovered the weakness.'

'As did your gift as a physician.' He took a moment to admire his favourite registrar, encased in plastic, and tiny. 'I think you may have saved his life, Doctor Manson.'

'I'll call oncology,' she said, not acknowledging his praise.

'He's too sick for chemo.'

'Radiation?' she asked.

He nodded. 'Yes. But I think we need to consult.'

'Who do you recommend?'

'I'll talk to my friend, Professor Hull.'

'You know Professor Hull?'

'We studied medicine together at Cambridge.'

The sun was setting as Magdalena opened the door to Wax Polish.

'Is that it? Two Waitrose bags and a suit carrier?' She looked at Trevor's meagre possessions sitting on the pavement.

'I have an Amazon Kindle, so no heavy books. I have an iPhone and charger for banking and emails, and my wallet. I'm the Jack Reacher of Hawksmead.'

'And I'm Lee Child. Get in, Mr Reacher.'

Trevor lugged his stuff into the pristine salon and Magdalena closed the door behind him. He followed her up the stairs to the bijou flat. On the dining table was a multicoloured bouquet of fresh flowers in a vase.

'Thank you for bunch,' she said, gesturing to them.

'Marks and Spencer at its best. I have no idea what they are, but they look lovely.'

She paused and smelt the bouquet. 'Roses, hypericum, irises, lisianthus, and a couple I don't know. Thank you, Trevor. Now I make tea then you help give final wipe to salon.'

'Is tomorrow a busy day?'

'Every day busy when working alone.'

'Why not get some help?'

'On my own I make profit.'

'Take a lesson from Harper Dennis. I was making money until Tina left. Sure, the wage bill went down but so did my profits. There's a balance to be struck.'

'Since pandemic, there's been no balance.' She reached for the kettle and switched it on. 'I have big debts. Very expensive.'

CHAPTER SIX

Saturday, 4th September

Eleanor woke and knew instantly something was wrong. Her vision was blurred and there was a terrible stabbing pain in the side of her back. She took a deep breath and coughed. The rattling sound shocked her. She'd been in touch with Lady Cornfield several times in the week to check that she and the baby were all okay. Could she really have caught the virus when out on the walk with Ron? She'd hugged Christina, who had been infected by the pilot during the helicopter flight, but she'd hugged her out in the open. On the other hand, she may have caught it the previous Monday when she made an inadvisable foray into The Falcon to celebrate August Bank Holiday. In fact, she had no idea where she'd caught it, but she was definitely within its grasp.

What about her lovely new friend, Ron? They'd had dinner together a couple of times in The Old Forge and even shared a little kiss. Was he also infected?

She hauled herself out of bed and almost staggered to her bathroom. There would be no reopening of the Olde Tea Shoppe anytime soon. Worse; her godson was coming to stay in preparation for his entry into the prestigious Undermere School of Dramatic Art. She was looking forward to his company although she was in no doubt that having a young man to live with her would have its challenges. But she didn't care. She wanted his youthful energy to fill her home.

The cough came again, and it was deep and harsh. Her body was in the grip of something evil; a disease her defences did not recognise and had no weapon to fight. What was she to do? Where could Joel stay until it was safe for him to live with her? She was determined not to let him down. She entered the passcode on her phone and swiped the screen.

'Hello Eleanor.'

'Audrey.'

'Who is this?'

'It's me.'

'Eleanor? You sound terrible. Are you all right?'

'Not really.' Eleanor coughed, then squeezed out the words. 'I need help. Is your spare bedroom free?'

'I'm coming over,' Audrey said.

'No!' Eleanor took a pained breath and coughed. And coughed again.

CHAPTER SEVEN

Sunday, 5th September

The day after her arrival in Hawksmead, Cadence Clearwater slid open the sash window in her bedroom and saw, beyond the hanging sign of a falcon in flight, what she had always imagined England to be... bow-fronted cottages lining a narrow, twisting lane on a gentle hill.

She smelt a whiff of baking bread carried on the early morning air. Where was it coming from? Her toned tummy rumbled and despite a strong desire to sleep-off more of her jetlag, she hurried to the bathroom.

Normally, she would spend a bit of time applying body lotion and face creams after a shower, but she was hungry and wanted to locate the freshly baked bread. She looked at her two suitcases and knew she should unpack. Instead, she slipped into a stretch pair of jeans, a loose tank top and a light sweater and checked herself in a full-height mirror fixed to the reverse of the wardrobe door. Happy, she grabbed her shoulder bag and denim jacket.

As she entered the bar, only a few lights were on to complement weak daylight penetrating multicoloured stained-glass windows depicting country life from eons ago. She heard Ted grunting from behind the counter and with a little trepidation she leaned over to take a peek. A trap door was open, and a lightbulb revealed wooden steps leading to a cellar.

'Hello?'

Ted appeared at the bottom of the steps. 'Good day. Did you sleep well?'

'Yes. Thank you. I thought I'd go out and find some breakfast.'

She watched Ted grab the handrail and haul his bulk up. He ducked his head as he emerged through the trap door. 'Heather would be more than happy to scramble some eggs.'

'That's very kind but I think I need to get some air.'

'I forgot to give you a set of keys.'

'That was my very next question.' She watched Ted cross to an old-fashioned till. A bell dinged and the drawer shot open.

'Here we are my dear. The long key is for the side passage gate. This key is for the side entrance. And this is your room key.' He handed her the three keys joined by a steel ring.

'Would you mind showing me the side entrance?'

'It's easy to find. When you approach the pub, instead of entering via the double doors to the public bar, turn right down Pilgrims Way where you'll see a wooden gate. Use the long jailer's key to open the gate, please lock it behind you, walk along the passage, sorry there is no light, until you come to a door. Use the modern key to unlock. There's a knob on the reverse. Please twist it to double-lock the door when you're inside.'

'And the third key,' smiled Cadence, 'is my bedroom.'

'Not that you need it as you are the only guest and we wouldn't enter your room, apart from for cleaning and to change the linen every Monday morning.'

'No problem.' She looked at the keys in her hand. 'Do I go out the back way, now?'

'The pub is not open to the public until twelve noon

on Sundays. But, I'll let you out the front.' Ted lifted the counter flap and weaved his way around battle-worn tables to the main entrance doors. He threw back two heavy bolts, twisted two locks and pulled open the right-hand door.

'About time!' said a rough-sounding voice.

Cadence saw an old man with a bloated face standing on the pavement.

'We're not open, Vincent,' Ted said.

'Except, as I see, to Miss Fit of Solana Beach,' she heard the old man respond.

'It's not Miss Fit,' Cadence said. 'It's Miss Fitness. And I won it a long time ago.'

Ted looked intently at Vincent. 'And how do you know this little nugget?'

'A name like Cadence Clearwater is catnip to the dark web.'

Ted stood aside. 'Come on. Get in.' He almost pulled Vincent through the door and then pushed him into the main bar. He turned to Cadence. 'My apologies. He's a nice guy and harmless. He must have overheard your name. I'm sorry.'

'No problem. I'm off to the bakers.'

'Unfortunately, it's closed Sundays.'

'But I could smell freshly baked bread through my window.'

'That'll be Heather.'

'Heather?'

'My wife. She always bakes first thing. Her pork and apple sandwiches are...'

'I don't eat meat,' Cadence interjected, 'and certainly not pork. Pigs are super clever. They understand what's going on.'

'What about mutton? They're not so smart.'

Cadence knitted her brows. 'Are you talking about sheep?'

'My apologies. Most of the food we serve is meat-based. But you're right. Meat production is bad for the planet. I'll let Heather know and she'll come up with vegetarian alternatives.'

'Thank you.'

'What about fish?'

'If it has a heart, I don't eat it. I don't believe in eugenics.'

'Eugenics?'

'Ranking beings by intelligence.'

'There's a greengrocer down near the station that is open on Sundays. You can buy fresh fruit there.'

'Great. I plan to check the local train service to Undermere.'

'Good idea. By the way, Heather and I are delighted you chose to stay with us. We hope you'll come to think of our pub as a home from home.'

She smiled and touched his arm. 'Thank you. My first riotous party is tonight.'

His belly laugh accompanied her as she stepped out into the morning sun and headed down the little town's main street. This was the first time she'd travelled overseas and although she watched British TV, it still felt surreal being in England.

Joel Redmond couldn't believe how late it was. He had slept well in the little cottage and had been the last to use the bathroom. He'd heard the elderly couple get up at the crack of dawn, which puzzled him. They didn't have jobs so why the early start? And it was Sunday. Joel liked to sleep in when he could. The journey up from London had tired him, compounded by the stress of watching his mother pack his case for the term ahead, and then meeting total strangers on the station platform who had treated him like a homecoming prince. By the time he felt ready to walk down the steep cottage stairs and find a hot drink it had gone eleven.

The tall man stood by the entrance to the kitchen. 'It's a little late for breakfast and a little early for lunch. But, young man, it's the perfect time for brunch. Are you up for bacon, sausages, tomatoes, toast from home-baked bread, two fresh-farm poached eggs, washed down with freshly-squeezed orange juice and a cup of tea, or coffee if you prefer? My first cup of the day has to be tea, but it is always swiftly followed by coffee from our new Nespresso machine. A birthday gift, delivered by Amazon.'

Joel didn't know how to respond. 'I... I...'

'Go through that door into the sitting room,' Malcolm gestured, 'and I'll see you in the dining room in a minute.'

Joel entered the little sitting room, full of knick-knacks, old-style furniture, paintings of dogs and horses, framed embroidery, silver and porcelain objects, and a large wooden mantelpiece above a fire grate resplendent with logs. He walked in his socks on soft wool carpet through an archway into a dining room with French windows leading out to a small but pretty garden with a pergola, and neatly tended beds with shrubs including lavender. If he stood on tiptoe, he could see over the rear stone wall to the vast moorland wilderness. On the rosewood dining table was a single place mat with horses, hounds and a laughing fox, accompanied by silver cutlery, two coasters and a white linen napkin.

Malcolm called from the kitchen. 'Tea? Or coffee?'

'Coffee please.'

Almost instantly, Malcolm came through carrying a pot of coffee. 'The Nespresso machine is good for single cups, but nothing beats a full pot of ground coffee.' He put the pot down on a mat and hurried back to the kitchen from which unbelievably tasty smells were emanating. A moment later, Malcolm returned with a porcelain cup and saucer, and a small matching jug of milk. 'Please help yourself. Hold the lid when you pour. Back in a minute.'

Joel was puzzled. Where was his wife?

'Audrey has taken a few groceries over to your godmother,' Malcolm said from the kitchen. 'She won't be going in, just leaving the bags on the doorstep. I fear, Eleanor has caught whatever is currently going around.'

'At least the vaccine will stop her getting really ill.'

'She's not had it.' Malcolm entered carrying a dinner plate with a classic English breakfast beautifully laid out.

'You mean the booster?'

'Any form of inoculation. She had the virus in the first wave, so felt she had her own inbuilt immunity.' He put the delicious meal on the mat in front of Joel. 'Orange juice?'

Joel was stunned. He'd never seen a breakfast like it.

'Back in a tick.' Malcolm scuttled back to the kitchen. Seconds later he reappeared with a glass of orange juice, which he placed on a coaster. 'Tuck in. There's tomato ketchup, HP sauce, salt and pepper. Just help yourself.'

'Thank you so much. This is amazing.' He pulled his phone out of his trouser pocket and lined up a shot.

'What are you doing?'

Joel smiled at Malcolm. 'It's for my Instagram followers. I'll get a load of weird emojis for eating meat, but I like to be controversial.' He clicked and tapped the screen then put the phone on the table and picked up a knife. 'I should do a video of me breaking the egg, but I can't wait.' He stabbed a perfect, yellow dome and watched the yoke spread. He cut off the end of a sausage and dipped it in. 'This tastes so good,' he said, munching. 'Thank you.'

'My absolute pleasure.' Malcolm poured coffee into two cups, holding the pot lid in place. 'So, are you all set for tomorrow?'

Joel swallowed and reached for the orange juice. 'I think so. They told us what to bring. I just hope my mum packed it all.'

'How old did you say you are?'

'Nineteen. Just.'

'And your mother still packs for you?'

'If I do it, everything comes out creased.'

Malcolm laughed. 'I'll have to show you the techniques.'

'Don't worry, it doesn't matter if it's creased when I go home.'

They heard the front door open and close. 'Hello?'

'We're in here,' Malcolm called back.

Joel put down his knife and fork, wiped his mouth on the napkin and got to his feet as Audrey came through via the kitchen. 'Ooh coffee. Any left?'

'Of course. That's why I made a pot.'

She looked at Joel, standing. 'Did you sleep well?'

'Yes, thank you.'

'Sit down, please,' Audrey said. 'You must treat this as a second home. I think you're going to be here for quite a while.'

Joel sat down but didn't pick up his knife and fork. He looked at Audrey who drew up a chair, opposite. 'Is she very sick?' he asked.

'It has hit her quite hard. She spoke or, rather, croaked to me from an upper window. She's pretty wretched. Hopefully, it will only last a day or two. I'll definitely keep an eye on her.'

'So will I,' Joel said. 'She's really special.'

Malcolm handed Audrey a cup of coffee. 'Yes, she is,' he said.

Audrey turned to Malcolm. 'By the way, her new friend Ron showed up with a bag of goodies. He said he'd bought top of the range personal protection equipment and so could go in and cook for her. I left her leaning out of the top window arguing with him.'

'It's good to know there's someone else looking out for her,' Malcolm said.

Joel nodded; his mouth too full to speak. Finally, he managed to swallow. 'I am a bit puzzled.'

Both Malcolm and Audrey looked at him, questioningly.

'I don't understand the difference,' he said, 'between inoculation and vaccination. I s'pose I could look it up.' He reached for his phone.

'No need to consult that little contraption, dear boy,' Malcolm said. 'Standing here before you is an English master who morphed into a copywriter.'

'Wow. You must know a lot.'

Audrey spluttered from the far side of the table.

'More than some appreciate,' Malcolm said. 'I shall explain whilst you eat your breakfast.'

Joel picked up his knife and fork.

'In the olden days,' Malcolm continued, 'long before any of us were born, people used to graft plants together to make a new, stronger one. The word inoculare is Latin for to graft. The word derives from oculus which is Latin for eye or bud. You did study Latin, I take it?'

His mouth full, and resisting a smile, Joel shook his head.

'If ever a language is not dead, it's Latin,' Malcolm added.

'Those poor schoolboys,' Audrey said. 'How they must've suffered.'

'On the contrary. My classes were very popular. I shall continue. Anything grafted is to inoculate. When seeking a cure for smallpox, British scientists implanted pathogens into healthy people through a small break in the skin to help them build resistance to the disease.'

'Darling,' Audrey interjected. 'Joel is eating.'

'To conclude,' Malcolm said. 'Cows suffered from cowpox, but farmers discovered that cowpox actually immunised farmers from smallpox. The virus that caused cowpox was known as vaccinia which derives from the Latin word for cow, vacca. Hence the word vaccination.'

'I'm still a bit puzzled,' Joel said.

'Aren't we all,' Audrey responded.

Joel put down his knife. 'What you're saying is, people were inoculated against smallpox and, later, vaccinated against smallpox.'

Malcolm clapped his hands. 'You've got it in one.'

'Thank God for that,' Audrey said.

Joel picked up his knife and fork. 'I still don't understand the difference,' he said. 'But what I do know is, this breakfast is brilliant.'

Malcolm reached for the coffee pot. 'I trust you'll

inform your Instagram followers to that effect.'
Mouth full, Joel smiled and nodded vigorously.

CHAPTER EIGHT
Monday, 6th September

It was barely seven in the morning when Magdalena first saw her. She had got up early to make final preparations for opening Wax Polish and was cleaning the etched glass on the salon door. The emotional punch she felt seeing the young woman out for an early run was the same feeling she had when she first met Tina at Harper Dennis. She was happy with Trevor. They had good sex. She wanted to marry him. The last thing she needed was to fall in love with the long-legged, honey blonde, running with such great ease up Hawksmead High Street.

'Can I make you breakfast?'

She looked at Trevor standing on the stairs in a T-shirt and boxer shorts. He was a kind, good-looking man for his forty-eight years; taller than Magdalena, and she was tall, quite well-muscled and most important of all, no beer belly. His chest, now smooth, felt good to her fingertips.

'That would be lovely. Mushrooms in fridge. And tomatoes. On toast would be good. No egg. No added salt, please.'

'Coffee?'

'Green tea. In cupboard above sink.'

'Fifteen minutes?'

She smiled. 'You good husband-to-be.'

He laughed and went back upstairs.

She switched on the salon lights and the brightness of the white walls, white shelving and white marble-effect floor pleased her. She checked her phone and selected a music list for her white Sonos speakers. All her equipment and supplies were sanitised and ready to go. Even so, she felt nervous. She always did at the beginning of the week especially as she worked alone. Would she be overwhelmed with customers, or would she be twiddling her thumbs and going even more broke?

On that Monday morning, his rucksack packed and his tummy full of Malcolm's scrambled eggs on toast, Joel caught the bus to Undermere School of Dramatic Art, expecting at least a couple of fun days if not an entire freshers' week, to get to know other first-year students, play a few party games, down a few drinks. He could not have been more wrong. USDA was not a university; it offered only two undergraduate courses: either a BA (Hons) in technical theatre, film, TV, and radio; or training to be a professional actor. Joel sauntered into his new home through the modest main entrance and the clock turned back to when he first went to big school. The atmosphere was tense, excited, and loud. Second and third-year students eyed the new intake, often making raucous and outrageous comments but offering no guidance as to where to go or what to do. Following others, he found his way to a changing room where he could stash his rucksack in a metal locker.

Long fingers at the end of a languid hand gripped his arm. 'Better hurry, sweetie. The show's about to begin.'

Joel looked into a smooth-skinned, smiling face with perfect teeth, full lips, and sculpted eyebrows. 'What show?'

After a mad rush down the street, dodging people hurrying about their business, Joel and his new friend, who he thought was male but couldn't be sure, were panting for breath when they slumped into the stalls of the Rickman Theatre and looked up at the stage where he had auditioned for what seemed an eternity.

A welcome by the school's principal, a former Shakespearean actor known to all as Sir Larry but officially Sir Lawrence Baehre was followed by little speeches from the school's faculty; a ragbag of former thespians, Joel considered well past their sell-by dates. At the end they were each handed an information folder covering all aspects of life at USDA including items Joel thought were totally irrelevant to becoming a film star, most notably identity and gender, although Ethan, his new friend, was clearly non-binary. Later he discovered that male and female students changed in the same locker room, albeit at different ends and he wondered aloud at the lack of privacy.

'Dear boy,' Ethan said, sotto voce. 'This is theatre. Back stage there is no male and female changing areas. If a star is a bit fussy there may be a screen but getting naked is what we're all about.'

'Really?' Joel was stunned.

'As an actor, you cannot say no if a script requires you to get up close and personal with a complete stranger,' Ethan said, getting way too close for Joel's comfort. 'Of course, these days an intimacy co-ordinator is de riguer to ensure untouchables remain untouched. I must admit, there are many times out clubbing I wished for an intimacy co-ordinator.'

The excited fresh intake of students all dreaming of success in a highly competitive profession were summoned to Studio Two for their first class. Joel stood at the back in his new exercise joggers and sweatshirt, with bare feet on old linoleum. To one side was a battered upright piano; and fitted to two corners were old-style speakers with wires trailing to a compact disk player sitting on a table next to a pile of CDs in plastic cases. Had the school not discovered Spotify? Full-height mirrors lined the walls and there were three tall windows with opaque glass panes.

Facing the class was June Dearlove. She was ridiculously elongated with short, lank, dark hair and a full mouth with big teeth separated at the front by a wide gap.

'Stand with your legs shoulder-width apart,' Miss Dearlove said, 'and shake the tension out of your arms, your hands, your shoulders.'

Everyone jigged and tried to shake out their mostly imaginary tension.

'Now follow me.' She pressed Play and Poker Face, an old Lady Gaga song, emanated from the speakers. 'Hands up, reach for the ceiling, stretch, stretch, sway to the left, stretch, stretch, and to the ceiling, now to the right.'

Joel loved looking at the girls at the front who wore leggings, providing many a happy view, especially the beauty from the railway station. If he'd been smart, he'd have guessed why a stunning Californian had come to this part of the world. She was tall, with fabulous hair casually curled into a sort of twist, held in place by a plastic bulldog clip. He'd deliberately avoided catching her eye as he knew he had to play it cool, a lot easier said than done. He felt ashamed of his lust, but he knew he wasn't alone. Several of his fellow male students jostled to be in the back row. Were they all guilty of classic male prurience, or was it fear of being singled out?

Lady Gaga suddenly stopped. 'At the back. Pay attention.'

Joel was jerked away from his romantic reverie and felt the piercing eyes of Miss Dearlove on him. 'Sorry, my mind was elsewhere,' he stammered.

'If you don't want to be here, there are plenty of others waiting for the call.' Miss Dearlove looked at the whole group. 'Theatre is tough, it requires total concentration. It also requires trust. Trust in your comrades. Trust that when your back is turned, they will not leer at your butt.' She turned her penetrating gaze back to Joel. 'Is that clear?'

Joel felt blood surging through his veins as the young women who stood at the front of the movement class almost as one, turned to see the subject of Miss Dearlove's ire. This time there was no avoiding catching the eye of the girl from the station. But it wasn't her who smiled and winked. It was his new best friend.

When his mother said goodbye to him at King's Cross Station, she told him what to expect. 'For the first time in your life you will know what it's like to be a girl. You will feel eyes on you; you will feel the casual touch of a man with the power to make or break your career. He may be a lead actor, married with children; or he may be a theatre or film director who can turn you into a star. Many pretty boys have succumbed to the unwelcome gaze of a great director wearing Gucci shoes and tight jeans.'

'Don't worry mum. I can look after myself. I'll be fine.'

His mother kissed and hugged him. 'I'm going to miss you.' She pulled away. 'Don't forget your annual check-up. Whatever you've got on, it's mandatory.'

Clean Bandit halted mid verse and Joel was yanked back to his movement class, which felt more like a warm-up for *Strictly Come Dancing* than acting as he knew it.

'Young man, what's the matter?' Joel felt Miss Dearlove's penetrating stare.

He mumbled, 'I'm an actor not a dancer.' The class turned as one to stare at him.

'Really?' Miss Dearlove folded her arms. 'And what is Ryan Gosling? An actor or a dancer?'

'He's a film star,' Joel replied. There were a few suppressed giggles. *Touché Miss Dearlove*, he thought.

'Was he born a film star, or did he have to work his socks off as you must do?' She took a breath and encompassed the whole class with her penetrating gaze. 'If you don't work 'til your soles bleed, there are plenty of others who are prepared to. You have succeeded in getting into one of the most competitive drama schools in the world and yet only a few of you will actually make it in what is an unfair, unkind, and unscrupulous business. We are here to help you attain the tools to survive and thrive with the very best.' She turned her attention back to Joel. 'I have yet to meet an actor who has not needed to dance at some point. And it's not just about dance. It's about posture, how to walk, how to run, how to sit down and get up.' She sighed. 'My God, you have so much to learn, and yet you have wasted the first hour of your first day at drama school.' Much to Joel's alarm, she weaved through the students in front of him and came right up to his face. 'Wasting your own time is a crime. Wasting the time of your fellow students is an unforgivable sin. Do it again, and you will be out. Do I make myself clear?'

'Yes Miss Dearlove.' Could his face be any hotter, or redder?

She returned to the front of the class. 'Right, let's shake the tension out. Legs apart. Arms loosely by you side. Now shake.'

The floor vibrated as the whole class pounded their feet and shook clammy relief out of their fingertips.

At the same moment Joel was being roasted by Miss Dearlove, his godmother had never felt worse. Despite being consumed by an overwhelming virus, Eleanor was embarrassed to be nursed by a man she had only, really, just met. She watched as Ron, dressed to the nines in protective plastic including a Perspex visor, medical-grade face mask, plastic apron and latex gloves, carried a tray with chicken soup and great hunks of white bread he had baked himself in her kitchen. She knew she must look as terrible as she felt and yet this man, who was slim and fit as a butcher's dog, fussed around her. She needed a shower. She could smell her own stink - this time the virus had left her with full taste and smell, but she was too weak to get out of bed, a bed that was soaked and stained and would be heading for the tip if she managed to survive.

'Ron, you must go.' It hurt her throat to talk. 'You've done more than enough. You'll need to isolate, just in case.'

He stood still and looked at her. 'Until I met you, I cared for no one, not even meself. I had nothing. I'd lost the only person I loved and had no desire to live. You have given me purpose. Letting me help you at this terrible time is helping me. But, my dear, anytime you want me to go, just say the word. The last thing I want is for you to be anxious.'

'How was it?' Malcolm asked.

Joel looked at the elderly couple standing in the hallway of their pretty, terraced cottage, their expressions, expectant. 'Fine, thank you.'

'You managed to get the bus back all right,' Audrey stated. 'They are so infrequent.'

'I came by Uber. My mum's card is attached to the account.' Joel slipped off his shoes. 'I'll go and get changed and have a shower... if that's okay?'

'Oh, of course,' Malcolm said.

'It was only *fine*, was it?' Audrey asked. 'Your first day at Undermere School of Dramatic Art, arguably the greatest drama school in the world, and you rate your first day as *fine*?'

Joel knew he was going to have to give them more. 'It was better than fine. It was amazing. Unbelievable. Beautiful.'

'Beautiful?' the elderly couple said in unison.

'Well, one person in particular. You remember the girl we saw entering the pub? The one I spoke to on the station platform? Today, I discovered she's in my year.'

'Did you have a chance to chat?' Malcolm asked.

Joel half-laughed. 'Every guy in the entire drama school, not just in my year, wanted to speak to her. She's mega.'

'You're judging her by looks alone,' Audrey stated, flatly.

Joel felt her keen stare. 'Yes, but not entirely.'

'I know exactly what you mean, Joel,' Malcolm said. 'I first met Audrey on a train. Her looks, her style, the way she moved... I was completely entranced.'

'Precisely,' Joel answered, fired up that the old man understood. 'Yes, she is amazing, stunning, incredibly... *wow*... but it's not just that.'

'It's what comes through,' Malcolm added, 'after the initial attraction. It's the way she speaks, the way she laughs, her turn of phrase.'

'She only said a few words at the station. Not quite a phrase.'

'At least you had a chance to talk to her, today,' Audrey said.

Joel was quiet for a moment. 'I... I didn't get a chance to talk to her, today.'

'Why not?' Audrey probed.

He shrugged. 'Didn't get a chance.'

'Were you being cool?' Audrey asked.

Joel had no response to her question. His mother had warned him about predatory men, but she'd given him zero advice on how to attract the attention of girls. He had friends who were girls from school, but he was, much to his total embarrassment, completely inexperienced when it came to dating.

Malcolm interrupted his thoughts. 'Joel, it took me a lot of courage to ask my late wife out on a date. When I first asked Audrey, my whole body shook with fear that I would blow it. And I did. But if you and this young woman are meant to be, it will happen.'

'Not necessarily,' Audrey cut in. 'Remember, faint heart never won fair lady.'

'What?' Joel was perplexed.

'Confidence is the key to success in all things,' Audrey emphasised.

'Or the ability to fake it,' Malcolm added.

'Do you think I've blown it already?' Joel asked, almost pleadingly.

The elderly couple both laughed.

Audrey stepped forward. 'Joel, to succeed, you need to understand how women think. I can teach you.'

'But she's American. They think differently.' Joel looked from one chuckling face to the other.

'Have a shower,' Malcolm said, still smiling. 'And then come down and join us for a cup of tea and a slice of my Victoria sponge. Dinner will be a bit later.'

'Thank you.' Joel placed his shoes at the end of the row. 'I know I have a lot to learn.'

'I can assure you, Joel,' Malcolm said. 'It's a lifetime's work.'

'Whereas, most women,' Audrey added, 'take about five minutes to learn how men think.'

Joel looked at Malcolm who gave him a conspiratorial wink.

'You've not blown it, Joel,' Audrey said, touching his arm. 'Frankly, she's lucky you're interested at all.'

He gave her a tight nod and hurried upstairs, feeling a little happier.

'Ambulance service.'

'My friend's really sick. I mean ill. Really ill. She has to go to hospital.'

'Is she breathing?'

'Barely. She needs oxygen.'

'Is she conscious?'

'No. She looks comatose.'

'What is your name and address?'

My name is Ron Smith. Her address is the Olde Tea Shop, Hawksmead High Street... I dunno the postcode.'

'An ambulance has been dispatched. Please stay on the line. Is there easy access?'

'There's a door off the High Street to the left of the tea shop. I'll go down and open it.'

'Open the door and then return to the patient. Stay on the line.'

Ron hurried down the stairs and opened the door

to the street. Despite it being early evening, there was little passing traffic. He put the hall light on to help draw attention to the open door. By the time he returned to Eleanor, he could feel sweat dripping into his mask. He yearned to take it off but didn't dare. Instead, he took her hand.

'Stacy, my love. My wonderful daughter. If you have any power at all, please use it to spare my new friend, Ellie. I loved your mother. You know that. And I love you, Stacy. And I know you would like Ellie. She's special. And I don't want to lose her.'

The wail of an ambulance siren attracted his attention and he sniffed hard. Within a minute, two paramedics in full PPE were in the room. He stood back as they swiftly examined Eleanor. The female paramedic turned to him. 'Are you her husband?'

'No. A friend. I've been looking after her but instead of getting better, she's getting worse.'

'My colleague will get a chair from the ambulance so we can carry her downstairs. When we've gone, air the entire flat and scrub all the surfaces. Everywhere aerosol droplets can land. Keep your PPE on whilst you're doing it.'

Ron nodded.

'And take a test, every day for the next few days.'

CHAPTER NINE
Tuesday, 7th September

Studio One was different to Studio Two; worn carpet covered the floor and heavy drapes lined the walls. Metal chairs with wooden seats were placed in rows and after a bit of shuffling, most of the new intake of female students sat at the front, and the young men, with one notable exception, sitting behind.

Joel grabbed a chair as close to his first love as possible but far enough back to avoid the icy glare of the formidable Miss Maynard, who was explaining how important voice and speech is for an actor, especially when performing on stage. She looked about his mother's age and matched his mother's stare that could turn the bravest of souls to stone. His mind wandered as he likened her to the training sergeant in the old movie, *Full Metal Jacket*, although she hadn't grabbed anyone's balls yet! Still, early days. Joel laughed at his own joke and to his horror, Miss Maynard stopped talking and the whole room turned to look at him.

Shit.

'Step forward and bring your chair,' the training sergeant commanded, and he could swear he felt his balls shrivel. Reluctantly he picked up his chair and, like a dead man walking, weaved his way to the front of the class and found himself standing next to Cadence. He sneaked a downward glance at her, but she studiously kept looking straight ahead.

'From now on you will sit at the front,' Miss Maynard said, 'until I get tired of you.'

Joel placed his chair at the end of the front row and sat down next to Ethan.

'Everyone stand,' Miss Maynard said, 'and move your chairs to the side of the room.'

The students followed her instruction and hurried back to where they'd been sitting.

'Right. Legs, shoulder-width apart.' Miss Maynard stared at Joel who was slow to move. 'That goes for you, too, laughing boy.'

He felt his heart hammer with embarrassment. How had he let this happen? He was locked in the stocks and rotten fruit was being thrown at him.

Miss Maynard continued. 'Breathe in, feel the air flowing into your lungs and expanding your diaphragm. Open your ribs right to the bottom of your ribcage; hold, hold and gently release through your mouth and nose.'

Joel began to relax. It was only the second day. Masses of time to establish a good reputation.

'Young man.' Joel looked at Miss Maynard in horror. 'Come here.'

What? She wanted him to stand right in front of her? He shuffled his reluctant feet and stood a little way from the scary teacher. She stepped towards him and placed a hand on each of his shoulders, then turned to the class. 'You will never see a great stage actor take a breath.' She looked at him, standing way inside his exclusion zone. 'Breathe in to three, hold, hold, and gently release.' Her hands pressed down on his shoulders. 'And breathe in again to three. Take it right down and fill your lungs. Nothing should move apart from your lower ribs and diaphragm.' She looked right into Joel's eyes. 'Certainly not your shoulders.' He felt his breath quicken. 'And again.' The whole

103

room breathed in. 'Right.' She took her hands off Joel's shoulders and spoke to the class. 'Select a partner and place your hands on their shoulders. Take it in turns.'

Joel looked around for a partner, hoping to bag Cadence.

'You, stay with me.'

His head snapped back to Miss Maynard.

'There are twenty-one in the class,' she said. 'So, it's your lucky day.'

Joel could have sworn he heard a couple of his new male friends, snigger.

Ron Smith had taken every precaution he could when he cleaned the surfaces in Eleanor's flat. Luckily, antibacterial cleaning products were readily available at Beckley's, a full-service convenience store near Hawksmead Station. He was surprised to find they still operated a traffic light system at the entrance, no doubt introduced at the height of the pandemic to restrict the number of customers. He was especially annoyed when he saw a broken crock of a bloke jump the lights and hobble right up to the till to buy Irish whiskey. Had the old man not seen Ron standing by the red signal? In his former self, Ron would have had a few words, but he no longer had the fight. All he wanted now was to help his new friend as best he could ...and lead a quiet life. If there was one thing events had taught him of late, it was to live and let live. Not that anyone would believe that of him if they looked under the very big rock that hid his past.

He inspected Eleanor's flat and smiled with satisfaction. It looked spotless. He was old school and believed cleaning was women's work but, since being widowed and especially following the death of his daughter, he'd become adept at shopping for himself, cooking for himself, cleaning for himself, and had even learned how to load a washing machine unaided. Yes, Ron Smith was inordinately proud of what Ron Smith had achieved.

A few doors from the Olde Tea Shoppe, Magdalena was counting her receipts after a day full of laughter and good business, especially when compared to no business during the dark days. Her customers seemed perfectly happy to chat and drink while they waited for her to give their nails, faces and legs, expert treatment. She'd been so rushed off her feet she'd had no time to eat a sandwich or go to the loo and really needed her former assistant, Paulina, to return from Poland. She decided to give her a call.

'You come back,' Magdalena demanded in Polish.

'No. I open salon, here,' Paulina replied with far too much excitement.

'Where you get money for salon?'

'British Government. I register salon in UK, but open in Lublin. Get big grant. Clever, eh?'

Magdalena was speechless, and furious with herself for not taking advantage of all the British Government handouts during the pandemic.

'You get money, too?' Paulina asked.

'Oh, yeah, yeah,' Magdalena lied. She ended the call as quickly as possible and checked her phone to see what government grants were still available. *Nothing.*

'Hi,' a voice said with an accent straight from the movies. Magdalena looked up from her laptop and saw standing by the open door, the epitome of beauty, American style - long blonde hair, wide-set eyes, straight nose, full mouth, perfect boobs, slim waist, narrow hips, long legs. Her visitor smiled and Magdalena added perfect teeth to the list. 'My name's

Cadence. I live at the pub. You know it?'

All Magdalena could do was nod and stare. Where Magdalena was exotically rounded with a hint of Romany, this girl was sleek and lithe. She knew of only one other woman who could hold a candle to her.

'Er yes, of course,' Magdalena said, her voice cracking as she stood. She cleared her throat. 'You want wax?'

Cadence smiled. 'A job would be better.'

'Here?'

'I think you could use my help.'

'What skills you have?'

'I trained at a salon in Solana Beach.'

Magdalena reached for her phone. 'What name?'

Cadence seemed to hesitate.

'You make job up?'

'The salon is closed.'

Magdalena put the phone down and looked at Cadence who for the first time seemed lacking in confidence, her hand resting on her flat stomach. After a moment, Cadence carefully closed the door.

'Search for *Shooting at Spa, Solana Beach*.'

Magdalena took a breath and picked up her phone. 'Shoot at spa, let's see.' She swiped her phone's screen. 'A lone robber shot and killed the owner of Clearwater Spa, in Solana Beach on Saturday, stealing the day's takings. The owner's teenage daughter was severely injured.' Magdalena felt her mouth go dry as she stared at Cadence. 'Your mom is dead?'

'Almost two years so I may need a little practice. I could do your nails, now.'

Magdalena couldn't help glancing at her own hands. 'Yes. Why not? You like tea? Coffee? Wine?'

Cadence smiled. 'I'm good, thanks.' She slipped off

her shoulder bag and slung her jacket over a chair.

'I sorry about your mother,' Magdalena said.

'It's why I'm here,' Cadence responded as she washed her hands in one of the basins. 'You don't have a constitution giving every idiot the right to carry a gun.'

'And you? You were shot, too?'

Cadence dried her hands on a soft, white towel. 'It's all in the past.' She looked around the salon. 'Nice place.'

'You're hired. When can you start?'

'Take a seat,' Cadence commanded, gesturing to one of the workstations.

Magdalena smiled and sat in the client chair.

Cadence sat opposite her. 'Hand please.'

She offered her left hand and felt a great surge from within as long, slim fingers examined each of her nails.

'Not bad,' Cadence said as she picked up a bottle of nail-polish remover and a circular cotton pad. She worked quickly and precisely, removing lacquer from all ten digits. She took a moment to select an appropriate emery board and filed and shaped Magdalena's nails. The awkward silence was mercifully filled by the sounds of Classic FM, playing through the salon's speakers.

'Good work. No need to do more,' Magdalena said.

Cadence ignored her instruction and searched through the many bottles stored on the station. She pumped cream into her palm and proceeded to massage each of Magdalena's hands with the most delicate, yet firm touch. The sensations were exquisite and within barely a minute, Magdalena felt a ripple rising from her toes, building through her ankles, climbing up through her thighs until she gasped, unable to contain the overwhelming explosion.

'Are you okay? Have I hurt you?'

Magdalena took a few deep breaths then looked at Cadence. 'It's a hot flush. I had Covid.'

'You're not ill?'

Magdalena took another breath. 'Long Covid. My nerves. Not infectious.' She pulled her hands away from Cadence and stood up. The door to the salon opened and Trevor walked in. He paused and looked from Magdalena to the young American.

'I hope I'm not interrupting.'

Magdalena felt a hot flush burn her cheeks. 'No. This is Cadence and she's going to work here.'

'When I'm not at school.'

'School?'

'Drama school.' She grabbed her jacket and shoulder bag. 'You know, the academy in Undermere.'

'You're an actress?' Trevor asked.

'Actor.'

He smiled. 'I stand corrected.'

'I'd better go. I have a speech to learn.'

'You know,' Magdalena said. 'Barman in pub. He was actor. He help you learn lines.'

Cadence nodded. 'I'll call by after school each day and see if you need my help.'

'Saturday, usually chock-a-block,' Magdalena said.

'Then I'll see you Saturday, if not before.' She looked at Trevor. 'Good to meet you.'

He held the door open and both he and Magdalena watched the extraordinary young woman as she strode off into the early evening twilight.

CHAPTER TEN
Wednesday, 8th September

Massimo Bisterzo fitted a Perspex visor over his double-masked face and looked at the alien staring back at him. The only way he could get through the day as a Consultant Physician in Intensive Care was minute by minute. He couldn't think for a moment about how life used to be. All he could do was take care of his own physical wellbeing for the good of his patients.

He stepped out into the main corridor and headed for his unit; his security pass gave him immediate access to the war zone. He had fought the virus through its many manifestations but just when the world was finally relaxing and returning to normal, there had been another surge. In the early days of the pandemic, people believed that those who became seriously ill usually had an underlying weakness – they had smoked, were morbidly obese, had diabetes, heart disease, cancer. But not with the latest variant. This time, the obvious targets were often spared and the fit and healthy, felled.

Doctor Manson approached him. She had been on all night and looked like it. 'Big problem,' she said.

He followed her to an Intensive Care bay and saw the shape of a woman. Massimo pulled a couple of blue latex gloves from a wall-mounted dispenser and approached the patient. Despite her mouth and nose being covered with an oxygen mask, she looked familiar. He examined her chart. 'Eleanor Houghton,' he said.

'Do you know her?'

He looked at Doctor Manson. 'I think I met her once. Opera.'

'Oprah? As in the talk show host?'

'Opera as in Puccini. She's a singer.'

Doctor Manson looked at the patient. 'What are we going to do if paxlovid doesn't work? Try another antiviral?'

'Dialysis.' He handed her the chart. 'Set it up, now.'

'Haemofiltration?'

He shook his head. 'It's acute kidney injury. We cannot delay.'

Unaware of his godmother's critical condition, Joel made a point of standing at the front of the stage-fighting class. He was light on his feet and considered sword fighting a discipline in which he could really shine.

Cy Plant seemed old to Joel despite his almost elastic muscles attached to a lean and wiry frame. 'There are many forms of fighting on stage, film and TV,' Plant said, his diction, overly-precise in Joel's opinion. 'For a fight to work, for it to look real, it requires the same level of accuracy in execution as an actor speaking one of Shakespeare's sonnets.' His voice sounded so rich in tone, it cloyed Joel's ears. 'There is never, and I repeat, never a time when you should adlib a fight. A sword, even a blunt one, can kill. Second: never devise your own fight routine. Every fight must be arranged by an experienced arranger. Mistakes will happen, but it is up to every one of you to protect your fellow actor. You are not opponents, or enemies. It is drama. Pretend. Make believe. Even on film, where it all looks so real, it is fake. Never forget that. If I see anyone putting another student at risk, it will be instant dismissal from this academy. There will be no warning. No yellow card as in football. Straight to red. There are plenty of other actors waiting in the wings. Do I make myself clear?'

Nobody answered or moved. Joel considered Cy Plant with his leathery face and lank, long hair a tad over-dramatic.

Mr Plant picked up a broadsword from a battered wooden table with metal legs and looked at his students. 'Joel.'

Thud went Joel's heart. Had Mr Leatherface read his mind?

'Would you go over to that crate and hand out the swords?'

Joel nodded and went over to a large, scarred wooden box with rope handles at each end and a heavy, hinged lid. He picked up one of many battered swords and handed the hilt to the first in line. When he saw who it was, he tried to catch her eye, but she was focused on the weapon. It took Joel over a minute to hand out all the swords until he was left with a two-handed broadsword with a long hilt and an impressive blade. He had to use both hands to lift it.

'Everyone got a sword?' Mr Plant, asked. 'Good.'

'I have been left with this beast,' Joel said, and immediately regretted his petulant tone.

'Partner me and I'll show you how to use that big boy.'

Was he joking, calling it a big boy? Joel looked at his fellow students and not one was sniggering or even trying to hold back a grin. He dragged the sword across the cracked linoleum to the front of class.

Mr Plant lifted his own stage sword, which was a lot newer than the ones Joel had handed out. Looking sinewy and way too athletic for his clearly ancient years, Mr Plant assumed a classic fencing on-guard position with his right foot in front of the other and his sword held high and parallel to the floor. 'Romeo and Juliet, Act One, Scene One, fight. Look at me... this is how you will never start a fight on stage. This is a fencing stance. Forget it. Your fight arranger will direct you to stand face on, sideways, even with your back to your opponent.'

'Excuse me, sir.' A chubby young man with spectacles who Joel hadn't spoken to yet, tentatively raised his hand.

'Name?'

'Mr Plant, sir,' came the reply.

'Your name, man,' Cy Plant said. 'Believe it or not, I know my own. What's yours?'

This time, Joel spotted a few suppressed smiles.

Red faced, the student responded, 'Rick Hanbury.'

'Your question Mr Hanbury?'

'Are there any masks we can wear? I'm a bit worried about my glasses.'

Mr Plant rested the tip of his sword on a section of wooden floor bereft of lino. 'Have you seen a Shakespeare play or any play or film where the actors in a swordfight are wearing masks?'

Rick Hanbury took a moment to think. 'No sir.'

Cy Plant looked around the class. 'Lesson one. The safety of Mr Hanbury's glasses is in all your hands.'

Various students glanced at each other.

Plant stamped his booted foot and he achieved one hundred per cent attention. 'Every single cut and thrust you make will be planned and rehearsed in slow motion. Think of it like a ballet. Each dancer knows exactly what the other's move is going to be.

Stage fighting is not real; it simply has to look real. Of course, accidents can happen. For example...' Mr Plant turned to Joel. 'Mr Redmond, hold your sword at an angle. You have a heavy, long, two-handed sword and I a lightweight blade. It's an uneven fight but the scene requires it. My character arcs his blade to slice off your head. Your character, realising that he cannot move his heavy sword in time to parry the blow, drops down on his haunches and the blade merely slices the air. Let's do it.'

The two faced each other and Mr Plant made an exaggerated loop so that Joel had plenty of time to duck.

'Good,' Mr Plant said.

Joel relaxed and looked at Cadence who did not even glance in his direction. Out of the corner of his eye he saw Mr Plant swing his sword. He had no time to duck or parry the blow. The blade flashed in the fluorescent light and stopped inches before chopping Joel's neck.

Mr Plant looked at his students whilst keeping the scarred steel close to Joel's throat. 'An actor makes a mistake. He forgets to parry the attack stroke. Does the actor get injured or killed because he forgot one of his moves?'

Cadence raised her hand. Mr Plant lowered his sword and looked at her. 'Sir. I believe it's incumbent on the actor making the stroke to the head to stop the blow, as you did.'

'Exactly.' Mr Plant turned back to Joel. 'Do not move,' he growled before emitting an ear-crunching yell as he swung his sword above his head and brought the tip to a halt by Joel's nose. He dropped the blade and looked at the students. 'The health and safety of your fellow actor is always in your hands. No play, no film is worth the death of an actor. Of course, there can be accidents, but safety, safety, safety must be the constant dialogue in your head.' He turned to Joel. 'Put the beast back in the box and use my sword.' He passed the sword hilt to Joel and turned to face the class. 'We work in a world of make-believe. Never ever forget that.'

Joel tossed the two-handed sword back into the battle-worn box and regretted his action as the clatter of the blade was much louder than he'd anticipated. He felt the whole room staring at him.

'Of course,' Cy Plant continued. 'If you're on stage at the National and blood is drawn, you do not drop your weapon and shout, "Ow, my finger!". You carry on unless your finger is no longer attached to your hand. In that case, you may pick up your finger, briefly address the audience, and depart the stage.'

Seated at a circular, scarred table in the old-style kitchen of her childhood home, Christina took her husband's hand. 'How are you feeling?'

'Lucky.' His surprising response was followed by a wintry smile.

'Lucky?' She was flummoxed. 'We both still have the virus.'

'I am lucky to be sitting with the woman I love in this dated kitchen with its pine cabinets, chipped vinyl worktop and all-in-one gas cooker.'

She laughed. 'It's not as though my parents couldn't afford an update. Of course, a pine kitchen was a major selling point when they bought the house in the 1980s.'

Abel's phone buzzed and he took it out of his pocket. 'It's a text from Graham's wife.' She waited patiently whilst her husband read the message, then put the phone face down on the table. 'The cancer is small,

Stage One. Almost undetectable. The plan is to cut it out and whack him with radiation so there's no recurrence. The prognosis is good.' He sniffed.

She squeezed his hand.

He looked at her. 'He's my friend. Yes, I employ him, but he is my friend.'

'How are you feeling?' Gary asked as he entered the kitchen and headed for the kettle.

Christina looked up. 'Baby's fine. But, Abel and I both scored two stripes. You?'

'I've just tested positive, again, too.' He half-filled the kettle and returned it to its electrical plate before tapping the switch. 'I don't know what name they're giving this new variant, but it should be called Regan.'

'Reagan as in Ronald?' Abel asked. 'President of the United States?'

'He means Regan as in The Exorcist,' Christina said, almost laughing.

'Now I'm completely lost.' Abel rocked back in his chair.

'My brother used to love horror movies,' Christina said. 'When I broke up with some creep, Sam thought the best cure for a broken heart was blood and gore – by the way, I didn't have a broken heart, it was my ego, and it was only slightly bruised. Anyway, Sam thought he would take my mind off the creep by scaring me half to death. One of the films he made me watch was The Exorcist where this young girl called Regan is taken over by the devil and green vomit shoots from her mouth. The DVD is probably still lurking in this house.'

'It's certainly lurking within me,' Gary said, as he poured boiling water onto a teabag. 'My guts are completely churned up.'

'Let's watch it,' Abel said. 'I could do with a bit of distraction.'

'I'll probably run out of the house, screaming,' Christina said.

Gary opened the fridge door. 'Uniform is outside at the front to ensure we don't leave. They're taking Regan very seriously.'

Abel got up from the table and looked through the kitchen window into the rear garden. Hector was chasing a rabbit. 'Do our neighbours have any pets?'

'The house next door keeps a couple of fluffy bunnies. I'm surprised the fox hasn't got them. He's pretty clever.'

'I think Hector has.'

Gary dropped his cup of tea in the sink and dashed out of the kitchen. A few seconds later they watched as he ran into the garden and chased after the dog.

Christina eased her bulk up from the table. 'Tea?'

'I've never had rabbit stew,' Abel responded.

'Oh, don't say that.' She picked Gary's broken cup out of the sink. 'My parents' best Royal Doulton. Thank you, Hector.' She dropped the pieces in a flip-top plastic bin.

Abel turned away from the window. 'Any whisky?'

'My father kept a secret stash of Glenfiddich for my mother. She always said she liked a couple of fingers in the evening.'

Abel roared with laughter.

'I was about sixteen before I understood the joke.'

He sat back down, still laughing. 'What wonderful parents you had.'

'They were pretty special.'

He got back up from the chair and wrapped his arms around her.

'They would've loved you,' she said, and she kissed him on the lips. 'But not as much as I do. Is it breaking the law if two Covid cases get a little variant?'

He chuckled. 'I think it's now the law that we do.'

They kissed again.

'What about the baby?' he whispered.

'Having a nap,' she whispered back.

Ron Smith paid the taxi driver with cash and got out of the Ford Galaxy. He adjusted his mask, put on a pair of horn-rimmed spectacles and entered the slowly rotating carousel door. He shuffled, impatiently, in his own section until he could escape into the reception area of Undermere General Hospital. He knew where to go having made one seismic visit during his daughter's final hours before he pulled the plug on her life-support.

Despite his near three score years, Ron liked to think of himself as sharp as a boxer, but taking the stairs two at a time whilst wearing a mask was not such a smart move and he was gasping for air by the time he reached the Intensive Care Unit.

He was approached by a senior member of the nursing staff, who pointed an infrared thermometer at his forehead. 'My name's Gavin. How are you feeling, today?'

Ron looked at the young man. 'Just fine, sonny.'

'And who are we visiting?'

'Eleanor Houghton.'

'Are you a relative?'

Ron took another deep breath. 'I'm not a relative, but I am a very good friend.'

'I'm sorry, sir. Only close relatives can enter the ICU.'

Ron was prepared for this and pulled out a British passport. 'This is my friend's. I wouldn't have it if she and I weren't real close. I was the one who called the ambulance.' Then came the exaggeration. 'I live with her.'

Gavin took the passport and looked at Eleanor's photo. He handed it back.

'Please sanitise your hands then follow me. We have to get you kitted up.'

'That bad, eh?'

'fraid so.'

'How's she doin'?'

'Professor Bisterzo will be able to give you a full account. He'll be available, soon.'

'Just give me the bottom line.'

Gavin stopped walking and looked at Ron through his Perspex visor. 'The virus appears to have shut down her kidneys. Acute tubular injury.'

'Can you restart them?'

'Professor Bisterzo is best placed to answer that question.'

'I'm asking you. I'm not interested in rank.'

Gavin paused a moment. 'We are able to treat the virus and Eleanor is responding, but we're not sure what exactly caused the rapid decline. Whatever the reason, the damage to her kidneys is serious.'

'What's the answer? Dial assist?'

'Yes. Dialysis,' the nurse emphasised the word, 'is the only long-term solution.'

'What about a kidney transplant?'

'Unlikely, at her age. It's a long list.'

'She can have one of mine.'

Trevor was seated at his desk in his estate agency, Harper Dennis, updating properties on his website and hoping for a lunchtime rush, or even a trickle. Somehow, he'd managed to keep his business afloat during the pandemic thanks to the grants he'd received from the British Government. For a lot of the time, his only employee had been on furlough.

'How did you fill your days, Max?' he'd asked the young man on the first day back.

'You know, YouTube, gaming. I bought a new Xbox. It's so fast.'

What was not so fast was his employee's work rate. It was as though all that time bingeing on YouTube videos and hour upon hour gaming on his Xbox had turned his grey cells to mush. But he did have his uses and was only paid the legal minimum wage.

Trevor pushed back his chair and stepped towards the agency's large window with its display of properties for sale and rental. Through the glass he watched the comings and goings of the almost bustling town of Undermere. In recent times his thoughts had become more and more reflective and often floated back to when his estate agency was thriving, when he was still married to Olivia, and when Tina – or rather Lady Cornfield – still worked for him.

'Boss.'

Trevor jumped. He was so absorbed by his thoughts he hadn't noticed the door opening.

'Sandwich.' Max tossed a paper bag onto Trevor's desk. 'You owe me…'

Trevor interrupted. 'Take it out of petty cash.'

Max pulled open a drawer in Trevor's desk and removed a metal tin. He opened the lid. 'There's only a few pence in here.'

Trevor removed a five-pound note from his wallet.

'What about yesterday?'

'Remind me, tomorrow.'

Max snatched the note from Trevor's fingertips. 'You should learn to pay your debts on time. And pay proper wages.'

Trevor was about to retort when someone caught his eye. He stepped closer to the window and saw a young woman waiting for the green man before crossing the street. It was the American he'd met in Magdalena's salon, he was sure. She was just the kind of person that could really generate sales. He tried to remember her name. It was one of those weird American monikers.

The lights changed and Trevor watched the young woman stride across the road. He was taken by her long limbs, thick blonde hair, and unadorned beauty.

'Back in a sec, Max.' He opened the agency door and called. 'Candace! Candace!'

She strode up to him and gave him a megawatt smile. 'Hi, how are you?' The simple phrase with its American cadence was laced with promise.

'I'm well, thank you. Could I have a word?'

She looked a bit surprised and shrugged. 'Sure.'

He pushed open the agency door and held it. Max hurried up to her. 'Are you looking to rent?'

'Thank you, no. I'm perfectly happy where I am.'

'Candace, would you like a cup of coffee?' Trevor asked.

'It's Cadence and 'erb tea would be lovely. I was just going to the health food shop to buy a pack.'

'Max will get it for you.'

'Will I?' Max asked, annoyed.

'I need some for the cupboard. Clients love it.' He looked at Max. 'Two packs of mint tea.' He turned to Cadence. 'Is that all right?'

'I can get it,' she said, and she reached for the door

handle.

'Perhaps you and I could have a quick chat,' Trevor said, 'while Max goes to the shop.'

Max stared at Trevor, his eyes flecked with flint. 'And with what do I buy it?'

Trevor took out his wallet and removed his bank card.

'What's the PIN?' Max asked.

'Tap.'

Max snatched the card, gave Cadence a quick up and down, opened the door and slammed it shut behind him.

'Interesting guy,' she said.

'Come and have a seat.'

She didn't move but she did cast her eyes around the agency. 'Not many customers.'

'It's mostly online these days. They usually only come in to sign contracts if they're renting, or to pick up keys if they've completed on a purchase. It's not how it was, face to face, which is a pity.' He smiled at the young woman, hoping she couldn't detect any signs of classic male lust.

'I know what you're thinking,' she said.

Had she read his mind?

She smiled. 'You want me to work for you?'

'No. Yes. I mean it would be great.'

'I already have a job at Wax Polish. You know, with your friend.'

'What about the holidays? Or are you going back to the States?'

'No.'

He watched as she wandered around the agency looking at unoccupied desks and chairs, and a meeting area with sofa and coffee table. She opened a door and peered into a small kitchen.

'What happened to your agency?' she asked.

'The pandemic happened.'

She looked at him. 'You have the aura of a successful businessman - nice watch, quality suit, but something happened that was more fundamental than the virus.'

'How old are you?' he asked.

'Nineteen.'

He smiled and shook his head. 'How did you get so wise?'

'My mom raised me as a grown-up.'

He admired her easy way. 'I once had a negotiator just like you. Her name was Tina.'

'What happened?'

'She got married.'

'Why did she leave her job?'

'Two reasons,' Trevor said. 'I didn't make her a partner and her husband joined the Met Police, in London.'

'I'm not looking to make partner or get married,' Cadence said. 'My ambitions lie elsewhere.'

'Great. Why not work here when you're not needed at Wax Polish?'

She nodded and smiled, and he bathed in her radiance. 'It still doesn't explain,' she said, 'why you let your business go.'

'You are smart, just like Tina. She could always tell when I was holding something back.'

'You don't have to tell me.'

'I invested my wife's inheritance in a bunch of properties in a city called Hull, without her knowledge, and lost most of her money. We broke up, I took my eye off the business, and here I stand.'

The door banged open, and Max strode in. He tossed

a paper bag with the packs of tea on Trevor's desk. 'Don't expect me to make it,' he said.

Trevor opened the bag and gave a green box to Cadence. 'On me.'

'Thank you.' She looked at the name. 'Pukka. Three Mint Organic. Perfect.'

Their attention was drawn by the hiss of a Coke can opening. 'Screw this!' Max yelled. He leapt away from his desk as brown liquid squirted and bubbled from the can.

Trevor shook his head. His dire need for Cadence to help was all too obvious.

She reached for the door handle. 'Thank you for the tea.'

In Undermere General Hospital, Ron Smith was aware that his contrived persona was slipping the more stressed he became. Fortunately, the Italian doctor sitting across the desk from him in Consulting Room Two seemed oblivious to it. Arrogant bastard. Probably thought he was above it all.

'Tell me, doc, what does it take?'

'As part of the HTA, Human Tissue Act, you will be interviewed by an independent assessor,' came Professor Bisterzo's accented response.

'A psychiatrist? A shrink?'

'Donating a kidney is a big step to take, with some risk. It's important to be sure you understand what's involved.'

'Why don't you tell me?'

'I'm not a transplant specialist.'

'You must have some idea,' Ron said, his old self bursting through.

'First, we have to crossmatch your blood with Eleanor's.'

'What? Mix our blood together to see if we kiss 'n' cuddle or come to blows?'

'Something like that.'

'No problem. I ain't scared of needles.' Ron gave Bisterzo the benefit of his best smile. Of course, the doctor couldn't see it through Ron's mask.

'There are other tests,' Professor Bisterzo continued, 'to ensure you are suitable as a donor, such as HLA typing.'

'HLA typing? Is that something I have to do with both hands?' Ron winked and pretended to type on an imaginary keyboard.

Professor Bisterzo took a breath and pressed on. 'HLA stands for human leukocyte antigen and is a form of genetic matching. There are parameters when it comes to matching, and HLA testing provides an indication. Of course, it's not fool proof.'

'In my experience, nothing is when it comes to medicine.'

Professor Bisterzo looked intently at Ron through his Perspex visor. 'It's a very good thing you are doing for your friend. She will have a much better prognosis receiving your gift of a kidney than one from a deceased patient.'

'If all goes to plan and we are compatible, what are her chances?'

'The science these days is very good. Ninety-five per cent of living transplantations function satisfactorily after a year. But, there are no guarantees. Sometimes, a kidney doesn't work, even if it's a good match, and has to be removed.'

'Removed?'

'They are the exceptions. The chances are, all will be well and Eleanor will be able to lead a near-normal life, for a while... thanks to your generosity.'

CHAPTER ELEVEN
Saturday, 11th September

Cadence Clearwater felt good, albeit a bit chilly. Her room had heating, but the single iron radiator took time to warm up, and it was still early in the day. She liked her landlords, the pub managers Heather and Ted, although Heather did keep trying to persuade her to eat unhealthy British fare, laced with animal fats and sugar. Cadence was determined to adhere to her strict no beating heart rule. Once, whilst flicking through the channels on the TV in her room, she saw Gordon Ramsay eat a snake's heart that was still beating. A long time ago, even before the incident that had changed everything irrevocably, she had decided to take control of her life and live and let live all the world's animals, apart from bugs, of course. She hated mosquitoes and spiders. An essential item was her spider catcher; a clever tool with long nylon hairs that safely caught the creepy little creatures for disposal outside, unharmed. Mosquitoes weren't so lucky. The females may have tiny hearts, but Cadence made an exception for them.

'I'm digging out some recipes from the internet,' Heather had informed her. 'Perhaps it's time for The Falcon to offer a vegetarian menu.'

'Isn't a falcon a bird of prey?'

'Yes, they do eat other birds.'

'That's nature, I guess.'

'But the ones around here dine mostly on mice and rats.'

'You have rats?'

'Just a few.'

Cadence laughed at the memory as she slipped on a pair of black, easy-fit trousers given to her by Magdalena, and a white tunic top with a mandarin collar. Attached with Velcro was a fob watch protected by a rubber surround.

'No wristwatch, bracelets or rings,' Magdalena instructed when she handed Cadence her uniform.

'The ring was my mother's. I never take it off.'

'Let me see.'

Cadence extended her hand.

'Mmm, nice ring,' Magdalena said. 'Put on chain round neck. You have chain?'

'I have chain.' Cadence perched on an upright padded chair and put her hands to the back of her neck.

'I help,' Magdalena said.

'Thank you.' Cadence half-turned and felt Magdalena unclasp her fine gold chain with its crucifix.

'You Christian?'

'Yes.' Cadence slipped off her late mother's ring and threaded it through the chain.

'Let me.' Magdalena connected the ends. 'I am excited for Saturday.'

Cadence looked up at her new boss. 'So am I.'

'My customers will love you.'

Cadence smiled at her reflection in the wardrobe mirror as she relived the conversation. She liked Magdalena and was looking forward to a day far removed from drama and, more importantly, far away from the intense gaze of a certain young man.

A few hours later that Saturday, Eleanor, no longer in the grip of the virus, looked at Audrey who was dressed in plastic PPE, wearing a mask and specs under a Perspex visor. 'I don't really know him,' Eleanor said. 'And now he wants to do this amazing thing. Why?'

'Why do people donate blood?' Audrey asked. 'They get nothing more than a mug of hot chocolate and a bag of crisps.'

'Kidneys don't renew themselves like blood.'

Audrey grasped Eleanor's hand between her latex-covered fingers. 'Take the gift. Now is not the time for holding back.'

'There's no guarantee we'll be a match,' Eleanor said. 'I mustn't get ahead of myself.'

'What do we know about the chap?' asked a tinny voice.

Eleanor picked up Audrey's phone from the bed and looked at Malcolm who was sitting in the Honda.

She took a moment to answer. 'I know he's had a recent great loss and has no family. Or no family he cares about.' She gave a little shrug. 'We met on the humpback bridge and just clicked. I like him.'

'But,' spoke the tinny voice, 'would you give him *your* kidney after such a brief acquaintance?'

The phone slipped from her fingers. She knew the answer to that question.

Abel reached down for a brown envelope sitting on the hallway mat in Rise House and ripped it open. He read the contents as he strolled into the kitchen, then spoke to the former couple seated at the table.

'Negative. We're all negative. It's official.'

Gary looked up from his phone. 'That's good. As much fun as it is living with you, both, I think I prefer the two husbands – less complicated.'

Christina closed her magazine and rested a hand on

her mound. 'The baby just kicked, clearly insulted.'

'It goes on to say,' Abel continued, 'that under Government Statute, we are to remain in isolation until a second test also returns a negative result.'

'So, we still can't go out,' Christina responded.

Abel dropped the document on the table with the envelope. 'It doesn't look like it.'

She sighed. 'They're really taking this new variant seriously.'

Gary stood and flicked on the electric kettle. 'Hector's not going to be happy.'

'He's not the only one.' Abel stared out of the window into the rear garden and watched Hector gambolling about.

Christina stood beside him and touched his arm. 'At least we're okay.'

He turned to his wife. 'Yes, we are. We are the lucky ones.'

'When's the second test?' Gary asked.

'They'll inform us in due course.' Abel put his arm around his wife's shoulders. 'I'll pull a few strings to hasten it up.'

Gary placed a mug of steaming instant coffee on the table and pulled out a chair. 'I've been thinking,' he said.

'About our next binge-watch on Netflix?' Christina asked.

'I've been thinking about that man we saw with your friend Eleanor. Does he remind you of someone?'

'I can't say he does,' she replied.

'Are you sure?'

'Yes.'

'Are you sure he doesn't remind you of a person you once met?'

Abel lost his patience. 'Stop being obtuse, Gary. Tell us who you think he is.'

'I will.' He picked up his coffee. 'In the fullness of time.' He took a sip. 'God this doesn't get any better. My taste buds are still screwed.'

Abel turned back to the window. 'Hector's having fun.' He smiled at Christina. 'One of your dolls must've fallen from your bedroom window.'

'What?' She moved her bulk and pressed against the windowpane just as Hector, his mighty jaws clamped around a blonde Barbie doll in a sparkling, mini dress, took his trophy into the kennel.

'It's Sophia.' She turned away from the window. 'He can have her. I never liked her, even when I was six.'

'What did she do to incur your wrath?' Gary slurped some more instant coffee... and winced.

'I named her So-*fear* but she insisted on being called So-*fire*. We discussed it but she refused to listen.'

'She had every right to decide how her name was pronounced,' Abel stated.

'I think I prefer SoFire to SoFear,' Gary added.

'I agree,' Abel said. 'To me, she comes across as a very attractive, feisty young woman.'

'Oh, there's nothing attractive about SoFire,' Christina said. 'Apart from her baby-blue eyes, lightly curled blonde locks, and super long legs.'

Abel and Gary exchanged glances.

Christina placed her hands on her hips. 'Trust me. You wouldn't like her. She's a smoker.'

Both men burst out laughing.

'I'll explain.' She reclaimed her chair and sat down. 'I made a little packet of my dad's favourite brand of Dunhill cigarettes and SoFire smoked them all.'

It took Abel a lot of effort to get out his next

question. 'Anything else you didn't like about her?'

'She'd only wear haute couture. She refused to put on the tie-dye dress I made for her out of my mother's headscarf. She insisted on Valentino.'

'As in Rudolph?' Abel asked.

Christina gave him a fake withering look. 'As in Valentino Garavani, as if you didn't know.'

'So, let me get this straight,' Gary said. 'This pretty young woman annoyed you because she preferred SoFire to SoFear, she liked to smoke your dad's cigarettes, and she had good fashion sense.'

'Sounds like my kind of woman,' Abel said. 'Apart from the smoking, of course.'

'There's more,' Christina said.

Both men looked at her.

'She had a big problem with Ken.'

'Ken?' Abel and Gary said in unison.

'He was supposed to be her boyfriend, but she refused to sit with him in the pink convertible. It ruined Christmas.'

Both men roared with laughter.

'Now you understand why Hector's welcome to her.'

Abel bent down and kissed his wife. 'I love you.'

Gary went up to the window and a moment later banged hard with his knuckles.

'What is it?' Christina asked.

'I think Hector's just buried SoFire.'

CHAPTER TWELVE

Tuesday, 14th September

What was making her smile? Once again, Joel had tried to engage Cadence in relaxed banter and had failed, miserably.

'Hi, what's cookin'?'

She'd looked at him as if he'd just spilt his coffee over her white jeans.

'Settling into old Blighty, okay?' he said, playing the classic Brit.

She ignored his question and asked him one. 'Do you play poker?'

'Poker?' If he'd been smart, he would've seen what was coming. 'Sometimes,' he said. 'Do you?'

'When I open a new deck, the first thing I do is toss out the jokers.' And with that she'd turned her back. Minutes later, he was still holding a full cup of cooling coffee, trying to find an upside to his interaction with the most desirable woman he'd ever seen. So, she played poker... perhaps he did have one card he could play.

'Joel?'

He looked at Emma, a fellow student. At any other time, he would regard Emma as a sparkling jewel, perfect in every facet, but Cadence had lifted the bar to heights he could never have imagined until he saw her on that train. 'Hi Emma, you okay?'

'Good, thanks. Just now, you had a strange look on your face. Sort of Romeo-like.'

'Romeo? I think not fair maid.'

Emma touched his arm. 'Will you help me with my

piece, later? We're meant to learn it.'

'Off by heart?'

She laughed. 'That's what actors do, you know. We have to learn lines.'

'Yeah, sure, when? I may be busy.' He saw a flicker of disappointment in her hazel eyes.

'You know, Denzel has already nabbed her.'

'What are you saying? Nabbed who?'

'Cadence, to work on pieces. What did you think I meant?'

'Yeah, okay, at lunch. We'll go to Mere Park.' He looked at her. She was pretty. Really pretty. Just not Cadence.

'Actually Joel... I think I'll work my piece with Lilly.' She turned away and did not give him a backwards glance. He stood near the top of the stairs and wondered how he could ever handle a career as an actor, when he was clearly useless at dealing with people. Several senior students brushed past hurrying to various studios.

'Women, they always eff you over.'

Joel turned to Ethan. 'Hi, Emma just told me we've got to learn our pieces,' he said. 'Have you chosen yours?'

Ethan moved in close. Too close. *'But soft, what light through yonder window breaks? It is the east, and Juliet is the sun. Arise, fair sun, and kill the envious moon, who is already sick and pale with grief that thou, her maid, art far more fair than she.'*

'Oh my god, you know it, already.'

Ethan slid an arm around Joel's shoulders. 'My dear boy, every day you should memorise Shakespeare. Your brain is a muscle; it needs training. Suppose you get a call from the Artistic Director at the Royal

Shakespeare Company. It's Hamlet. You're perfect for the role, but can you learn the lines in four weeks?' He looked at Joel squarely in the face. 'Could you?'

'I... I don't know.'

Ethan moved in closer, almost within kissing range. 'You don't know?'

Joel smelt warm, mint-refreshed breath. 'I take your point.'

Ethan pushed Joel away and laughed. 'Don't worry... you'll get work. Perhaps not Shakespeare, but the soaps love pretty boys like you. Instead of Romeo saying to Juliet... *O, speak again, bright angel, for thou art as glorious to this night, being o'er my head, as is a winged messenger of heaven.* Instead, you'll say: *Juliet, you look fit. Sick babe.*' Ethan laughed at his own joke and ruffled Joel's hair. 'You'll do all right.'

Suitably patronised, Joel watched Ethan as he deliberately sashayed away. Annoyed as he was, he vowed to follow Ethan's advice and learn a little Shakespeare every day.

'You and Miss Houghton are not a match.'

Ron looked at the doctor in shock. He was sitting on a padded chair in Consulting Room One, sideways on to a large desk. 'Are you sure?' Ron asked. 'You've double checked?'

'I printed out the report for you.' Professor Bisterzo slid a buff-coloured file across to him, but Ron didn't take it. Instead, he slammed his fist on the desk's wooden veneer and got up from his chair.

'Mr Smith, one moment.'

Ron rubbed his bruised hand as he considered the masked Italian, still wearing operating scrubs.

'The good news is... you are a match for another patient.'

'Really? Well thanks very much.'

'That is excellent news for Eleanor.'

Ron placed his hands on the desk and leaned towards the surgeon, disregarding social-distancing etiquette. 'And how is that excellent news for Eleanor?'

'It bumps her up to the top of the transplant list.'

The Italian now had Ron's full attention.

'You donate your kidney to a stranger who is a close match to you, and Eleanor receives a kidney from a live donor who is incompatible with their chosen recipient. It's called paired kidney donation.'

'Let me get this straight. I donate to a stranger and a stranger donates to Eleanor.' Ron sucked in air through the fabric of his mask. 'And this kidney swap happens at the same time?'

'There may be a short gap.'

'Does Eleanor know?'

'I thought you'd like to tell her.'

'What's Abel doing?' Gary asked as he slumped down on the sofa in Rise House and surveyed the untidy sitting room. 'I heard him shouting upstairs.'

Christina looked up from her kindle. 'He's going crazy trying to keep all his business plates spinning. The manufacturing plant in China has doubled its prices. If he doesn't accept the new deal, he'll be forced to break contracts with his customers in the USA.'

'That's the price of doing business with a totalitarian state like China,' Gary said as he picked up a copy of the Financial Times. 'We should wake up and manufacture our goods elsewhere, or even in the UK.'

'Abel is having a rethink about his entire operation,' Christina said. 'He has good people, but global turmoil has wreaked havoc with transport and it's keeping him awake at night. Me, it's just heartburn.'

Gary tossed the pink newspaper onto the messy coffee table. 'I know you're worried. We all are. The world's not in a happy place. But, we've got to make the best of it.'

Christina placed a hand on her mighty mound. 'As long as we stay well, whatever happens financially, we'll be fine.'

'I'll be fine,' Gary said, 'when Frank Cottee is behind bars.'

'You're convinced it's him?'

He nodded. 'I am. It all makes sense.'

'And Eleanor?'

'She'll be okay.'

'Audrey says that it's life or death for her. Without Mr Smith, she won't see her next birthday.'

'Another kidney will come along.'

'Gary, what you endured was hell. But it's been more than two years. We all have to move on.'

'That's easy for you to say. You weren't traded like an African slave to a criminal gang. You weren't chained to a bed at night and forced to work in the freezing cold.'

'Hurting Eleanor won't give you back a single day.'

He took in a deep breath. 'Coffee?'

She pointed to the mound.

He went into the kitchen and flicked on the kettle. One thing for sure, isolating had increased his caffeine intake. Or maybe it was living in such close proximity with his ex-wife and her annoyingly decent husband.

Abel joined Gary in the kitchen and looked out of the window. 'Bugger. Will it ever stop?'

Standing side by side, they stared into the rain-sodden rear garden then up at the billowing, dark grey clouds.

'No one was better than Graham at predicting local weather,' Abel said.

'You're gonna miss him until he's ready to fly again.'

'There was one occasion when he got it wrong. I wasn't with him.'

'He admitted his mistake?'

Abel nodded. 'He got lost in low cloud flying down the River Thames. Nearly hit a crane, was fortunate to find Battersea Heliport, and then lost the tail rotor to a flock of birds. Fortunately, his innate skill brought the helicopter down, safely.'

'What's the latest?' Gary asked.

'They caught the cancer, early. I've arranged a private ambulance to take him to the Royal Marsden in London.'

Gary nodded.

'His prognosis is good.'

'The virus was the trigger?' Gary asked.

'Seems that way.'

'Like cigarettes. It's why I gave up smoking... and Tina hated it.'

'Since the fire,' Abel said, 'she won't even light a candle.'

'Her birthday's in a couple of weeks. There'll be twenty-seven of them.' He turned to Abel. 'What does a man buy a girl who's got everything?'

'A card. A real birthday card. Not an e-card. Not an Amazon animated voucher. Just a card with a personal message written in ink.'

Gary laughed. 'And that from the man who took her to Florida just to swim with dolphins.'

'You should've seen her. The speed she went through the water holding the dorsal fin, incredible.

And all that kissing.'

'I don't need the details, thank you Abel.'

'She was kissing the dolphin. They were in love. Well, she was with him.'

'Flipper gets all the girls.'

They both laughed.

'You look pensive,' Abel said. 'You're sure Ron Smith is your man?'

'I'm puzzled. The man I knew, the criminal who lived in a vast house in Essex, with razor wire, guard dogs, ex-convicts for staff, and would have had me killed if it weren't for his daughter, that man, Frank-the-Punch Cottee could never become Ron Smith, kidney donor.'

'I agree. People's fundamental nature doesn't ever really change.'

'You're wrong.'

The two husbands turned to Christina who had entered from the sitting room. Her hand rested on her large mound as she eased her way onto an upright chair.

'Nature is only part of who we are,' she continued. 'Events push us one way or another.' She looked down at her bundle. 'Like the birth of a child. Come feel.'

Both men moved, then Gary, a little embarrassedly, ushered Abel forward. He rested his hand on her abdomen. 'I just felt her!'

'I assumed you were having a boy,' Gary said to Christina.

'We don't know for sure,' she said. 'We asked them not to tell us at the scan.

'Actually,' Abel interjected. 'I think it is a boy. He just kicked.'

'Girls play football too.' Christina placed her hand

over her husband's.

The doorbell rang and Gary left the kitchen. A few moments later he returned, ripping open an official-looking envelope. He took a moment to read the contents. 'Negative. We're all good.'

Christina clapped her hands. 'Excellent. I'll let my brother know, he and his hubby can come home.'

'I'll tell Hector,' Gary said as he handed the document to Abel. 'He's going stir crazy, stuck in the garden.'

Abel read the contents and dropped the sheet of paper on the kitchen table. He beamed at Gary. 'Vacation over. It's time for our phoenix to rise from the ashes.'

Undermere School of Dramatic Art was proving to be a bit tougher than Joel had expected when he swaggered his way through the long audition process. It wasn't expressive movement, voice and speech, acting for camera, Alexander Technique, stage combat, or even how to convey desire and intimacy; it was his obsession with Cadence that he now realised was out of control. The harder he tried to attract her attention, the smaller he felt. Other students could chat with her, discuss the true meaning of a play's text, tell jokes, laugh, be normal... but he couldn't.

At dinner with Audrey and Malcolm he blurted out his true feelings. 'I don't know what to do. I think about her night and day. It's driving me crazy.'

'We've all been there,' Malcolm said. 'Have some wine. It helps.'

'No thank you and, with respect, I think it must be quite a while since you... what was the word in your day? Since you and Audrey walked out together. Courted.'

Audrey cackled at the end of the table.

'What Audrey is trying to express in her unique way,' Malcolm said, 'is that she and I first walked out, as you so delicately phrased it, about six years ago.'

'Oh.' Joel was shocked.

Audrey reached across the table and patted his hand. 'Malcolm and I were both widowed when we met.'

'So, you're, like, sort of, mates, good friends,' Joel stumbled.

'No. On the contrary,' Malcolm said, his voice firm, almost authoritative.

'Malcolm!' Audrey gave him a cold smile. 'Details are not necessary.'

'Quite.' Malcolm smiled back. 'Suffice it to say, I felt about Audrey as you do for your young American friend.'

'Really?'

'Yes. Like you, I felt lost. I felt she was beyond my reach, until a quirk of fate brought us together.'

Joel digested this latest revelation. 'So, what you're saying, is that I should wait for a quirk of fate?'

'Absolutely,' Malcolm said emphatically. 'And it's not something that can be rushed. Pushed for. It's a bit like fly fishing.'

'Fly fishing?'

'Yes. All you can do is create the perfect environment. It's up to the fish whether the fly floating on the surface is appealing or not.'

Audrey cleared her throat. 'What the old man to your right is trying to say, is that you should focus on drama and becoming a great actor. If she likes the look of you, she'll bite. If she doesn't, you'll still be a great actor who will definitely appeal to other fish.'

'I don't want other fish. You've not seen her, well not really.'

'Believe you me,' Malcolm said. 'There is barely a man on this earth who has not felt as you do now. Let me tell you about Mary, who had blonde hair, the sweetest nose, and...'

'Really Malcolm,' Audrey interrupted. 'Do you think Joel needs to hear about your teenage angst?'

Joel turned to Audrey. 'I don't mind.'

'Fine,' Audrey smiled. 'As long as I can tell you about my first love.'

'And who was that?' Malcolm asked, with a twinkle.

'Paul McCartney.'

'I think I've heard of him,' Joel said.

'I think the whole world has, dear boy,' Malcolm added.

Joel turned to Audrey. 'What happened? Did a quirk of fate bring you and Paul McCartney together?'

Both Audrey and Malcolm burst out laughing, much to Joel's puzzlement.

CHAPTER THIRTEEN

Wednesday, 15th September

'You stink!'

On hearing Christina's exclamation, Gary looked over his shoulder. She was sitting in the rear of the VW Golf beside Hector, whose breath Gary was almost used to. 'Please, Tina. You'll offend him. You know how sensitive he is.'

From the front passenger seat, Abel pulled a monogrammed handkerchief from his top jacket pocket and covered his nose and mouth. Slightly muffled he said, 'Hector takes morning breath to a whole new level.'

Gary slowed the car as he approached the humpback bridge at the north end of the little town. Suddenly, he jammed on the brakes, hurtling Hector forward so his mighty slavering jaws came between him and Abel. 'Sorry about that, there's an idiot standing on the bridge.' He looked through the windscreen at an unmoving figure wearing a trilby hat, who was peering over the parapet at the water below. 'I think it's the same man we saw with Eleanor up at the school.' He tooted the car's horn and they saw the man jump, clearly startled.

'Nice one, Gary,' Christina said from the rear as she pulled Hector back into place. 'Give him a heart attack.'

'I wanted to see his reaction,' Gary said. 'You can tell a lot about people when they're startled.'

The man turned his back to the crawling car as he rummaged in his coat pocket and pulled out a black face mask. He fixed the elastic over his ears and pressed his body against the low side wall, to give room for the Golf to pass.

'I think I'll have a word,' Gary said. 'There's something about his manner that's suspicious.'

'Once a policeman, always a copper,' Abel commented.

'Why not set the dog on him whilst you're about it?' Christina added.

'You win.' Gary floored the accelerator and the Golf leapt forward, pushing them all back into their seats. The car bounced as it came off the humpback bridge.

'Take it easy, Gary,' Christina yelled. 'I'm not due, yet.'

'You know who he is, don't you,' Gary stated as they approached a rusting school sign directing cars to turn right at the next junction. The Golf sank on its suspension as Gary swerved into the mile-long drive and accelerated along the pitted tarmac to the burnt-out ruin of the old school. He swung the car around the gravelled apron, rubber tyres spitting out stones until they came to a halt.

'Frank Cottee,' Gary stated. 'That's who it is.'

Abel turned to him. 'Who are you talking about?'

'The man on the bridge is Frank Cottee. I know it's him.'

'How can you be so sure?' Christina asked.

'Same height, same demeanour, and he was standing where his daughter had her fatal accident.'

Abel took a deep breath. 'You know, every time I see this place it takes me right back to that night. The sooner it's demolished the better.'

Hector barked ferociously from the rear seat.

Abel laughed. 'Hector clearly agrees with me.'

'What do you think I should do?' Gary asked.

143

'Give the green light to the clearance contractor,' Abel said as he opened his door.

'I mean about Cottee?'

Christina touched her former husband's shoulder. 'I know he made you suffer but can't we move on?'

'He's a criminal. He needs to be put away.'

'Isn't losing his daughter punishment enough?' Christina asked. 'How does it help putting him away?'

Gary got out of the car and opened the rear door. He grabbed Hector's heavy leather lead but lost grip as the dog knocked him aside and cantered off, barking excitedly.

'No, it's not enough,' Gary shouted as he slammed the door.

Abel opened the opposite door and took Christina's hand as she got out. He closed the door and put his arm around her shoulder. They walked away from the car towards the remnants of the former boarding school.

'It's not just me who suffered,' Gary called. 'There are many innocent people who were victims of his crimes.' He slipped into the driver's seat, fired up the engine and the front wheels spun on the gravelled surface. He skidded to a halt. 'Take care of Hector,' he called through the open driver's window. 'I'll be back, soon.'

'Our bags are in the boot,' Abel shouted, but Gary didn't choose to hear as he roared off, his front tyres spinning as the rubber fought for traction. In his rear-view mirror, he saw Hector galloping after him as he accelerated down the long drive.

Creating a new identity whilst on the run is never easy unless you're well prepared, as Ron had been. Deep in his criminal heart, he had always known there would come a time when he would have to say goodbye to Frank Cottee and become a new man. In fact, Ronald Edward Smith had lived a parallel life to Frank Cottee for more than three decades. The man had credit cards, bank accounts, National Insurance number, passport, and had paid tax to HM Revenue & Customs. Most importantly, Ron Smith was registered with the UK's National Health Service, so when he offered to pair his kidney with a stranger, he had a medical record going back years.

Was living as Ron Smith full time changing his personality? His character? When his daughter had been on life support after her car accident, Frank was so angry, so bitter, that instead of donating her precious organs, he ripped out the cable to her ventilator and watched her die together with her lifesaving spare parts. And then he met Eleanor on the bridge and had fallen for her hook, line and sinker. For a few brief hours he saw hope for a happy future and then Covid snatched it away. His decision to give her one of his kidneys was a no-brainer for Ron Smith, if not for Frank Cottee. She was a decent, kind, beautiful woman who deserved nothing less than a second chance. Ron smiled. Once he'd donated his kidney to whoever was to get it, for a week or two, he and Eleanor would only have one decent kidney between them.

He laughed. Life really was full of surprises.

Gary knew he was driving too fast as he rounded another bend on the Old Military Road. Up ahead he could see the humpback bridge, the northern gateway to the little town. He slowed as he approached, hoping to see the man, but the bridge was all clear. He felt his stomach flip as he bounced the old white car down on the far side and took the S-bend slowly at the top of Hawksmead High Street. He scanned the pavements to the left and right, passing familiar shops that had either done well during the pandemic or were forced to close. At least Abel's grand scheme for the old school on the moor would help rejuvenate the town. His phone rang but he let it go to voicemail.

Disappointed at not seeing the man from the bridge, he turned into Hawksmead Station car park and swung back onto the High Street. He drove at a steady pace past The Falcon, Eleanor's Olde Tea Shoppe, Merlin's Hardware Store, Wax Polish the beauty salon, the Old Forge restaurant, and on past Hawksmead's bow-fronted cottages that often featured in television dramas. At the top of the town was Hawksmead's Memorial Garden, created by Audrey's husband, Malcolm.

'There are places to sit in there,' Gary vocalised to himself. He turned right into the short driveway that led to the walled garden and brought the car to a gentle halt. Taking care not to slam the driver's door he walked through the ruins of the old boarding house. The garden was an oasis of calm, with wildflowers, young trees, benches, picnic tables, and a memorial stone dedicated to the lives of five teenage boys who lost their lives whilst attending the school on the moor. It was also where Gary married his beloved, Tina. What a fool he had been.

Sitting on one of the benches was the man he had seen on the bridge, still wearing his trilby hat. Gary decided to risk all and approach. The grass muffled his footsteps, so he was able to walk right up to the bench without the man appearing to notice. His hat prevented Gary seeing his eyes, and the rest of his face was covered by a black mask.

'Frank.' He put weight behind the name. 'Frank Cottee.' The man on the bench didn't appear to have heard. Gary sat beside him. 'Hello Frank.'

'I do apologise,' the man said, his voice slightly muffled by the mask. 'Were you speaking to me?'

Could Gary detect East London mixed with Essex in the man's disguised vowels and consonants? 'You remember me, Frank?' He looked intently at the man seated beside him. No response. He tried a harder approach. 'My name's Gary and I slept with your daughter.'

The man laughed through his mask. 'I don't have a daughter and my name is Ronald Smith.' He got up from the bench and Gary mirrored him. 'This is a beautiful garden,' the man said.

Gary persevered. 'Your daughter's life ended at the bridge. Is that why you were standing there?'

The man faced Gary. 'A friend of mine is ill, gravely ill. And the only way I can help her is by donating one of my kidneys to a complete stranger.' He looked at the garden. 'What do you think I should do?'

Gary took a moment before replying. 'Clever. Nice deflection. I always respected you, Frank. I even liked you. You're a smart guy. But you don't fool me, mask or no mask.'

'Young man, I'm here for peaceful contemplation.'

'Well, you can peacefully contemplate from a prison cell.' He gripped the older man's arm and was surprised by the size of his sinews. He was without doubt Frank-the-Punch, former boxer and wanted criminal. 'Frank Cottee, I am arresting you for the kidnap of an undercover police officer, and countless other crimes including bribery of officials, extortion, protection, theft, and...'

The older man wrenched his arm free. 'This Frank Cottee you speak of clearly did you a disservice, but I am not he. I suggest you spend a few moments in this garden to ease your troubled mind.' He strode away.

Gary called after him. 'It's only a matter of time, Frank.' The man didn't break step.

Roff! Roff!

Exhausted. Staggering. Lungs heaving, Hector, the great hound of a dog, collapsed at Gary's feet. He knelt down and hugged the panting beast.

His phone rang. He checked the screen and connected. 'It's okay. Hector's here with me.'

'And so are our bags,' said his former wife.

'Hang on. I'll bring them to you.'

'Too late.'

He looked up as the chop-chop sound of a helicopter faded away.

Massimo Bisterzo, head of the Intensive Care Unit, was wrapped up in his protective equipment and feeling very uncomfortable, not just because he could feel trickles of sweat down his spine but because he had to explain a difficult procedure to a patient he liked. There was something about Eleanor Houghton that had really got under his skin. Was it his Italian masculinity that could not fail to notice she was an absolute beauty? Not young, but like a ruby rose with velvety petals darkening at the edges, and sufficient thorns to keep him on his toes.

'Thank you, doctor,' she said.

'It is very good news.'

'When can you go ahead?'

This was the tricky bit. 'We have to wait.'

'What for?'

'Mr Smith has to donate his kidney, first. It goes by age and his recipient is about half yours.'

'Half my age? Well, thank you very much Professor Bisterzo. I shall be singing the joys of anno domini for the rest of the day.'

'We call first-time mothers over thirty-five, geriatric.'

'I guarantee I am not pregnant!' She broke into a smile. 'So, where do I wait? Here or can I go home?'

He took a long breath. 'You can go home but you will need to come in for haemodialysis three times a week.'

'Do I need any medication? According to my phone, potassium can be a problem?'

'HD deals with the increase in potassium. You don't need meds.'

'And calcium?'

'Same answer. It will be checked, monthly.'

'Wonderful.' She threw off the bed covers. Her gown was rucked-up and Massimo couldn't help but notice that she had inadvertently exposed herself. 'Whoops!' She grabbed the sheet. 'Please forget what you've just seen although it must be preferable to my colonoscopy!'

Massimo smiled under his mask. 'When the moment comes and you receive the call from the transplant team, please do not have a last cup of tea or slice of cake. Bring all your medicines in a bag together with a few personal items to while away the time post-procedure.'

'As Mr Smith is ready to go, hopefully I'll get the call, soon.'

Massimo pressed on. 'Pre-op you will have to undergo a few tests just to make sure no new medical conditions have arisen and to check that the donor's kidney is still a good fit for you.'

'Assuming I'm all good – God I hate that expression... but assuming that I'm ready to go, what's next?'

'I am not part of the transplant team but they'll connect your new kidney to your blood vessels and ureter and close you up.'

'What about the old kidney?'

'It's sold for dog food.'

'What? I hope you're joking.'

'Don't worry, you get to keep your old kidney.'

'In a jar?'

'They always leave natives in. Your transplant goes in the lower abdomen to the left or right of the iliac fossae. To spare Google, the iliac fossa is the concave area within your hip. Your new kidney is attached to the iliac vessels and, lastly, connected to the ureter.'

'Post-op?'

'You will feel a bit groggy and there will be a bit of discomfort.'

'Painkillers?' Eleanor smiled. 'I love a good painkiller.'

'Don't we all,' Massimo chuckled. 'We will give you medication to prevent your immune system from rejecting the new kidney.'

'How soon will I start feeling normal again?'

'As soon as your kidney leaps into action you will feel better.'

'Leaps?'

'A medical term. Seriously, we will keep a close eye on you to ensure the medication is working as it should. You may need dialysis if the kidney takes a while to get up to speed.'

'How long will I have to stay in hospital?'

'About a week. We may have to deal with a urinary tract infection.'

'Give it to me doc. What else should I expect?' She picked up her phone from the bedside cabinet. 'I suppose I can Google it.'

'Don't. All you'll read is worst case scenarios.'

Eleanor scrolled her screen. 'Blood clots?'

'Blood clots can occur and are usually dealt with by medication.'

Eleanor turned back to her phone. 'Arterial stenosis, whatever that is?'

'It's a narrowing of the arteries and can cause a rise in blood pressure. A simple stent solves the problem. Please, stop looking.'

'What else have we got? Blocked ureter, leakage... ooh, here's a good one.' She looked up at him. 'Rejection.'

'And you may get knocked down by a car on Hawksmead High Street.'

'Yes, you're right.' She replaced the phone on the bedside cabinet.

'However,' Massimo cleared his throat.

'Here it comes. The body blow.'

'Immunosuppressants do leave the door open to infections and an increased chance of developing diabetes, or gaining weight, losing bone density, and a number of incidentals including cancer.'

'Since when has cancer been an incidental?'

'Balanced with the benefit of having a replacement kidney they are all incidentals, an annoyance at most, and treatable if they occur.'

Eleanor lay back and closed her eyes.

'So, have a rest,' he continued, 'and I'll be back a bit later when we can decide whether it's best for you to wait at home or here in hospital.'

Later that same day, in the kitchen of Mint Cottage, Eleanor's godson found himself cornered as he made a mug of instant coffee.

'Invite her for dinner,' Audrey stated.

'Won't she think it a bit weird? We're students. Money is tight.' He poured milk from a small, floral jug into his coffee and focused on stirring. 'She'll turn me down and everyone will know.'

'Invite her to dinner, *here*. For a bit of home cooking.'

Joel glanced at the Aga stove. 'She'll still think it's weird.'

'Faint heart never won fair lady.'

Fear squirmed his guts and his mouth went dry. 'She's vegetarian. Very fussy about what she eats.'

'Malcolm has an extensive menu.'

He placed the full mug on a small circular tray. 'Would you excuse me?' His voice cracked and squeaked, and he dry swallowed. 'I have work to do.' He edged his way around her.

'It's your life, Joel.' She leaned over the tray and gave him a peck on the cheek. 'Don't underestimate how special you are.'

Several miles away from Mint Cottage, in the Earl Beatty, a secluded pub in the rural village of Motspur, Gary looked over a pint at Detective Inspector Scanlon.

'It's him,' Gary said. The two men were of similar age and had trained together but were never friends. Dave Scanlon had scraped through the exams whereas Gary had been as adept with the written as he had been with the practical.

'What if he is?' Scanlon said. 'You blew it when you

approached him. He'll be long gone now.'

'No, he won't. He's donating a kidney.'

'A kidney?' Scanlon rocked back in his seat. 'A kidney? Then it's definitely not Frank Cottee. He may, at a pinch, donate a kidney to his daughter, but as she's dead it won't do her much good.' He hooted at his own joke.

Gary leaned forward. 'There's a woman in Undermere General Hospital who caught Covid and needs a new kidney. Frank appears to have fallen for her.'

'And how did you come by that tasty nugget?'

'I still have my informants.'

'Yeah, and I still have my virginity.'

Gary laughed. 'I've been isolating with my former wife and every day she chatted with someone who is a close friend of the woman who needs the kidney.'

Dave grinned. 'So, you do have a snout.' He chuckled. 'When's the transplant due to take place?'

'Well, there's the thing. They're not a match so they're doing a paired transplant. Eleanor, the woman, is receiving a kidney from a stranger. In return, Frank is donating to someone else.'

'So, we nab him after the op?'

'Too risky. He may not recover from the operation.'

'Let's hope he doesn't.'

Gary took a deep breath. 'Dave, he needs to pay. He needs to suffer. He needs to rot in prison.'

'And dying's not enough for you?'

'If he donates a kidney, he'll get sympathy from the court. He'll get medical treatment outside of prison and could easily escape. More than that, he'll be regarded as some kind of hero, not the murdering scumbag he is.'

Dave removed an e-cigarette from his pocket. 'And what about the person who was due to receive Cottee's kidney? Do they go hang too?'

'There'll be other donors.'

'You're right. It's about time Cottee was collared, assuming this Ron Smith is him.'

'He is, I guarantee it.'

'I'll arrange a warrant.' Dave placed the e-cigarette between his lips and pressed the battery button several times. 'Damn, out of juice.'

'Time to give up?' Gary asked.

'The same could be asked of you and Frank Cottee,' Dave said. 'And we know the answer to that question.'

CHAPTER FOURTEEN
Thursday 16th September

'Joel.'

He looked at Pamela Maynard, considered to be the finest drama teacher in the land and felt his muscles spasm, his stomach twitch, and his throat contract. Hot blood spread through his veins seeking to cool at the surface of his skin, turning his neck and face bright red for all the class to see. Beads of sweat appeared from nowhere and trickled under his arms, down his spine, and through his eyebrows. Worse. He caught Cadence looking at him and tried to read her impassioned expression.

'Stand over there and deliver what you've prepared,' Miss Maynard commanded.

He cleared his throat. 'It's in my bag.'

'Where it will remain.'

'Er yes.' His voice cracked. The strands in his vocal cords felt tight and scratchy. A condemned man, he weaved his way through fellow students to where Miss Maynard directed him to perform.

She spoke to the group. 'Stepping onto a theatre stage is easy. But, more often than not, you will be asked to audition in surroundings that are anything but conducive to a good performance. It could be via Zoom on your phone or laptop. It could be in an office, with a desk; or a boardroom with executives in suits all staring at your breasts.'

'I'll be all right, then.' Conor laughed at his own joke, taking the attention of the group away from Joel, much to his relief although he found Conor annoyingly handsome with his bright blue eyes fringed by dark lashes.

Miss Maynard took back control of the class. 'Until you are established as an actor, almost all your waking time will be taken up trying to get work. You have talent but to succeed you have to offer so much more.'

'Like breasts?' Conor laughed again.

'Being an actor is a people-business and people come in all shapes and proclivities. Traditionally, women have been the victims hence the hashtag MeToo movement that resulted in the jailing of Harvey Weinstein. But, Conor, below the radar, young men have also suffered.'

'Yeah?' responded Hailee, a student Joel often like to hide behind. 'Miss Maynard,' Hailee continued. 'A man coming on to a man is an equal contest. A man coming onto a person who menstruates is not.'

'You're right, Hailee,' Miss Maynard said. 'But it's not just about physical strength, it's the power of one over another.' She looked at Joel. 'At this moment, I could take any one of you aside, be inappropriate and give you a problem. You could report me. Or, you could go along with what I want and gain an advantage over the competition. Because, believe you me, you are competing. You are in a fight for the roles that will showcase your talent to agents, directors and producers. So, will you report me? Or will you let me get my wicked way to gain a perceived advantage?'

The group was silent. Embarrassed. Miss Maynard pushed on. 'You're in Cannes. At the film festival. You're there to promote a student film when you get an invitation to meet an Oscar-winning producer. His company is based in a suite at one of those grand hotels on the Croisette. He has a touchy-feely reputation, but he also has the power to make you a star. All excited, you go to his suite. There are assistants, other people, you feel comfortable. Gradually, they disappear until it's just you and him. He sweet-talks you about Hollywood, the movie industry and how big you're going to be. He gets a bit too close, but he wants to fly you first class to Los Angeles for a screen test. His hand is on your leg. He plans to introduce you to a top agent, to directors whose movies he has produced. Now he's telling you how much he likes you. You have a choice. You can run out and shatter the dream he's just spun, or you can give him a little sugar. What do you do?'

Hailee raised her hand. 'I don't care about his sweet tooth, he's not getting my sugar.'

The group laughed.

Miss Maynard smiled. 'He's not interested in your sugar, Hailee, he wants Joel's sugar. He's gay and he likes pretty boys.' She looked at Joel who felt his whole being shrink before her gaze.

'I'm not gay,' Joel spluttered.

'It matters not a jot. To him you're prime beef and he has the power. Do you give him what he wants and get from nowhere in your career to somewhere, or do you scamper away?'

Everyone looked at Joel. He cleared his throat. 'I would explain to the producer that although I really appreciate what he can do for me, unfortunately it's not my predisposition.'

His fellow students laughed.

'And you think that will put him off?' Miss Maynard asked.

'Wouldn't it?'

'What would your response be?' Conor asked.

Miss Maynard paused a few seconds. 'I would walk out, if I could, but it may be too late. Suppose I am tiny, petite, and he is big and heavy. He forces himself on me and I give up fighting. If I have to have sex, then I may as well get the screen test and the Hollywood agent. Except, when he's finished, blown his load, all his sweet inducements evaporate to be replaced with a threat. If you say anything, to anyone about what's just happened, he'll make sure that none of the top agents, directors and producers will ever hire you. Worse than that... he'll let people know that you're selling your body to all comers to get ahead.'

For a moment, there was shocked silence.

'What is the answer, Miss Maynard?' Joel asked, his voice, reedy.

'Integrity. Never give anyone a single granule of sugar to get ahead. Even if he's the Artistic Director of a major theatre company.'

'But if you're in a hotel suite all alone,' Hailee said. 'What are you supposed to do?'

'You have to judge the situation but, when the last assistant leaves, you suggest that the conversation continues in the bar whilst making your way to the door. If he says no, you thank him for his time and go with your integrity intact.'

'Without an agent? A screen test? A career?' Conor could not conceal his smirk. 'Surely, it's best to let them think you might come across, rather than shutting the door completely?'

Pamela Maynard waited until she had their full attention. 'Your body does not have to be bait to hook an agent or a film role. You are lucky. The business is much more evenly balanced these days in terms of men and women. It's still male dominated – straight and gay – but since hashtag MeToo, men are much more cautious.'

Joel put up his hand as though in school. 'Not every man is like that.'

'No. But it takes a lot of machismo to make it in this profession and, unfortunately, some of that drive can spill over into abusive behaviour.' She addressed the whole class. 'You can have a producer with many great films to his credit and multiple Oscars, who is witty and intelligent, and yet so deeply flawed he cannot control his sexual urges.' She turned back to Joel. 'I believe, Mr Redmond, you have a little Hamlet to share with us.'

Joel had hoped he'd escaped the humiliation. 'Er yes, no, my mind's gone blank.'

Miss Maynard waited a moment then spoke to the whole class. 'Getting the job is about ten times harder than playing the role. When your agent gives you details of an audition you are at the start of a running race for which there can only be one winner. How can you make sure it's you that gets the role? Simple. You make the director, the casting director, the producer, the star of the show want *you*, and nobody else.'

'I get it.' Everyone waited for Cadence to say more. She didn't.

Miss Maynard smiled. 'Cadence, please share your thoughts.'

'I would prep all the people with influence, so I know something about them, and the production company, and I would prep the script.'

'Good.' Miss Maynard turned to the class. 'To beat the phenomenal odds, you need to prepare.'

'Fail to prepare,' Conor said, 'and prepare to fail. Is that the mantra?'

'There's truth behind every cliché,' Miss Maynard said. 'If you're given a scene, learn your lines. Get advice from an older actor. Practice in front of anyone who will listen. The more you do that the less self-conscious you'll be.'

'As you said, Miss Maynard,' Conor cut in. 'We all know our stuff. We're all good. Won't our blazing talent shine through?'

Several in the class sniggered.

'In the main entrance hall,' Miss Maynard said, 'there are several boards fixed to the left-hand wall as you walk in. It's a list of students who received our highest accolade for excellence since our school was founded in 1925. It's our victor ludorum. Look at the names and see how many you recognise. Google them. At least half of the ones still alive are no longer in the profession, and they were the ones we regarded as the most likely to succeed. It's a lottery, but you can beat the odds if you truly appreciate that *getting* the job requires one skill, and *doing* the job another.' She picked up a glass of water sitting on a battered, pedestal table, clearly a prop used in numerous productions. 'To spare you years of angst, and poverty, I recommend that you quit now, save your student loan, and study for another career. But I know that none of you will listen to me, and rightly so. After all, many highly successful actors were standing right where you are now just a few years ago.'

'Shall I do my speech?' Joel asked.

Miss Maynard smiled. 'Next time. And without the book.'

A great weight was lifted off his shoulders. He'd only read half the play, and hadn't learned much beyond *To be, or not to be: that is the question.* Now he had a chance to study like he'd never studied before.

Joel's godmother slipped her arm through Malcolm's and tottered down the wheelchair-ramp to one side of the main entrance to Undermere General Hospital.

'The car's not far,' Malcolm said. 'Audrey parked it as close as possible.'

'Thank you so much for collecting me and for inviting me to stay.'

'I'm sure your godson would be more than happy to move into your flat whilst you convalesce. Afterall, it's just a few steps from The Falcon.'

'Joel likes to drink?' Eleanor asked.

Malcolm laughed. 'Not at all. It's where the love of his life is located.'

'I had no idea,' she said. 'Please don't be offended by my wish to be at home.'

'I won't, as long as you promise to call if there's anything you need.'

'I'll be fine. And Ron will be staying with me.'

'I hadn't fully appreciated the closeness of your relationship.'

'We care for each other but the only organ I've touched in recent memory is the one in the Methodist Church.'

Malcolm chuckled. 'It's not my place to pry.'

'He's a good man, as are you.'

'I try to be, although I'm not in his league. My kidneys are not going anywhere.'

'If Audrey needed one, I'm sure you would oblige.'

'If Audrey needed two, I would oblige. But I'm twenty years older than your friend.' He spoke as he guided Eleanor, gaunt and frail, past a parked car towards the silver Honda. 'What your friend is doing for you is truly honourable but entirely understandable.' He opened the front passenger door and helped ease her into the car.

She looked up at him. 'Understandable? Really?'

'Completely.'

'That's very kind of you.'

'I'll just go and pay the ticket.'

'Let me.' Eleanor reached for her handbag as Malcolm gently closed the door. She turned to the driver who was fast asleep behind the wheel. 'A certain drama student wearing you out, dear Audrey?'

Her friend didn't stir.

CHAPTER FIFTEEN

The California sun was dipping to the pale horizon. Not that she would see it until she stripped off her dark blue tunic, slipped into her spandex rash guard, and peeled on her bright pink and yellow neoprene wetsuit. She would delight in the hot golden sand scorching her soles until plunged into the unpredictable Pacific. One ankle leashed to her long surfboard, she would lie flat for a few minutes of powerful paddling to reach her ocean buddies, who sat and chatted about nothing and everything as they waited to catch a perfect ride. She had become expert at barrelling a giant wave as it curled around her, adjusting her speed with the twitch of her board or running her fingertips through the surf, choosing the moment to make a rapid exit by shooting from the barrel, kicking out over the crest and sliding down the back into calmer water. Sometimes she'd see a shark, even a juvenile great white, lured to the shallows by abundant fish, especially stingrays and tuna.

Her mom opened the salon door to let out the final customer after a long but fun day of plucking, threading, filing, waxing, and listening without judgment and often without comment. Cadence heard things no teenage girl should know but as an only child, she'd had to grow-up fast. Real fast, not the fake fast of social media, but the kind of maturity that a deep insight into marriage, cheating, financial woes, and all manner of problems that two people and the world can generate. There were always a few

surprises at **Clearwater Spa, Solana Beach,** and that
Saturday Cadence had enjoyed a big one. She was used
to tall women but there was something about Serena
that made her truly special. The shape of her long
limbs was amazing but, up close, it was her beautiful
face with eyes as dark as bitter chocolate fringed by
long lashes that every woman desired. She was in to
reshape her brows, to have her lip hair lasered, and
her arms and legs waxed. 'And whatever else, sweetie,
shakes my booty,' she said with a husky voice and a
smile that revealed perfect pearly teeth.

Cadence worked on Serena's nails and felt the
strength in her large hands at the end of long arms,
ideal for paddling a surfboard, she thought. She
guided Serena to a secluded section of the salon where
there was a couch with a fitted roll of paper, and the
waxing workstation with heater and assorted tubs,
tubes, strips and wooden spatulas. The tall woman
placed the strap of her shoulder bag over the back of a
chair followed by her studded, denim jacket.

'Just got to get some supplies,' Cadence said, and
she headed for the storage room. The contrast with
the salon was immediate. It was lined with metal
shelving screwed to stud walls, decked-out with
numerous boxes and bottles. She picked up a tub of
hypoallergenic wax and headed back to the salon.

Waxing Serena's arms took quite a bit of time
and extra dollops of the bright blue wax. Each time
Cadence ripped away Serena's hairs she admired the
woman's fortitude. Did she not feel it? To reduce any
adverse reaction such as swelling and itching, Cadence
massaged each arm with CeraVe moisturising cream.

'Smooth as a baby's tush.' Serena smiled as she
stroked her waxed skin. 'And now the main event.' She

stood and slipped off her floral cotton skirt to reveal narrow hips at the top of legs that seemed to go on forever. But Cadence didn't want this session to go on forever, she wanted to hit the surf, and checked to see if her mom, who she referred to as Gwyneth when they were working together in the salon, could take over. A quick glance through a gap in the curtain told her it was an emphatic *no*. In fact, Nicola, a former beautician who had recently given birth, had been called in by her mom to provide a little back-up at the nail bar.

Serena lay on the couch and Cadence cast a glance at her white underwear that concealed very little.

'I know what you're thinking,' Serena said. 'And, you know what, you're right. Would you help me?' Her thumbs slid under the satin briefs.

'No!' Cadence answered with a touch more vigour than she'd intended.

'I thought you offered a full service?' Serena said with an edge to her voice.

'I don't do Brazilians. I'm too young. I'm only sixteen.' She spread a large dollop of hot wax on Serena's thigh. 'Come back another time and my mom'll depilate you to buffed perfection.'

Serena rested her head on the vinyl pillow and closed her eyes and swallowed. Cadence, for the first time, saw her laryngeal prominence. Now it made sense. She ripped off a strip of hardening wax.

'I'll cash up,' her mother said after the last customer left. 'We did good work today.'

Cadence lifted the side vent of her tunic and pulled out a wad of ten and twenty-dollar bills. 'Look at this.'

Her mother grinned. 'You're my golden ticket, sweetheart. I knew it as soon as I first saw your chubby face all covered in gunk.'

'Mom!'

'It's yours.'

'It's ours. Put it in the safe with the rest.' She proffered the cash.

'Keep fifty. It's too late to surf. Go see a movie.'

'I'm gonna shower, play Distrust with my friends online, and fall asleep on the couch.'

'You plan to wait up for me?' her mother asked. 'To check I get home safe?'

Cadence grinned and opened the till. It too, was stuffed with greenbacks. Many customers liked to pay cash rather than have their partners see just how much their beauty-maintenance was costing each month. 'It's a privacy issue,' her mother explained.

'Don't worry, mom. I'll clean up. You get ready for your date.'

'Are you sure, honey?'

The bell above the door tinkled.

'Did you forget, something?' Gwyneth asked.

Cadence glanced up from counting the day's takings and watched as her mother walked towards the open door.

'I did forget something.' Serena pushed Gwyneth back into the salon with her perfectly manicured hand.

'Hi Serena,' Cadence said, as a ripple of fear stiffened her sinews.

'Sweetie, put all that cash into a bag and give it to me.'

'Why would I do that?' Cadence asked, laced with defiance.

'Cadence.' There was a tremor in her mom's voice. 'Do as the man says.'

The slap was fast and brutal. Her mom smashed into a mobile beauty station and they both crashed onto the tiled floor, scattering boxes of acrylic nails, powder, liquids and glue; bottles of cleanser, varnish remover, and moisturising creams; and pots with files, clippers, and hundreds of cotton buds.

Cadence rushed forward to help her mother. She looked up at Serena. 'Why? Why are you doing this? It can't be for surgery. You've already transitioned. I saw that.'

'Silicone sweetie. Tucked behind my fake foo-foo lies a monster.'

'Give him the money, Cadence,' her mother said, gasping for breath, through lips smeared with blood.

'Do as your mom says,' Serena growled.

Cadence gathered up all the dollar bills and offered the wad to Serena who snatched the cash in her long fingers and put it in her shoulder bag. She observed the teenage girl. 'I like my schlong, but I want a sweet sugar plum like yours, honey. And that costs.' She smiled, then headed for the door.

'You'll never be like me!' Cadence shouted.

Serena stopped and rested her head on the door's opaque glass. 'You don't understand. You don't know what it's like. You TERFs never do.'

'She didn't mean it,' her mother spluttered. 'You've got the money, now go.'

Cadence took a few steps towards Serena as tears flooded her eyes. 'Your DNA is all over the salon. You cannot transition that.'

'Stop it, Cadence,' her mother pleaded.

Serena dipped her hand into her bag and pulled out a small revolver with a snub barrel, steel cylinder, and a black grip.

Cadence saw the muzzle flash but could not remember hearing the bang.

CHAPTER SIXTEEN
Thursday 16th September - Evening

Joel came down the steep cottage stairs. It was good to have a break from Shakespeare. He knew the bard was exceptional, and he was enjoying Hamlet, but it was damned long and so tough to learn, even just one speech.

Malcolm, who was preparing an early supper, called from the kitchen. 'How're you getting on?'

'Fine, thank you.'

'Don't you just love Shakespeare? There are so many brilliant phrases we use in common parlance.'

'Yeah, I was surprised he used so many clichés.'

'What?' Malcolm entered the hall wearing a butcher's-style, striped apron. 'Four hundred years ago *brevity is the soul of wit* was an original thought.'

'Was it? How do you know Shakespeare hadn't heard a bartender spout those words in a Southwark tavern?'

'He may have done, but the fact there are so many quotable lines in every single play he wrote, surely proves the man was a genius?'

'If there are that many, please prove it by quoting a few.'

'All right I will.' Malcolm returned to the kitchen and checked the oven.

'Smells good,' Joel called from the hall.

Still wearing his apron Malcolm returned holding a plant pot containing fresh coriander. He held it up and said, '*Alas, poor Yorick! I knew him, Horatio: A fellow of infinite jest.*'

'Don't you mean, *Alas, poor Yorick, I knew him well*?'

'A common misquote young man. What about this? *The lady protests too much, methinks.*

'Wrong again,' Joel said. 'It should be *Methinks the lady doth protest too much.*

'Young man, methinks you're winding me up.'

Joel assumed the stance of a great theatre knight and with a vibrato in his voice he declaimed: '*O, what a rogue and peasant slave am I for doing such a thing.*'

'Yes indeed, Sir John.'

'My dad worked with him.'

'Really? Your father worked with the great Sir John Gielgud?'

Joel was about to reply when he heard a car pull up.

'That'll be Audrey with our guest for dinner,' Malcolm said.

'Guest?'

'Music may be the food of love, but sometimes one needs to eat.'

'Am I dressed smartly enough?' Joel looked at his blue jeans and old T-shirt with its faded slogan – *Gamers Rock at Chess.*

'You look just dandy.'

The front door opened.

Joel turned and stared in horror at Cadence who was wearing a simple dress under a lightweight raincoat. She was ushered into the narrow hallway ahead of Audrey.

She smiled. 'Hi Joel.'

'Hi.' Joel looked at Malcolm who grinned.

'*There is a tide in the affairs of men,*' Malcom said, in a sonorous tone, '*which taken at the flood, leads on to fortune. Omitted, all the voyage of their life is bound in shallows and in miseries.*'

'Julius Caesar, Act four, scene three,' Cadence responded as Audrey closed the door behind her.

'You know the play?' Malcolm asked.

'Yes. I saw the film with John Gielgud playing Cassius, James Mason, Brutus, and Marlon Brando as Mark Antony. Black and white. A bit staged but definitely well done.' She turned to Joel. 'I'm sure you can get it on Netflix.'

Audrey sniffed the air, theatrically. *'Methinks dinner is ready.'*

'Everyone's an actor!' Malcolm laughed.

Cadence turned to Audrey. 'Thank you for inviting me. Early on in the pandemic I caught the virus and for almost a year I had no real taste or smell. And then I had the vaccine and bam, it all came back, and I love it. Even bad smells smell good.' She touched Audrey's arm. 'But this is a good smell. I can tell you're a very good cook.'

'I can assure you,' Audrey said. 'Malcolm's the good cook.'

Without a smile, Joel added, 'Men *can* do some things, you know.'

Silence. The halt in conversation was agonisingly awkward.

Cadence looked pointedly at Joel. *'Swear not by the moon, the inconstant moon, That monthly changes in her circled orb, Lest that thy love prove likewise variable.'*

Malcolm cleared his throat. 'Juliet to Romeo I do believe.'

'And look how that turned out,' Joel said, bitterness edging his words.

Cadence slipped off her coat and Audrey hung it on a hook. 'Romeo was impetuous,' Cadence said to Joel. 'He was too quick to rush to judgement. They could've been happy.'

'So, Shakespeare got the ending wrong?' Joel asked, his tone tinged with sarcasm.

'Absolutely,' Cadence said. 'Juliet would never have stuck a dagger into her belly.'

'Why not? Romeo was dead. Poisoned. She had nothing left to live for.'

'That's where Shakespeare tripped up,' Cadence responded. 'Juliet was pregnant.'

'Pregnant? Where's that in the text?'

'Nobody knew except for her.'

'Not even Shakespeare?'

'Oh, he knew,' Cadence said. 'But he also knew if Juliet were with child, she would never have killed herself. He had to keep it quiet.'

'What a fool,' Malcolm exclaimed. 'A tiny tweak to the ending and he could've called his next play *Romeo's Baby, the sequel*.'

They all laughed ...with relief. The tension was broken.

'Please go through.' Malcolm gestured to the open door into the cottage's front room. 'Dinner is about to be served.'

The next morning Cadence handed Joel a green envelope. 'Would you give this to your friends?'

He swam in her blue pools of bliss. Several students from the year above jostled them as they hurried to their classes up the concrete stairwell.

'It's a thank you,' she said.

'I'm glad you had a good time.'

'You're lucky.'

'It's a fluke I'm there. I was meant to stay with my godmother in Hawksmead, above the Olde Tea Shoppe, but she caught the latest variant.'

'I like the people who own The Falcon. In fact, everyone I've met here has been real kind.'

'Aren't people kind where you live?'

She paused. 'Yeah. Of course. Most of the time.'

He took a breath. 'Can I see you, outside of school? Maybe a drink in your pub?'

'Joel.' Her slim fingers touched his cheek. 'We can be lifelong friends. I hope that's enough for you.'

CHAPTER SEVENTEEN

Sunday, 19th September

Trevor rolled away from Magdalena and sat on the side of the bed.

'What is problem?' she asked.

Through the window they heard cheerful church bells peeling from St Michael's belfry.

'What is it?' she asked again, resting her hand lightly on his bare shoulder. 'You have second thought?'

He turned and looked into her richly exotic face. 'I love you, Mags, but I saw the way you looked at Cadence yesterday in the salon.'

'She good worker. Polish ethic.'

He nodded. 'Today, she's spending a few hours working for me.'

Magdalena threw back the covers and stood by the bed in all her beautiful nakedness. 'Why she work for you?'

And God created woman. Trevor felt a stirring. He took a breath. 'She asked for a job. I gave her one.'

'But you too old for her.'

'What about you? Are you too old for her too?'

She smiled and sat down beside him on the bed and rested her head on his shoulder. 'I like her, but she not lesbian.'

'Is she threesome material?'

Magdalena slapped his thigh then cupped his face in her big hands. 'I am still your number one, yes?'

'As long as you'll have me.'

She smiled and he looked at her beautiful teeth

framed by her generous lips, so kissable. 'We make good couple,' she said, and she pushed him down onto his back. Within seconds he had entered heaven.

Cadence timed it perfectly. The service in the Methodist Church at the top of the quaint town ended and within minutes she had flagged down the number 68 bus and been delivered to Harper Dennis in Undermere. Trevor had given her the code for the door, so she didn't need a key to open-up.

Once in the agency, she had carte blanche on how best to use the time. Her first job was to put the lights on and make it look welcoming. Then, she made a cup of peppermint tea, switched on Trevor's computer, and settled down to studying the properties currently for sale and to rent ...or to let as Trevor insisted on describing it. She loved looking at the photos, especially the old properties that were so small compared to the average American home, yet so idyllic.

Standing alone in the agency, she swiped her phone's screen and tapped the WhatsApp icon. Just a few special people had access to the chat entitled Cadence in Wonderland. She took a selfie and thumbed a quick message: *Yesterday a beautician, today a realtor, tomorrow an actor ...well, maybe.*

Her darling Aunt Angela had delayed her mother's funeral until Cadence was well enough to attend, albeit in a wheelchair and accompanied by a medic. Cadence never got to meet her mother's date, although her aunt told her that many of the flowers filling her hospital suite were from the man.

'Why didn't he come to the funeral?' Cadence asked.

'He didn't want to impose,' Aunt Angela explained.

A bedroom was made available for Cadence in her

aunt's home while she recuperated. Despite having three of her own children to raise and an absent husband, her mother's sister took on the role of mother. She had to change the bandages on incoming and outgoing wounds and to attend the fresh wound the surgeons had to make when they realised the damage to her colon was too great to repair.

'It's shower time, girl.' Her aunt would say the words accompanied by jazz hands.

'I'll just wash.'

'You can shower. I checked with the hospital. In fact, they recommend it to decrease the risk of secondary infection.'

'I'm scared.'

'It'll feel nice. There'll be no pain.'

'I'm scared to look.'

Her aunt took her hand. 'I know you are, but you're healing, baby.'

Cadence knew there was one wound that would never heal. It would hurt until the day she died.

The front door to Mint Cottage opened and Audrey stepped into the hall. She heard Malcolm call out as she hung up her coat and kicked off her shoes.

'My darling,' he said. 'Would you cast your mince pies over my plan for the fête, or should I say country fayre?'

She entered the dining room and stood beside Malcolm. Spread out on the table was an A2-sized roll of paper, held down at the four corners by a ceramic pot of marmalade, a sterling silver cruet set, an ammonite fossil, and a bottle of HP sauce.

'How was church?' he asked.

'A little bit quiet without our organist, but we sang our hearts out. Although there was one hymn to which everyone seemed to have their own tune.'

Malcolm chuckled. 'And our dear Reverend?'

'Wonderful as always. His theme this week was the power of prayer.'

'Or lack thereof.'

Audrey ignored her husband's comment and looked at the plan. 'I wondered what you'd been doing in the library.'

'The children's section has a fantastic choice of crayons and a big worktable.'

'And how is our favourite librarian?'

'She's thinking of retiring.'

'She'll miss earning no money. What will she do with her day?'

'When she saw my unrivalled idea for a late-summer fayre,' Malcolm said, his voice brimming with fake pride, 'she promised to make an appearance.'

'There could be a stall selling old library books, suitably sanitised, of course.'

'I'll mention it to her,' Malcolm said. 'Although humping dusty tomes from the library will be no easy task. I think the paper and card recycling bin is a more sensible solution.'

'Tell that to the authors!'

Malcolm laughed.

Audrey slid on her spectacles and examined the colourful illustration of Hawksmead's Memorial Garden. Bordering the top in blue was the river with its stone bridge. Below was a small meadow with intricately drawn shrubs and trees leading to the remnants of the former school boarding house, mostly coated with ivy and clematis. At the bottom of the paper, was the high brick wall that provided a semi-circular border between the garden and the Methodist Church graveyard where Christina's parents were buried. Between the ruins of the boarding house and the high brick wall, Malcolm had illustrated stalls in the finest detail.

'Sweetheart, this is extraordinary,' Audrey said.

'Thank you. I try.'

She laughed. 'So, what have we got? A bouncy castle? Who's going to be in charge? After all, it can't be a free-for-all.'

'That's an old joke and, yes, everything is going to be free. That's the whole point.'

She looked closely at the illustration. 'What's that? A farmers' market stall?'

'I want everyone involved,' he replied.

'Candyfloss? So bad for children's teeth. And toffee apples as well?'

'It's a fayre. It would be wrong not to include them.'

Audrey pointed at a four-legged beast. 'And what is that?'

'It's meant to be a suckling pig. I thought we could have old-fashioned bowling with wooden bowls and arches. Whoever gets the highest score, takes home the piglet, or at least a prime joint from the local butcher.'

'What about a veggie prize? People could bowl for a basket of vegetables and let the pig live.

'Set herbivores against carnivores?' Malcolm asked.

'It would sharpen up the competition.'

'I like it. You and I could both have a go and win roast pork and all the trimmings.' He squeezed her shoulder. 'Brilliant idea, my darling.'

She pointed to a raised platform. 'Disco dancing?' She looked at her husband. 'Are you sure?'

'Silent disco dancing. You wear headphones. It's

hilarious to watch.'

Her finger moved. 'Tombola. Good. I'll sort out some prizes for that.' She continued to scan the illustration. 'Oh, that is excellent.'

'What is?'

'The donkey. I love the smell of donkeys. It reminds me of when I was a child in Broadstairs. One donkey ride would use up an entire week's pocket money, but it was worth it just for the feel of the hair, the creek of the saddle, and the wonderful smell.'

'So that's why you give so generously to the donkey sanctuary.'

'Ooh, I've an idea,' Audrey said.

'Yes?'

'What's the attraction called where you hit a big wooden mallet onto a metal prong thing and it propels a metal ball up a tube to a bell at the top?'

'Test your strength. I'll add it to the list.'

She looked back at the plan. 'Please tell me, no. You're not actually considering a carousel?'

'With carriages and horses. The children will love it. It'll be worth every penny.'

'Every penny of your pension you mean.'

'Of course. I'm eighty-one. I can't take it with me, and I know you're all right.'

'Valid point. I'm a bit too big for a donkey ride but I would love to ride a cock horse to Banbury Cross.'

'And you shall, my angel.'

'This is exciting. What else?' She scanned the plan. 'Coconut shy. Excellent. That's a classic. What have we here? Guess the weight of the dog?'

'Guess the weight of Hector the Heroic Hound.'

Audrey looked at her husband. 'Won't he scare the children? And how do you weigh him? He's enormous.'

'Gary will figure it out. He was very keen to take part.'

'Cake stand?' Audrey asked.

'Hopefully, Joel's godmother will be well enough to partake. Her Scottish shortbread is second to none.'

'By the way, where is our young thespian?' Audrey asked.

Eleanor looked up from her comfortable seat on the sofa in her flat above the Olde Tea Shoppe. 'Ron? What are you doing?'

He was standing by the window curtain and appeared not to hear.

She got to her feet and stood beside him.

'Keep out of sight,' Ron said.

'Why? What's going on?'

'There's a man down there with a dog.'

'It's Gary. I know him. I'll go and see what he wants.'

Ron gripped her arm. 'I know what he wants. He's already accosted me once. He thinks I'm someone else.'

'Let me talk to him.'

'No. I've a better idea.'

Tinkle went the old-style bell above the door to Harper Dennis and Cadence looked up from Trevor's computer. Her heart skipped. If things had been different, the person backlit in the doorway would've been her mate for life.

'Good day, sir. Are you looking to buy or rent?'

Joel smiled. 'Is there a third option?'

She laughed as she clicked her mouse a few times, stood, quickly looked around to make sure the agency was all neat and tidy and ready for the start of the new week, switched off the lights and ushered Joel out the door. She checked it was locked then put her arm through his as they headed for the bus station.

'How was your morning?' she asked.

'It was amazing.'

She looked at him. 'Really?'

'When I went to bed, I tried to learn some more Hamlet. When I woke, I knew it. Well, almost. My brain was working whilst I slept.'

'Your brain is always working.'

'If only.'

'Recite it to me.'

He turned to her as they walked. 'Now? Here? In public?'

'Being an actor is about performing in public.' She checked the time on her phone. 'But, if we hurry, we may just make the bus.' And, within minutes, the number 68 was taking them out of Undermere.

'Would you like to hear it now?' Joel asked.

Cadence looked at the backs of several heads sitting in front of them. 'Although you have a captive audience perhaps now is not the best moment.'

'But I want to perform.' He got up from his seat.

She grabbed his arm. 'Sit down, Joel.'

He laughed as he sat back down next to her. 'As if I would, he said.'

She looked at him. 'You constantly surprise me, Joel.'

'That's what my mum says.'

'I hope to meet her, one day.' She looked out of the window. 'I recognise that cottage.'

Joel leaned towards her, their heads, close. 'Malcolm and Audrey are really nice people. So relaxed. I can come and go as I please. They gave me a key and the alarm code.'

'She and I had a lovely chat before church this morning,' Cadence said. 'Did you know she was a model in the Swinging Sixties?'

'It doesn't surprise me.'

'Her first job was a three-week trip to Australia modelling clothes for Mary Quant.'

'Impressive.'

'You have heard of Mary Quant?'

'I'm sure she's very famous.'

'That's what I said to Audrey,' Cadence said, and they both laughed.

For ten minutes they chatted as the bus rattled along the Old Military Road over peaks and through the troughs, crashing into potholes, splashing through puddles and rivulets, and on until they passed a rusting sign warning they were approaching a junction for a school.

'Excuse me, sir,' Cadence called out to the driver. 'Could we get off here?'

'It's not an official stop,' he shouted back.

'Could you make an exception?' Cadence said as she hurried down the aisle towards the driver. 'I'm American.' She heard a few stifled giggles from fellow passengers as the bus slowed to a stuttering halt.

'Make it quick,' the driver ordered from behind his protective screen. The doors slapped open, and Cadence and Joel wasted no time jumping off. They watched the bus pull away.

'My landlord told me he went to the school up on the moor. I thought we should visit.' A few minutes later, they were standing at the end of the long drive. 'Buses used to stop here before the school closed,' she said.

For the next half hour, as they ambled, they discussed drama, their tutors, and the assorted delights of their fellow students, oblivious to the moor's natural earthy beauty. It surprised them both when they were confronted with the burnt-out edifice of the old school now cloaked by reinforced plastic sheeting.

Cadence was the first to comment. 'Ted, my landlord, said the fire could be seen for miles.'

'People must've died,' Joel almost whispered.

'According to Ted, nobody died, thanks to a dog.'

'A dog?'

'An heroic dog. Classic Hollywood.' She looked about her. 'Shall we explore?'

Joel stepped away. 'I think it's too dangerous to go in.'

'Not the school, the *moor*.'

They both stared at the vast expanse of undulating green and golden hues.

'We could take a shortcut to Hawksmead,' Cadence said.

Joel took a deep breath. 'My mother gave me two pieces of advice when I left home. One was not to walk on the moor. She said it's full of rocky escarpments, rapid streams, sucking bogs, and…' He paused.

'And what? Cougars? Bears?'

He shook his head. 'Sheep.'

Cadence burst out laughing. 'I thought you were gonna say ghosts! Ted told me this was built as a Victorian workhouse for the poor. Children often tried to escape the cruel regime by crossing the moor at night. Many died.'

'So, my mum was right to warn me,' Joel said.

She looked up at the sky. 'Perhaps it is a little late. We'll take the road back, although speeding cars are a lot more dangerous.'

He let out a pent-up breath. 'Phew. I really don't have the footwear for traipsing across the moor.'

She threaded her arm through his, and they headed back towards the start of the long drive. 'What was the second piece of advice your mother gave?' she asked.

'I blew that one before I even arrived.'

'Let me guess,' she said. 'Don't fall in love with the first girl you meet?'

There was no ready response.

'You should follow her advice,' she said.

'How are you, Sean?' Eleanor asked from the back of a minicab. 'I hear your taxi business is going well.'

The driver glanced over his left shoulder. 'Do I know you?'

'Sorry, it's the mask. We met many years ago when you and Tina came to tea at the old school boarding house. I helped Audrey serve.'

'Worst day of my life. It broke up our relationship.'

'You've just gone through a bloody red light!' Ron yelled.

'Sorry.'

'Forget sorry,' Ron said. 'Focus on the road.'

Eleanor squeezed his hand and spoke gently, but still loud enough for Sean to catch her words. 'Many years ago, Sean dated Lord Cornfield's wife, when she worked as an estate agent.'

'You let a good one go there,' Ron said.

'I didn't let her go,' Sean snapped. 'It was that house. It affected her mind. Her reasoning. It was possessed. Good thing it burnt down.' He swerved to avoid a cyclist.

'This is driving me crazy,' Ron said, vehemently.

Eleanor spoke to Sean. 'Would you mind turning round and taking the country route along the Old

Military Road?'

'It's a lot longer that way. It'll cost you more.'

'Turn round,' Ron said. 'Or we'll get another cab.'

A few minutes later their stomachs flipped as the car crashed down on the north side of the humpback bridge and accelerated along the thin strip of tarmac.

'There's my godson,' Eleanor exclaimed as the taxi roared past the young couple.

'Can't stop,' Sean said. 'I'll be late for my next job.'

Ron squeezed Eleanor's hand. 'He's with a friend. You don't need to worry.'

After a bumpy ride and splashing through many rivulets, they entered Undermere.

Sean spoke over his shoulder. 'Where would you like to be dropped?'

'Near the centre,' Ron replied. 'We'll take it from there.'

'You've got bags.'

'I'm aware of that, son.'

'I can drop you at your place.'

'Here, take this.' Ron tossed a couple of large notes onto the front passenger seat. 'Stop by the bus station.'

Christina, Lady Cornfield, put down her glossy Mayfair magazine and, with difficulty, reached for her phone, vibrating on the glass-topped coffee table. She took a few deep breaths then looked to see who was calling, and sighed. Living with her ex-husband in Hawksmead whilst they recovered from Covid had been harder than she admitted to herself, let alone to Abel. She loved Gary, and although she would never swap back, he would always have a special corner of her heart. She swiped the screen. 'Hi Gary, are you wanting Abel?'

'We've lost him.'

'Abel?' She pushed herself up and felt the baby kick.

'No, not Abel,' Gary said. 'I've not tried to get hold of him.'

'Who then? Hector?'

'Frank Cottee.'

She took a moment before responding. 'You can't be sure it's even him.'

'I am sure. I saw him without a mask looking down from the window in Eleanor's flat, but no one's there, now. They've both gone.'

'How do you know? Did you ring the bell?' Christina used the sofa arm to steady herself as she got up onto her feet.

'I broke in,' Gary replied. 'I'm not proud of myself but I had to know for sure.'

She closed her eyes and took a long breath.

'Did you hear what I said?' Gary asked. 'He's gone. They've both gone, and I've no idea where. I thought you might know.'

She looked out of the apartment window into the beautiful, lush garden at the centre of Berkeley Square. 'Gary,' she said. 'Are you telling me, you broke into my friend Eleanor's flat; the same Eleanor who caught this evil variant and now needs a kidney transplant? The same Eleanor who has found a friend prepared to donate a kidney to a third party, also suffering from kidney failure?'

'I have to find Cottee.'

'If you arrest Ron Smith you'll stop the transplant happening.'

'I have no choice.'

The baby kicked and she sought relief by sitting on an upright dining chair. 'Gary, you need to face the truth. It was you who destroyed our marriage, not

Frank Cottee. You were a serving police officer and you slept with his daughter. What he did was bad, beyond terrible, and I know you suffered, greatly, but it was a symptom not the cause. You have to move on.' She waited for a response. 'Gary?' She looked at her phone. He'd terminated the call.

CHAPTER EIGHTEEN
Saturday, 25th September – the day of the fayre

Malcolm pressed the button on his bedside clock and the screen lit up. It was time to shake a leg. He looked at his wife who was still deeply asleep. As he eased himself out from under the duvet a shaft of morning light pierced a gap in the curtains, bounced off a gilt-framed mirror and caught his eye. He smiled. It was going to be a sunny day. September – such a reliable month but one that could be full of dread. For a moment, he remembered how it felt to be a new boy at boarding school, far away from home. Even as an English teacher, when welcoming the new intake to the former school out on the moor he could not shake off the unease he felt in his gut. There was one boy who had attracted his attention. He was shy and excellent at English. But he had one big problem; when asked a question he couldn't get the words out. Boys in his class would make machine gun noises when he tried to say any word beginning with *W*. One day, he turned up to audition for the school play and read for the role of Cyrano de Bergerac's true love. There was no hint of a stutter as Roxane imbued the thirteen-year-old's entire being and Malcolm, the play's director, had no choice but to give the boy the role. It wasn't out of pity; it was simply because the boy was Roxane. During the long weeks of rehearsal, the young teacher grew overly protective and worried for the boy's wellbeing.

The play was a triumph, and parents believed that the girl playing Roxane had been brought in from another school. The following morning, Malcolm went to congratulate his star in the offsite boarding house at the north end of Hawksmead, but the boy misinterpreted Malcolm's intentions and ran away. He tripped on a raised floorboard and fell down a flight of stairs. For fifty years, Malcolm bore his secret guilt for the fatal accident until Roxane walked back into his life. He first saw her on the train to Hawksmead and was immediately entranced. Later, they had a chance to meet and get to know each other but their budding romance was crushed when Audrey revealed that she was the boy's big sister and had come to Hawksmead to learn the truth behind her brother's tragic death. It was not an easy path of discovery for either of them but, despite many emotional hurdles, Audrey was able to forgive the once young teacher and Malcolm was able to let go of the guilt he'd carried for so long. Five years on, he and Audrey were still happily married and relishing every moment of their time together.

He let her sleep.

'Do you mind if I go?' Christina asked, her arms not quite long enough to wrap around her handsome husband. 'I know Malcolm. He'll have organised a big festival for the people of Hawksmead and I want to be there to support it.'

Abel looked down at the large mound keeping them apart. 'You're a bit close to be travelling so far, aren't you?'

'It's my first. Dates are always a bit flaky. Anyway, if the bump wants to come out ahead of time, there's a Maternity Unit in Undermere General.'

'I've paid for the Lindo Wing.'

'Don't worry. I'll be back, tomorrow.'

'You're sure you're okay going by train? You could

take a chopper. I'll call Battersea Heliport.'

She kissed him on the lips. 'The train will give me a chance to read my baby book.'

'You've already read it.'

'I know. But I want to go through it again.' She pulled away from him. 'Ow, baby, that hurt.' She smiled at her husband. 'He's kicking and punching like a pro.'

'He? You're sure about that?'

'It's either a boy or Nicola Adams.'

Abel laughed. 'One thing I do insist upon.'

'Don't worry, my seat is First Class. I'm not that crazy.' She looked at her watch. 'I'd better book a taxi.'

'Sebastian's outside. He'll drop you at the station. I would come, too, but I've got you-know-what to sort out and the Chinese don't believe in weekends.'

'Roll up! Roll up! Ring the bell if you're strong enough.'

Malcolm looked at the mighty wooden mallet and the worn steel button. 'Do I look as though I can ring the bell?'

'You ring *my* bell,' Audrey said to her husband as she slipped her arm through his. She smiled at the grizzled man offering the battered mallet. 'You should feel his bicep.'

Malcolm chuckled. 'My darling, your lack of honesty does you credit.' He turned to the carny who was wearing an open-neck striped shirt, bright red waistcoat, and black and grey striped trousers. 'I would like to introduce you to Dick Fletcher who helped me organise the fairground attractions.'

The weathered man bowed his head and offered Audrey the mallet. 'Swing big and hit home me darlin' and it'll ring true for you.'

'Is that what you say to all the ladies?' She did not

reach for the long handle.

'I tell you what, Mr Fletcher,' Malcolm said. 'Why don't you show us how it's done?'

Dick cast a jaundiced eye over the old machine with its thermometer-style markings on a vertical wooden board. 'Challenge accepted.'

Malcolm and Audrey stepped back a pace as Dick parted his feet and took a deep breath.

'We're waiting,' Malcolm cajoled.

The heavy mallet head swung in an arc and Dick hammered it down with all his might on the steel button. A metal puck shot out of its cradle and flew up the graded board. It hovered agonisingly close to the bell, then gravity took hold and it slid back down.

'Give it to me,' said Ron Smith who was wearing a raincoat despite the sunny day, his trilby hat, and a black face mask.

'Follow through is the secret,' Dick said as he proffered the mallet handle. 'If you get the puck beyond halfway, you'll be leading the field.'

Ron took his time to position his hands on the wooden handle then looked at Dick. 'Follow through you say?'

'That's right.'

'What do I get if I ring the bell?'

Malcolm took a pace forward and spoke for all to hear. 'You get the admiration of every red-blooded male in Hawksmead.'

'And a cuddly toy of your choice,' Dick laughed.

'Best move back,' Ron said to Dick and Malcolm who merged into the gathering crowd of onlookers. There was silence as they watched Ron line up the mallet. He took a breath then swung it in a blur above his head. It crashed down on the button with such force, the metal puck shot like a bullet up the slide.

Gary heard the clang of a discordant bell cutting through the hubbub filling the Memorial Garden. Hector, held on a short leash, cocked his head and barked, scaring several people who reached for their children. A growing crowd was enjoying the extraordinarily good September sun. Free to all comers, everyone was in high spirits.

Gary reached for a tall man's arm.

'Did you see who rang the bell?'

'Probably a Russian,' he replied, his Irish lilt infused by Hawksmead's flattened vowels. 'They're everywhere.'

Gary released his grip. There was only one person he knew who had the strength, the skill, and the ego to risk showing off so publicly.

Cadence entered The Falcon from the street wearing her beauty-salon tunic and looked across the empty bar with its dark-wood furniture, polished for centuries by elbows and butts.

'Hello?'

A man's grizzled face rose from behind the varnished counter.

'Cadence.'

'Ted. Why is the bar bereft of the good folk of Hawksmead?'

'It is said that nothing comes for free, except, it seems, the Hawksmead Fayre where everything is free apart from drink and food.'

'Of course.'

'You should go,' Ted said.

The door banged open behind Cadence, and she moved quickly towards the bar.

'Unfortunately, I have to remain here,' he continued, 'for the likes of this gentleman.' He observed the approaching customer. 'Good day, Vincent'

Cadence watched the man approach the bar and half-sit on a wooden stool. 'The usual, Ted.' He turned a bleary eye to Cadence. 'And for you, Miss Fitness? What is your poison?'

'Turmeric infusion. Thank you for the offer.'

Vincent looked at Ted. 'You heard the lady. Put it on my tab.'

'Your tab is so old,' Ted replied, 'it's still in shillings and pence.' He placed a pewter tankard under a brass spout and pulled a long wooden handle.

'Well,' Cadence said. 'I'm off to get changed.'

'Will you go to the fayre?' Ted asked as light brown liquid gushed into the tankard until froth poured down its sides.

'I may have a nosey.'

'You'll enjoy it. But be prepared to go back in time.' He placed a circular paper coaster on the counter and carefully positioned the pint of ale.

'Aarrh, that looks good, my friend.' The old man smiled, revealing stained and crooked teeth.

'You should go, too, Vincent,' Ted said.

'I'd rather sit here and regale you with my unlimited supply of anecdotes.'

'Not quite so unlimited.'

'Right,' Cadence said. She did a light drum roll on the counter. 'I'll see you later.'

'Be careful girl,' Vincent said, and then belched. 'Pardon me.' He wiped his mouth on the back of his sleeve. 'Be careful how you go, my dear. Those pickpocketing gypsies get everywhere.'

Magdalena was in the process of turning the sign on her door from open to closed when she saw a face that stirred her soul. A person pulling an Aerolite cabin bag who meant so much to her and to many others in the little town. She opened the door. 'Just when you need angel, she is there.'

Christina grinned. 'Are you closing?'

'Not to you. I strip, I pluck, I thread, I file, I polish anything and everything you want, my sweet.'

'I was hoping we could go to the fayre, together. I'll pay for the loss of business.'

'Of course, I go to fayre. Wax Polish is tombola prize. Good marketing, yes? The Lord would approve.'

Christina laughed. 'Yes, Abel would approve.'

'So, Lady Cornfield. You like quick treatment?'

'I would love quick treatment but another time.'

Magdalena rested her fingertips on Christina's great mound. 'How long?'

'Two weeks, approximately. Hard to know for sure. It was a very busy time.'

'Lucky man. Your baby is most wonderful since birth of Jesus.'

Christina laughed. 'To me, that's for sure.'

'Leave bag here.'

'Oh, thank you. Great idea.'

Magdalena, reached for the extended handle and pulled the cabin bag into her salon. 'Wait one minute. I change.'

Gary almost barged his way through the throng of inquisitive people keen to see the traditional all-the-fun-of-the-fayre attractions. There was even a children's carousel and already a queue of excited little ones. *Guess the weight of the dog* had been abandoned as the combined weight of Gary staggering under Hector's immense bulk was too much for the scales, and Hector refused to be weighed on his own.

Gary spotted Eleanor doing great business at her cake stall but was shocked by the change in her appearance. Once a comfortably rounded beauty, she now looked thin and drawn although her eyes still sparkled as she handed over a paper bag full of scones, he knew she'd baked that morning.

'Eccles please Eleanor.'

She gave Gary her radiant smile and his resolve slightly weakened. 'How lovely to see you. And how is dear Hector?'

'I had to tie his lead to the towbar on my car. He saw a rabbit in the children's petting area and wanted to eat it.'

She laughed. 'Does he like cake?'

'He's a bit more of a steak and kidney kind of dog.' He paused. 'I didn't mean to mention kidney. How are yours?'

'They're okay but I do need a transplant.'

'Are you still living above the Olde Tea Shoppe?'

'I'm staying at Ron's to be near the hospital for when the call comes. He's due to donate any minute.'

'Is he at the fayre?'

'He didn't want to mingle with such a large crowd but refused to let me come alone, and he enjoys baking. You'll recognise him by his mask and trilby.'

Cadence was from a *one-horse town* in California but had seen large crowds, although she'd never been to a rock concert or to a football or baseball match. As she stood by the entrance to the Memorial Garden and looked at the seething mass of people, she was all for returning to the pub, or catching the bus to

Undermere to help in Harper Dennis, when she felt a hand take hers. Her shock immediately melted when she saw it was Joel. He smiled and she couldn't help but kiss him. She had promised herself never to fall for a boy, not because she didn't want to, but knew when the true damage inflicted by the bullet was seen, nobody would find her desirable. Losing her mother had broken her heart and she would rather die than have it broken again. She even wondered whether she could really be an actor. Nude scenes were certainly off the slate, that was for sure.

'You came,' Joel said.

She stepped back, annoyed with herself for giving away to her instinctive reaction.

'I came as an actor. To observe British people at play. Isn't that what Miss Maynard told us to do?'

Joel grinned. 'This is not *British* people – this is Hawksmead. Quite different.'

'I think it's typical of the way Americans see Britain… you know, lords and ladies, stiff upper lip, jolly good stuff, what-ho.'

Joel laughed. 'If America is happy to buy it, we're happy to sell it.' He took her hand again and she felt something move deep within.

Out of the milling throng beamed unnaturally white teeth. 'Tina, my dear,' spoke a rich, brown voice from a tanned and wrinkled face. 'Where have you been hiding all this time? It's years since you thrashed me on the tennis court.'

Christina produced her megawatt smile. 'Hello Jason. How are you and how is the beautiful Mrs King?'

'We are tickety-boo as I can see you are.' His eyes dropped to her mighty mound, now way too big to be referred to as a bump. 'Many congratulations.'

'Thank you.'

He opened his mouth to no doubt flirt some more when she was rescued by her wonderful friend, Audrey. 'Tina!' The elderly lady wrapped her arms as best she could around her. 'You are glowing my darling. Pregnancy clearly suits you.'

Christina pulled away and looked at her confidante. 'I am a bit top heavy.' She took her arm and turned back to Jason whose eyes were focused on her oversized boobs. 'Please excuse us. My friend and I are going for a little wander.'

'Be my guest.' He theatrically bowed. 'By the way, make sure you visit Eleanor's cake stall. After all, my dear, you are eating for two, or is it three?'

Christina and Audrey plodded through the throng, nodding to acquaintances and chatting to friends as they made their way towards Malcolm who was in animated conversation with Reverend Longden.

'May I borrow your car?' The voice was rough, East London. Both Christina and Audrey looked into flinty eyes peeking out above a black mask, shaded from the sun by a soft hat. 'I've 'ad the call.'

'To prayer, Mr Smith?' Audrey enquired with a twinkle.

'In a way,' he said. 'A young man has just arrived at the hospital and is waiting for my kidney.'

Audrey touched his arm. 'I'll drive you.' She fished in her handbag.

'It's okay, Audrey. I'll take Mr Smith,' Christina said. 'You stay here with Malcolm. I won't be long.'

'Are you sure?' Audrey's eyes dropped to the mound.

'I can't wait to get behind a wheel. Being chauffeured is so boring.'

Audrey laughed and handed over an electronic key

fob. She turned to Ron. 'You're doing a wonderful thing, Mr Smith.'

'Some, might say, not before time.' He looked at Christina. 'Shall we go?'

Christina kissed Audrey on the cheek. 'Where's the Honda?'

'On the High Street, by the church.'

'Tell Malcolm, I'll take care of his baby.'

Audrey smiled. 'And you take care of yours.'

'If you see Magdalena,' Christina said, 'please tell her I'll be back soon.'

'I don't wish to rush you, my dear,' Ron said, 'but there's a man making his way towards me I'd rather not meet.'

Christina turned her head and saw her former husband. Their eyes locked. She squeezed Audrey's shoulders. 'Could you detain Gary for us?'

'Go!' Audrey said.

Christina followed Ron as he hustled around children eating candyfloss and teenagers taking selfies in front of various Edwardian attractions.

She accepted his arm as they hurried down the drive to the High Street. Almost as one, they looked back to the Memorial Garden to see if they were being followed.

'We'd better get going,' she said. 'I know Gary. He's a bit too determined.' Ron's arm steadied her as she trotted her bulk towards the Honda. She pressed the fob and the lights flashed.

Ron opened the driver's door and held it for Christina, who edged her way in sideways, reached for the handle below the seat, and slid it back. Ron closed the door, and she adjusted her seat position, fitted her seatbelt and fired up the engine. He slipped in beside her.

'All set?' she asked as she adjusted the rear-view mirror.

'All set.'

In the mirror she spotted a familiar white VW Golf approaching. 'Bother.'

'What is it?'

She started the engine and moved the lever from Park to Drive. 'Put your seatbelt on. This could be a bumpy ride.'

'Don't forget you're pregnant.'

'I won't!'

The front wheels squeaked like a couple of mice and the Honda Jazz almost leapt forward. Christina pressed her foot and was surprised by how quickly they gathered speed down the slight incline. A swift left and right through the High Street's 'S' bend and on down past The Falcon, past the railway station and on towards the main road to Undermere, all the while ignoring the headlights on full beam behind them. Traffic lights ahead shone red and she knew there was a camera ready to catch the impatient. Amber joined the red and she drove the Honda out onto the main road, swerving hard to avoid climbing onto the pavement on the far side.

To complement the full beams in her rear-view mirror, there was constant blaring of the Golf's horn. Drivers heading in the opposite direction turned their heads to watch the car chase. Pedestrians shrunk back from the pavement kerb.

'You know why he's following us, don't you, Frank?' she asked.

'I have a very good idea.'

'What you did was wrong but what he did to your

daughter was also wrong.'

'And what he did to you was unforgivable.'

'Well, he's paid the price for his sins.'

'As have I for mine.'

'When you've donated your kidney, what will you do?'

'I intend to look after Eleanor.'

'I don't think Gary will let you.'

At that moment, the VW came alongside as both cars were forced to stop at traffic lights for a major junction. Christina looked at Gary who vigorously gestured for her to pull over. She nodded and pointed to a parking zone up ahead. The lights turned green, and the Honda shot forward, its nearside wheels scraping the kerb.

'What are you doing?' Ron asked.

'Pulling an old trick.' She watched as Gary eased the VW ahead of the Honda and came to a halt. In her mirror she saw blue and red flashing lights as a police patrol vehicle came to a halt behind her.

'It's all over,' Ron said, defeat in his voice.

'Leave it to me.' She watched as a police officer opened his door and approached her side window, which she lowered. 'My waters have broken. My contractions are every few minutes, and I'm trying to get to hospital. The man in front thinks I carved him up and has been chasing me, blasting his horn and flashing his lights.'

'May I have your name, please?'

'I'm Lady Cornfield, wife of Lord Abel Cornfield. This Honda belongs to Malcolm Cadwallader. He lent it to me to get to hospital. I'm fully insured to drive any car.'

'Go,' said the officer. 'I'll deal with the other driver.

Good luck.'

Christina reversed the Honda towards the police car then drove around the Golf just as Gary was getting out. In her rear-view mirror, she saw Hector poke his massive head through the passenger window, his teeth bared at the policeman.

'You're a smart girl,' Ron said. 'Just like my Stacy.'

Christina carried on as fast as she dared until she saw a turning for the hospital and a sign that read:

NO ENTRY
AUTHORISED VEHICLES ONLY.

'Had we better go to the main entrance?' Ron asked.

Christina gasped as stabbing pain took her breath.

'Are you all right, dear?'

She flashed the Honda's lights, cut across oncoming traffic, and drove at speed up the twisting, tree-lined drive coming to a juddering halt by Accident & Emergency. Sudden contractions prevented her from doing anything other than grimace and emit a high-pitched squeal.

'I thought you were telling porky pies to the copper!' Ron said as he released his seatbelt.

'I thought so too!' she gasped.

He hurried around the nose of the car and opened her door, took her arm and helped her out.

She looked down at a large damp patch where she'd just been sitting. 'Could you park the car, Ron?' she said, panting. 'They're brutal here if you don't park properly. In the boot, there'll be a Waitrose bag you can put on the seat.'

'Don't worry about that. I'll leave the key on the off-side front tyre. Best 'urry. Your baby's gonna be out a lot sooner than my kidney.'

Wonderful, thought Gary, as he drove away from

the police patrol car. He could now expect several speeding tickets courtesy of the flashing cameras; and he'd had to invoke the old-boy network to avoid being arrested for dangerous driving.

He was tempted to approach the hospital via the *NO ENTRY AUTHORISED VEHICLES ONLY* entrance where he knew Tina and the man he believed one hundred per cent was Frank-the-Punch Cottee had driven, but there was only so much jousting with authority even an ex-police officer could take in one day.

He stopped by the barrier to the main car park, tapped in his car's licence plate on the keypad and snatched the ticket. The barrier went up and he drove through the crowded carpark searching for a space.

Christina sat on one cheek as she was wheeled down a corridor to the Maternity Unit. 'I think the baby's coming out.' She opened her bag and reached for her phone. A few seconds later she heard her husband's wonderful voice and was about to speak when her muscles contracted and the phone slipped from her fingers.

'I'm looking for a man who calls himself Ron Smith.' Gary spoke into the intercom by the entrance to the transplant unit.

'You have to make an appointment,' came the distorted voice of a woman who Gary could tell was born thousands of klicks away from Undermere. 'This is a secure unit, with no visitors unless registered.'

'I'm a former police officer and unless you open the door, I will call my colleagues and they will break it down. Do you hear me?'

He waited for a response. It came from an unexpected direction. Two uniformed men, both immense bulks rested a hand on each of his shoulders.

The sun continued to shine brightly that glorious September afternoon. For visitors to the fayre, time stood still and for a while the joyous event cleared their minds of all the usual day-to-day worries. Audrey looked at the memorial stone carved with the names of five schoolboys including her darling brother, Robert. She remembered a church fête held in Plaxtol, a little village near Sevenoaks, where the organisers had persuaded Gregory Peck to be the guest of honour. At the time, he was a world-famous film star - classically tall, dark, and very handsome. Even though Audrey was only thirteen, she could see why her mother found him so attractive. She smiled at the memory. Today her husband was creating many wonderful memories for local children who thrilled in the same delights Audrey and her little brother had shared so many years ago.

'There's a lady giving tarot readings,' Joel said.

Cadence peered out from behind a giant wraith of pink candyfloss. 'Do you really want to know what's gonna happen?'

'Don't worry. Nobody can predict the future, not even tarot cards.'

'I do like mysticism,' Cadence said. 'In some ways, I want to believe.' She slid her arm through his. 'Take me to her.'

'Perhaps not. She does look a bit spooky.'

'Okay. You join the kids on the carousel while I have a reading.' And she headed off.

Joel took a breath. Could he have met anyone more unpredictable than Cadence Clearwater?

'He's the nicest man I've ever met, except for Malcolm,

of course.' Tears flooded Eleanor's eyes as she picked up a rock cake with a pair of tongs.

Audrey smiled. 'Well, very special people bring out the best in others. It'll be your turn next.'

'It didn't even hurt,' Eleanor said as she screwed up the top of a paper bag and handed it to a young boy.

'What didn't hurt?' Audrey asked.

'The vaccination. I've had this phobia about needles since I was a child. It was so different to what I imagined. I wish I hadn't waited. If I'd been braver, the virus wouldn't have affected me so much and my kidneys would be okay.' Tears rolled down her cheeks.

Audrey hugged her. 'You will get through this.'

Malcolm came up to them, pushing back strands of hair. 'Ladies, you are in the presence of a man who has won a pig!'

The old friends broke apart and Eleanor reached for a paper napkin and dabbed her cheeks.

'A joint of finest pork,' Malcolm continued, 'is waiting to be picked up from Malpass the Butcher.'

'Congratulations,' Eleanor said, her voice a little thick. 'What did you have to do to win?'

'I hit a purple patch and bowled rough-hewn balls through hoops to perfection. I also think the cataract surgery helped.'

'Perhaps we should send your surgeon the joint of pork?' Audrey suggested with a big smile.

'I also won this apple bobbing.' From behind his back Malcolm produced a toffee apple.

'Apple bobbing?' Eleanor asked. 'You stuck your face in a barrel full of water with all that spit and dribble?'

'Ah.' Malcolm took a pristine white handkerchief out of his pocket and wiped his mouth. 'I fear you have a very valid point, Eleanor. Which is why the apples were served with large hooks and each competitor used a sort of fishing rod to hook them out. I think my long arms helped.'

'So,' Eleanor said. 'You didn't bob for apples at all. It was hook-a-duck by another name.'

'Precisely.'

Overhead came the chop-chop of a helicopter.

'I wonder who that is,' Eleanor said.

'I know exactly who it is.' Audrey smiled and almost danced with excitement. 'Tina must be having her baby.'

'Good lord,' Malcolm exclaimed. 'Is she expecting?'

Eleanor burst out laughing. 'I love your man,' she said to Audrey.

'Right,' Malcolm said. 'Perhaps we'd better get along to the hospital. At the very least, we could pace the corridors.'

Audrey cleared her throat. 'About your car. It's already there.'

Abel watched the helicopter take off from the rear seat of the taxi he'd ordered whilst in transit from Battersea Heliport.

'So, you're the famous Abel?' the driver said, looking over his shoulder for longer than he should. He nearly missed the mouth of the long drive that led from the burnt-out building on the moor to the Old Military Road and had to swerve to avoid ending up in a ditch.

'The shortest route to Undermere,' Abel said, 'is not through a hawthorn hedge and across a corn field.'

The driver laughed almost maniacally, and Abel wondered whether he should bail out before the car gathered more speed.

'Good joke,' spluttered the driver.

'What joke?'

'About the corn field, Lord Cornfield.' The driver laughed again.

Was he insane? Abel kept his voice, calm. 'You know me?'

'Sort of. We have someone in common.' Again, the driver laughed. 'Someone we both know outside and in.' He giggled deliriously.

'And who's that?'

'Your wife.'

Abel took a moment to respond. 'Hello Sean. I hear you're married with children. I'm glad things worked out for you.'

'Really?' Their eyes met in the rear-view mirror 'As far as I'm concerned,' Sean continued, 'you're the receiver of stolen goods.'

Abel sat back in his seat. 'I suggest you keep your mouth shut and focus on the road.'

A minute of silence later, Sean turned right at the end of the drive and accelerated hard. Abel glanced out of the side window as they climbed a steep hill and for a moment his thoughts were distracted by the beauty of the wilderness.

'Undermere,' Sean said. 'Where in particular?'

'The hospital. Christina's in labour.'

Sean snapped his head round. 'She's giving birth?'

'Before I get there if you don't focus on the road.' Abel felt the car surge forward. 'Drive sensibly. It's not an emergency.'

'It should be my child. She was mine.'

'Christina belongs to nobody. You never owned her, and I don't own her now.'

'You only want her for breeding, to pass on your Lordship'

Abel drew in a deep breath. 'You still care for her,

that's why you're angry.'

'Wouldn't you be?'

'It's fine to be angry, but it's important to understand why you're angry. Until you do, you can't move on.'

'Move on? I'll never move on.'

'You have to get past it. At the moment, you're coming across as a dangerous psycho.'

Sean appeared to concentrate on the ups and downs, twists and turns of the narrow strip of tarmac, lit by the late afternoon sun.

'Listen to me Sean,' Abel continued. 'Are you listening?'

'Yes, I'm listening.'

'You have two choices. You can either wish Christina well and get on with your life while she gets on with hers, or you can stew in your own bitter juice.' He sat back in his seat and stared fixedly at the back of the younger man's head.

Sean skidded the car to a halt near the Rorty Crankle Coaching Inn. 'I wish her well, and the baby.'

'That's good to hear. Now get going.'

'But I don't wish *you* well.'

'Fine. Just get me to the hospital and we'll call it quits. You might even get a tip.'

Sean paused a moment. 'I don't want your money. Get out.'

'What do you mean, get out?'

'Get out of my car.'

Abel released his seat belt and leaned forwards, resting his hand heavily on the younger man's shoulder. 'Do anything to harm Christina, or the baby, and you'll see what a billionaire can really do.' He opened the door. 'I hope I never see you again.' He slammed it shut.

Tyres squealed as the taxi roared off and was soon lost from Abel's view. The sun was still up but it would be dark long before he made it on foot to Undermere. The pub car park was empty and the pub itself looked closed. Hawksmead Fayre was clearly a big attraction. What about a bus? No sign of one in either direction. He took out his phone and scrolled his contacts with his thumb.

Christina was the only mother-to-be in the delivery room. She had seen many births on TV but still found it embarrassing to have her inner sanctum probed by latex-covered fingers.

'Well done, Bettina. It won't be long now. Just keep breathing.' The Irish midwife's voice sounded muffled behind her mask and under the modesty sheet.

'My name's Christina and I need an epidural. I can't do without it.'

From between her legs the midwife answered. 'Yes you can, Bettina, and I'll help you.'

Another wave of contractions took over Christina's entire lower abdomen and radiated to her upper thighs. Why was she not in a private ward in St Mary's Hospital, London, enjoying a pain-free, elective caesarean? Why hadn't she been cautious? Not even Abel's vast wealth could save her from the stabbing, pulsing contractions that kept on coming. She'd never felt more scared, or more alone.

Gary hated taking the scenic route across the moor when travelling between Undermere and Hawksmead. The thin strip of tarmac offered way too many surprises and Hector would bark to be let out for a run the entire route.

The VW suspension made an unappealing crunching sound as the two nearside wheels struck a massive pothole he would've seen if he hadn't been looking at his phone. Also, Hector truly stank. Although Gary was used to the smell, the stench was even getting to him. As for the leather interior, the rear was scratched and scored, and long strands of dribble had left unappealing streaks all over the seats at the front.

In the late afternoon sun, the Rorty Crankle looked stunning. He would have like to stop for a drink, but it was not open, he was driving, and babies wait for no man. He swung into the carpark and saw Abel pacing around looking at his phone.

'Oh my God,' Abel said as soon as he opened the front passenger door.

'Cover your nose and mouth with one of your monogrammed handkerchiefs,' Gary said. 'Or there's a used Covid face mask in the glove compartment.'

Abel got in and slammed the door. 'Thank you, Gary. Let's go.'

'If I were still a traffic cop, I'd book Sean for just being a bastard.' He swung the ailing Golf around the deserted carpark and headed for Undermere. 'Where's your bag?'

'I was in too much of a hurry to pack. I presume you have our things from last time?'

'They should still be in the boot.'

'You didn't do our laundry? Hang them up? Air them?'

'Didn't cross my mind. Any news?'

Abel checked his phone. 'Not a single update.'

Gary glanced at him. 'You'd think she could at least text between contractions.'

Their banter was interrupted by an alarming crack and a sudden lurch as the two offside wheels hit a sink hole in the road.

'What was that?' Abel shouted.

Gary's answer was almost obliterated by a deeply unpleasant grinding. 'I think we've just broken the front suspension.'

'Are we going to make it?'

The hideous noise stopped almost as quickly as it came.

'We'll make it.'

The Golf limped through a sweeping left corner and the two men took a moment to appreciate the panorama. A chunk of sun was bitten off by the moor's famous jagged Ridgeway, a challenging walk for even the most intrepid.

'It is beautiful,' Abel muttered.

'Unless it's bucketing with rain and you're trying to escape from a load of menacing men with dogs.'

'Happy days.'

Gary gave a dry laugh. 'Yeah. Happy days.'

They both lurched forward, their seat belts snapping hard, as the nose over the offside front wheel slumped down accompanied by a sharp, metallic screech. The car spun and fell off the ribbon of fractured tarmac onto a slope, blanketed with moss and wild grass. A rear wheel slammed into a rocky outcrop and the VW Golf with its three inhabitants flipped over onto its roof. The windows crazed as sensors released blasts of nitrogen to inflate the front airbags. The car continued sliding on its roof as it careered down a steep incline then flipped onto its wheels and came to a sudden halt on its side, half in and half out of a rapidly flowing brook.

Joel Redmond sat down opposite heavily rouged, wizened cheeks, puckered lips, and kohl-lined rheumy eyes, partly obscured by a lace veil and topped by an absurdly youthful curly black wig. Madam Petralee wore a crushed velvet jacket over a long cotton and lace dress, decorated with beads and multicoloured satin ribbons. She was seated on a foldaway wooden chair in front of a deck of tarot cards, placed on a square-shaped Bridge table, inset with worn green baize.

Cadence stood a few feet away, an amused expression hovering around her eyes and mouth.

Thin fingers with bright red talons tapped the deck of cards. 'What would you like the tarot to tell you, today?' Her words scraped across smoke-damaged vocal cords.

Joel looked at Cadence who smiled at him and shrugged. He turned back to the faded blue eyes with flecks of green and took a deep breath. 'Will I be famous? Will I be rich?'

Madam Petralee picked up the deck and gently shuffled the cards, almost caressing them as she stared unblinkingly at the teenager. She placed the deck down in front of her. 'Give me your hand.'

Joel took a moment to digest the request then stretched his arm across the table. He felt her papery skin as her fingers guided his hand and placed it on top of the tarot cards.

'Do you feel it?' she asked.

He looked at her and felt way too connected. 'I feel the cards.'

'What are they telling you?'

'They're a bit sticky?'

She grabbed his wrist in her claw. 'The tarot never

lies.' She gave him back his arm and cackled. 'And your pulse always tells the truth.'

'What truth?'

'That you are already rich.'

'Am I?'

'You are young, healthy, educated, and you have a beautiful girlfriend. To be famous is a curse. Do not wish that upon yourself.'

'What about me?'

Both Joel and Madam Petralee looked up at Cadence.

'What does the tarot say about me?'

Madam Petralee turned to Joel who hastily vacated the chair. Cadence took his place and rested her right hand on the deck. 'What do you see?' she asked.

For a moment, Madam Petralee seemed a little flustered. 'I see a beautiful manicure.'

'I have a part-time job at Wax Polish.'

The fortune teller rested her scarred hand on the young American's.

'What do the cards tell you?' Cadence asked.

'We shall see.' Madam Petralee lifted her hand and Cadence removed hers. Bony digits turned over the top card and laid it down. 'The Magician. He represents many things but as I look at you, I see healing.'

Cadence stared back at her, impassively.

Madam Petralee turned another card. 'The Lovers. The path to true love takes many turns but yours is short and straight, should you wish to take it.' She turned another card.

'Death!' Joel shouted. 'Come on Cadence, let's go.'

Madam Petralee stretched across the table and gripped the young woman's wrist. 'Death represents endings and beginnings. It's about freeing yourself from the past and opening your mind to new opportunities, new dreams, new loves.'

Cadence pulled her hand free and got up from the chair. 'Thank you.'

'One more card.' Madam Petralee rested her fingertips on the deck.

'No,' Cadence said as Madam Petralee peered at the next card.

'What is it?' Joel asked.

Madam Petralee looked up at him, then at Cadence. 'Would you like to know?'

Cadence shrugged.

Madam Petralee placed the card face up on the table.

'The Tower,' Cadence stated. 'What does it mean?'

'It represents, love, loyalty, fidelity.'

'According to Google,' Joel said, using his thumb to scroll the text on his phone, 'the Tower foreshadows disaster. Something as massive as it is unexpected. It is a card that represents upheaval, destruction, chaos. Dreams, hopes, ambitions are replaced by the harsh light of realism.'

Cadence stepped back from the table. Joel reached for her, but she shrugged him off.

Madam Petralee gathered up the cards. 'If you believe that phone contraption, it will do you no good.' She looked fixedly at Cadence. 'The Tower card is tricky to read but when I look into your eyes, I see this is a time for starting again, for shaking off the shackles of the past, for renewal, for beginning a new chapter, or even a whole new story.'

Audrey touched her husband's arm. 'There's Hector.'

'Hector?'

'Hector. You know, Gary's dog.'

Malcolm, who was tall despite his accumulating years, peered over many heads towards the ruins of the former school boarding house. 'I can't see Gary.'

'I'm going to check he's all right,' Audrey said, and she strode off, weaving through the happy throng of people who seemed reluctant to leave the fayre despite the dipping sun.

Malcolm followed. 'Be careful,' he called after her. 'Remember, he's a beast.'

'A very brave beast,' she almost shouted over her shoulder.

Two young children were pulled away from the dog by their parents as Audrey and Malcolm approached Hector, now lying on his side, panting.

'There's something not right,' Audrey said as she knelt. 'I think his front leg's broken. And there's blood and bits of glass in his pelt.'

Malcolm folded his frame and eased his way down beside his wife. He pulled at a piece of glass embedded in the dog's short hair. 'It's from a shattered car's window.'

'He must've been hit.' She looked around her. 'Where's Gary? He was here when Tina took Ron to hospital in your car.'

'Do you have his number in your phone?' Malcolm asked.

'I don't believe I do. I only have the landline for Rise House.'

'I'll call an emergency vet,' Malcolm said. 'But first, could you do me the honour?'

Audrey struggled to her feet and, once standing, helped pull up her husband.

'Geez, my knees hurt,' he said as he took out his phone. Using his index finger, he jabbed at the screen. 'There are a few vets in Undermere.'

'Why not call the RSPCA?'

'I'm on their website now but can't find the number, just loads of gumph. You would think they'd make their number easier to find.'

Audrey eased herself down again and knelt by the panting dog. 'Hello Hector. You're a very brave boy.' She ran her hand over his patchy fur. 'There's a metal disc on his harness.' She reached for her handbag and removed a pair of spectacles. 'It's a mobile number. It'll be Gary's. I'll read it out.'

'I think I'll go home,' Cadence said to Joel.

Alarm clouded his face. 'I'll walk you.'

'You don't have to. You're having fun, plus you can get a ride with your elderly friends.' She flashed him her California smile.

'Perhaps I could buy you a drink in The Falcon?'

'Ted gives me free lemonade all the time.' She touched his arm. 'But it would be nice to have your company.'

He paused for a moment. 'I like you, Cadence.'

'I like you, too, Joel. You're a special friend.' She took his hand. 'Let's go.' They threaded their way through the dwindling crowd, in and around the ruins, but came to a halt when they saw Audrey comforting a big, black, ugly hound – clearly in trouble – and Malcolm talking animatedly on his phone.

They heard him say to Audrey. 'Because we know the dog, and his injuries aren't the result of cruelty, they want us to call a local vet. The question is, finding one.'

'There may be one here,' Cadence said. 'Amongst these people.' Malcolm and Audrey looked at her. She continued. 'You could utilise the public address system the mayor used to open the fayre.'

'Brilliant idea,' Audrey said. She reached for her

husband and he helped her up. 'I'll do it now.' The crowd of onlookers parted to give her a clear path.

'I'll try his owner again,' Malcolm said to Cadence and Joel. He tapped his phone and put it to his ear. 'Gary. It's Malcolm. As soon as you hear this message call me back. It's Hector. He's hurt.'

Gary was shivering. He was partly submerged in bitingly cold water as all heat bled from the dying sun. If he stayed where he was, he would not make it until morning.

'Abel.' His voice cracked. He cleared his throat. 'Abel,' he said with more force. Abel was above him, held by his seatbelt, and was dripping blood onto Gary below. He was breathing, but for how much longer?

'Abel. Wake up.' Where did he keep his iPhone? Had he dropped it during the crash? Gary's phone was in his pocket and washed by the brook for too long to be still working. He had to get help, or neither of them would see Christina's baby.

The contractions were coming every minute. Where was Abel? She should be listening to relaxing music. It was part of her perfect birth plan for the Lindo Wing. She'd called Abel over and over to see if he would answer, but as lovely as it was to hear his voicemail message, it had become as annoying as the midwife.

The contractions subsided and her phone rang. She felt around for it as her panic grew. 'It's on the floor. Can you get it for me? It'll be my husband.'

Fiona, the midwife, peeled off her surgical gloves, stamped the pedal on a bin and threw them in. She looked under the bed and picked up the phone. 'Don't be disappointed but it's someone called Audrey.'

'Oh God. I forgot. I borrowed her car. I'd better

answer.'

Fiona handed Christina the phone. 'You have about twenty seconds before the next contraction.'

Christina swiped the screen and put the phone to her ear.

'Audrey. I'm in labour. Your car is in the car park. Ron said he'd put the key on top of the offside front. Abel is supposed to be here by now... Arrrhh. Sorry. Arrrhhhh. Can you come... Hector? Where's Gar... Arrrrrrrrhhhhhhh.' She dropped the phone on the bed and gripped the bed sheet.

Audrey looked down at her husband comforting Hector. 'Who would Abel call to pick him up from the helicopter if not a taxi?'

'Gary,' Malcolm replied.

'Something must've happened en route to the hospital.'

'We need a vet for Hector,' Malcolm said, 'and we need a car to find Gary.'

'I have a car,' rasped a voice.

Audrey and Malcolm looked at Madam Petralee who pulled off her veil and black wig to reveal a scarred face and a patchy head with clumps of greying hair.

'My name's Dermot, and Hector was my brother's dog. I have a car. I'll find Gary.'

Malcolm struggled to his feet and stretched out his lean frame. 'You're the Irish traveller, aren't you?'

'Guilty as charged.'

'The fire up at the school,' Audrey said to Dermot. 'You saved Christina's life.'

'We all played our part, including you.'

'I can help,' spoke a young man's voice. The three looked at Joel.

'Count me in, too.' Everyone turned to Cadence. 'The

more eyes the better.'

'The young lady's right,' Dermot said. He looked at Joel. 'You have a phone?'

'Yes.'

'With the numbers of these good folks?' He gestured towards Audrey and Malcolm.

'Yes.'

'Then we should hurry. The sun's going down.'

Where was Abel? Their birth plans were in tatters.

'Come on Bettina. Remember to breathe.'

'It's Chris...' She couldn't finish her name. The contraction made her gasp as a watermelon opened her soul.'

'Baby's almost ready to come out,' Fiona said from beneath the sheet. 'Don't push. Take short, panting breaths. Don't push. Let your muscles relax. Your baby is coming. You're doing a wonderful job. That's it.'

Christina felt latex fingers slide past her baby's head.

'I'm turning baby a tiny bit, and...'

'Don't cut me!' Christina gasped.

'You don't need an episiotomy. You're doing just fine, Bettina.'

'It's Christina,' she yelled.

'A little push.'

Milk squirted from an exposed nipple, and she watched it arc through the air. 'My boobs are leaking!'

'That's perfectly normal... now push. Come on, Bettina, push.'

Christina heard a glopping, sucking sound, felt a phenomenal release followed by an overwhelming emotion she could never have imagined.

'Welcome to the world little one,' the midwife said.

A few moments later, Christina heard a sharp

cry and, seemingly within seconds, was holding a wrapped bundle.

'Does this car have any springs?' Joel glanced at Dermot who was driving a Mercedes 300SE at breakneck speed along the Old Military Road's narrow strip of tarmac.

'There's the Rorty Crankle pub where I took Lady Cornfield for lunch,' Dermot said. 'Of course, she was plain old Tina then. Not that she was ever plain.' The aged Merc crashed into a pothole and Cadence banged her head on the rear side window. 'Sorry about that, missy.'

'Wait!' Cadence yelled. 'Stop. I saw tyre marks just before that giant hole in the road.'

Dermot brought the car to a halt. He thrust it into reverse, zigzagged back along the road and skidded to a stop. 'Best wait here,' he said to Joel. 'The moor can be treacherous.'

'We'll all go,' Cadence said as she opened her rear door.

The dying sun had turned the moor into a patchwork of shadows as the three stood on the edge of the crumbling strip of tarmac.

'Look!' Cadence pointed at the moss-covered earth. 'Those marks look fresh.' They all peered at what seemed to be deep ruts in the peat.

'Let's go.' Dermot stepped onto the soft moor. 'Keep together.'

'I can see a sort of escarpment,' Joel said as he rushed ahead.

'Be careful, Joel,' Cadence called after him.

'Yeah, be careful,' Dermot echoed. 'Remember, *we* are the cavalry.'

They hurried down the gentle slope, running

around water-filled hollows and skipping over innumerable scattered boulders.

'There's a side mirror,' Joel shouted. 'And I can hear running water.' He pressed on then came to a sudden halt. Flanked by Dermot and Cadence he peered through the gloom down at the VW Golf, on its side and partly submerged in fast-flowing water.

'I recognise that car,' Dermot rasped, breathing deeply. 'It belongs to Tina. I pray we're not too late.'

'A little prick,' the midwife said. 'Just to help your womb contract and so we can deliver the placenta.'

Within seconds Christina felt sick. The room began to spin, and she vomited with no warning over the baby's soft blanket.

'What's happening?' It felt as though her whole body was turning inside out. Was there a second baby?

'Here we go,' said the reassuring voice. 'All complete. Take a look.'

Christina opened her eyes as she was presented with a great sack of bloody goop and a length of umbilical cord cut off at the end.

'Lovely,' Fiona said. 'All delivered in one neat package.' She placed the placenta in a steel dish.

'I'm a mess.'

Fiona smiled. 'If you can't be a mess giving birth, when can you?' She popped back under the sheet and Christina heard the midwife's muffled voice. 'It's all looking good. Well done mummy.'

Mummy! She was a mummy. She looked at the little bundle, wrapped in the soft, vomit spattered blanket, as tears trickled from the outside corners of her eyes.

'Bettina,' Fiona said. 'I'll leave you for a few minutes to let you get to know each other then I'll be back to weigh baby, take measurements, do a few checks, and give a little injection of vitamin K.'

'Injection?' Christina heard her voice come out in a cracking croak.

'It's good for baby. Reduces the risk of an internal bleed.'

'My recommendation is that we put him down,' the veterinary surgeon said, a slight Spanish lisp to her diction.

Audrey's mouth dropped open. 'We can't.'

Malcolm stepped forward and looked at the vet who was wearing loose fitting trousers with knee patches and a khaki jacket over a T-shirt. 'Give us the alternative,' Malcolm said.

'I can set his leg and stitch him up but his hip, I can't do anything about that. God knows how he got here.'

'Do everything you can to help him,' Malcolm urged.

'Please,' Audrey said. 'This dog is a true hero. I'm sorry, but at the very least we need a second opinion before ending his life.'

'I understand. You don't need to worry. I'll do all I can to help the perro feo.'

'We cannot move him,' Cadence said.

'Unless we lift Abel out of the way,' Dermot responded to the young American, 'we cannot get Gary out.'

'He needs a neck brace,' Cadence said, emphatically. 'Paramedics wouldn't move him without one.'

Dermot looked up the long slope to Joel who was standing on the edge of the road with his phone to his ear. 'I hope they're on their way.'

'Somehow,' she said, 'we have to get the other guy out or he'll die of hypothermia.' She looked in the semi-submerged car through the broken rear-door window and shouted above the cacophony of rapidly flowing water. 'Hello. Can you hear me?'

There was no response.

'Let me,' Dermot said.

Cadence moved out of the way.

'Gary, it's Dermot,' he shouted. 'Your friend from the old school.'

A weak voice responded. 'Dermot, you bastard.'

'Are you hurt?'

'I don't think so,' Gary gasped. 'But I'm completely numb. The problem is, if I get out, Abel will slide into the water. He's been unconscious since the accident.'

Dermot tried to open the rear passenger door. 'It's jammed.' He turned to Cadence. 'I'll climb through the window. Can you help me?'

Cadence supported Dermot's shoulders as he threaded one leg then the other through the open rear window.

'Lower yourself, slowly, or you could get hurt,' she said.

Before Dermot could respond, he slid from her grip.

'Dermot!' Cadence peered into the car. Her fingers felt sharp edges of glass. 'Dermot. Are you okay?'

'The water's freezin'. I'm standin' on the riverbed.'

'How can I help?' she asked.

'Lean in and reach for Gary. I'll hold Abel in place so Gary can pull himself out.'

'That sounds pretty complicated,' she replied.

'We've been in worse situations, believe you me.' He turned to Gary. 'Lower your seat back so I can lean across and support Abel, then crawl out.'

'I don't know if I can move,' Gary said, barely above a whisper.

'Think of the fire we were in and you'll soon warm

up,' Dermot said.

'Are you sure you're supporting him?' Gary asked.

'As best I can. Now, get out. And no acting the maggot.'

Eleanor sat beside Ron as he was prepared for the removal of his kidney in the pre-operative holding area. She was dressed from head to toe in protective plastic including a cap, mask, and Perspex visor. Ron was barely dressed at all. He was simply wearing a hospital gown as he lay on a wheeled stretcher.

'I feel a bit naked,' he said.

She squeezed his hand. 'I will never forget what you're doing for me. You're the kindest man I've ever met.'

Ron's face creased and his howl of laughter shocked the theatre nurse who was writing notes on his chart. 'It's redemption, my sweet. For all my many, many sins. Nah, that's not right. I'm doing it because I've fallen for yer. Whether you've fallen for me, or not, it don't matter.'

'We're ready Mr Smith,' a second nurse stated.

'What's on the menu? Devilled kidney?' he chuckled at his own joke as he was wheeled through a pair of swing doors.

In dying daylight, Joel ran and skipped over boulders down the hill to the semi-submerged VW Golf where Cadence was pulling on one of Gary's arms through the rear door window.

'Let me help,' he gasped as he reached for Gary's other arm.

'Go back,' Cadence shouted. 'They may not find us.'

'It's okay. I told them we are down the hill from the car.'

'Have you got his arm?' Cadence asked.

'I think so.'

'One two three, heave.'

Undermere General Hospital's many odours penetrated Audrey's mask as she followed three coloured lines painted on the hard floor to help direct people to various units. But she didn't need any guidance having been a patient after a near drowning in the River Hawk, and a second stay when she was injured in a fire that destroyed the old school boarding house.

The hospital may have saved her life, twice, but she did not enjoy walking its long corridors, skirting around sick people being pushed on trolleys and in wheelchairs. She remembered all too vividly feeling naked and pathetic when she was recovering from her burns.

Following a brief chat via intercom to the Maternity Unit she knocked on a door to a side ward and pushed it open. Propped up on pillows, was Christina as she'd never seen her before. When they first met six years previously, on the platform of Hawksmead railway station, Tina, as she was known then, looked more like the Head Girl from an independent school, but now she glowed with new-mother hormones.

'Audrey!'

'Ssshh!' Audrey looked over her shoulder. 'I convinced your midwife I'm your mother. A little long in the tooth, I grant you.'

'Thank you for coming. Abel should be here, but he must've got delayed.'

Audrey hid her anxiety behind a big smile and a face mask. 'Congratulations. May I see?'

'Her daddy will be disappointed he's not the first,

but come and have a look.'

Audrey stepped forward and peered over her mask at the little blotchy bundle. 'I can see both you and Abel.'

'Have you heard from him? I'm getting worried.'

Audrey took a deep filtered breath. 'We think Gary went to collect him after the helicopter landed but has had some sort of accident. Hector, although quite badly hurt, found his way to the fayre.'

'What about Gary?'

'We don't know. Dermot's gone to look for him?'

'Dermot? You mean the Irish traveller? He's back?'

'Surprisingly.'

'And he's gone to look for Gary?'

'With our lodger, Joel, and his American friend.'

'But why isn't Abel answering his phone?'

'You know what the signal's like along the Old Military Road. Don't worry. Gary and Abel will take care of each other. They'll be here soon, I'm sure.' She watched fat tears fill Christina's eyes. 'Do you have a name yet?'

'Yes, it's...'

Audrey held up her hand. 'Don't tell me! Let me guess.'

Christina used a corner of the bed sheet to wipe her eyes. 'I don't think you'll get it.'

'Well, Abel is a less common Biblical name.' She peered again at the new-born bundle, happily sleeping. 'I've got it! It's obvious. Your beautiful daughter is a perfect combination of you and Abel. Her name has to be Christabel!'

'Christabel?'

'I'm a genius.'

'Is Christabel even a proper name?'

'Of course it is. There have been many notable women called Christabel.'

'Really?'

'Christabel Pankhurst, the daughter of Emmeline Pankhurst.'

'The suffragette?'

'Absolutely. She went to prison fighting for our right to vote.'

Christina looked at her sleeping angel. 'Abel calls me by my full name. I think Christina and Christabel are a bit too similar.'

'You're right, of course.'

'We have chosen a name. If she'd been a boy, we would've called him Mark after my uncle. You know, your brother's schoolfriend.'

Tears now sprang to Audrey's eyes. 'That would've been wonderful.'

'But, as she's a girl, she'll be christened, Rowena.'

'Rowena? As in Ivanhoe by Sir Walter Scott?'

'No, as in Rowena Ravenclaw from the Harry Potter books.'

Audrey chuckled. 'Rowena is a lovely name. My best friend at ballet school was called Rowena.'

The baby cried. Christina put her little finger in her mouth and Rowena immediately started sucking. She replaced her finger with a nipple. 'Ooh, that hurts. She's a strong little thing.'

'I'm impressed,' Audrey said. 'It took quite a while before my boys latched on. I can see Rowena is a very determined young lady.'

'Who needs to meet her daddy.'

Dermot was standing in the fast-flowing icy water, half in and half out of the car, his feet part-buried in the brook's rocky bed. He needed both hands to support Abel. He'd tried letting go and leaving it up to the seat belt, but the inertia reel wasn't snapping tight. The airbags in front of the seats were now fully deflated. As the car rolled down the hill, Abel must've banged his head. Whatever happened, he'd had quite a knock.

'Abel. Wake up.' Dermot had shouted many times but to no avail. In fact, he wasn't sure that Abel was even still alive. Unless help came soon, he certainly wouldn't be.

'Ten, nine, eight, seven, six, five, four, three, two, one...' Ron was surprised he'd managed to count all the way back to zero. Shouldn't he be unconscious?

The young nurse lifted and locked-in the sides of the stretcher.

'I'm still awake,' Ron said but both the nurse and the anaesthetist didn't seem to hear, or were ignoring him.

A gas mask was placed over his mouth and nose, and he was wheeled into an operating theatre. The room was crowded with people wearing green scrubs, white gloves, white masks, and Perspex visors. Bright lights shone from the ceiling, reflecting in the shiny steel of a trolley where he saw a tray of terrifying instruments. He lifted his hand and tried to pull the gas mask off, but the anaesthetist forced his hand away. The nurse appeared in view with a massive syringe and thrust the needle into his arm. He felt the liquid travelling through his veins and was entirely paralysed. He couldn't move an arm, or leg, or even his head. Just his eyes could move, and he stared in horror as the surgeon picked up a scalpel from the tray.

'Which kidney is it?' he asked nobody in particular.

The nurse, still holding the massive syringe,

answered. 'Mr Cottee is a bad man. Many have died during the course of his long criminal career. To atone for his sins, he is donating all his organs, today.'

'Excellent,' the surgeon said. 'We'll start with his kidneys and save his heart 'til last.'

By the light of a police officer's torch, the paramedic fitted a neck brace to support Abel's head, helped by Dermot who had been in the freezing water for more than twenty minutes.

'That was the easy part,' the paramedic said, his voice dry, flat, reassuring. 'Until we can be sure he has no spinal injury, we cannot move him.'

'What?' Dermot yelled, his voice raspy, croaked, vibrating with cold. 'I cannot stay in the water. I'm freezing to death.'

'That's all right, sir. I'm going to secure the gentleman to the seat with a couple of straps. Hang in there for a few more minutes.'

Gary, who'd been stamping around in the growing darkness stepped forward. 'There's a leather dog lead in the boot of the car. I'm sure it's long enough to wrap around Abel at least twice.'

The paramedic turned to Gary. 'I doubt it's strong enough.'

'You've not seen my dog. He weighs more than Abel. It's definitely strong enough.'

'We can give it a go, assuming the boot will open. When the firefighters arrive, we'll strap him in, properly, and take him to hospital in the car seat.'

CHAPTER NINETEEN
Monday, 27th September

Audrey entered the main cafeteria within Undermere General Hospital and saw Eleanor with her head in her hands sitting at a corner table. It could only mean bad news. She took a deep breath through her face mask and felt her damaged lungs, tighten. A few seconds later, she pulled out a chair and sat down.

Eleanor reached for her handbag and searched inside but gave up. She looked across the table, her face ravaged by crying.

Audrey pulled a lace-trimmed handkerchief from her sleeve. 'Freshly laundered.'

Eleanor took it and dabbed her eyes. 'Ron is recovering well and so is the person who received his kidney.'

Audrey removed her mask and put it in her handbag. 'Go on,' she said.

Eleanor gave her nose a gentle blow. She looked at Audrey. 'I will boil your hankie.'

Audrey reached across the table and squeezed Eleanor's free hand. 'What's happened?'

'The living donor I was matched with has decided against donating a kidney.'

Audrey paused for a moment. It was a body blow that could cost Eleanor her life. She leaned as close to Eleanor as the table would allow. 'You're at the top of the list, thanks to Ron; someone else will come through.'

'I don't think I can last that long.'

Audrey took a breath. 'You can have one of mine. I'll

get them to test me.'

Eleanor smiled. 'My dear friend. You are truly beautiful, but...'

Audrey interrupted. 'I am not past it. I checked. Old dogs like me can still donate.'

Eleanor gave a wintry smile. 'My darling, it's not your age but your health. They will put you through innumerable tests. Forgive me for saying this, but even if we're a match, they won't risk putting you under the knife. Let's face it, this hospital knows what you went through.'

Audrey sat back in her chair. 'Is there no one in your family?'

'I blotted my copybook with my relatives when I was young and frisky.'

'What happened?'

'My cousin Karen and I grew up as sisters. Our mothers were sisters, and everyone took us for sisters as we looked so similar. We liked the same things including performing. We had a few rocky moments when we fell for the same teenage boy, but one way or another we each got the boy we wanted, or at least she did. Aged nineteen, we were both engaged within months of each other and, to save costs, we had a double wedding. I don't recommend it. Sharing such a special day even with your best friend may save a few quid but one bride inevitably takes more of the spotlight.'

Audrey smiled. 'And that bride was you.' It was said as a statement.

Eleanor nodded. 'I don't think my cousin quite forgave me. And I don't think I quite forgave my cousin for marrying the man I knew in my heart I wanted.

'Oh, that is sad,' Audrey said.

Eleanor gave a little shrug. 'Kenneth, Karen's husband, and I both went to The Guildhall School of Music and Drama; me on the music course and he as an actor. Although our paths often crossed, we managed to keep a respectable distance. During that time, Cousin Karen got a job working for a hedge fund, first as an assistant and later, when the partners with balls discovered she had a pair herself and the brains to go with them, as a fund manager. She had a gift for making money, enabling Kenneth to live well despite being a student.'

'When did you sleep with him?' Audrey asked.

Eleanor took a deep breath. 'In my imagination I slept with him every night but, despite flirting, almost throwing myself at him when we were both drunk at parties, he remained faithful to Karen, or at least to what she was putting in the bank. Anyway, during the holidays we muddled along as a foursome. Going out, having fun. Cliff, my first husband, who was eight years older than me, was an accountant with a good business brain and had to travel quite a lot, especially to the States. A few years after drama school I got a job at Her Majesty's Theatre in Haymarket, London.'

'Phantom?'

Eleanor nodded. 'In the ensemble. I didn't know whether it was lack of trying or lack of chemistry, that I didn't get pregnant. Meanwhile, Karen was popping them out like peas between making her millions.'

'Having popped out two myself, there is no aspect of birth that reminds me of shelling peas.'

Eleanor smiled. 'Technically, I was a first cousin-once-removed to Kenneth and Karen's three girls, but they called me Auntie Elle. I was always there for their birthdays, unless I was on tour. We were a happy family. My marriage to Cliff ticked along. His sex drive was not to my liking, but I didn't for one moment suspect he was having an affair, which he was, with an absolute stunner in Saskatchewan.'

'Saskatchewan?'

'Western Canada. That's all I know. All I needed to know.'

'You broke up?'

'Not quite. I wasn't worried about his affair. I'd just landed the lead in a tour of Phantom and was living the dream. My voice was at its peak, and I loved the show, the music, the company.'

'What happened?' Audrey asked, drily.

'Manchester in January is not a happy tour date. We were playing at the Palace Theatre, and Kenneth was on tour with Sleuth. We met up and...'

'...and an affair doesn't count on tour. Isn't that the showbiz mantra?' Audrey asked.

'It was definitely my mantra. We made up for lost time and were at it like rabbits. I loved him. Every part of him. I was prepared to sacrifice my whole world to be with him. I thought he loved me, too.'

'I'm sure he did.'

'Yes, but not as much as Karen's income, their kids, his homelife.'

Audrey squeezed Eleanor's hand. 'It's very tough being the other woman.'

Eleanor used the hankie to dab her eyes. 'Our respective tour dates forced us apart and every time we met at family gatherings, I yearned to be with him.'

'How did your cousin find out?'

'I fell pregnant.'

Audrey's mouth dropped open. 'I had no idea.'

232

'My husband was tested in Canada, unbeknownst to me, and discovered he was sterile. No little tadpoles. So, when I announced I was pregnant he knew it could not be him. He wound the clock back to Manchester and broke the news to Karen. He'd been looking for an excuse to break up our marriage and my pregnancy was the perfect escape. Karen challenged Kenneth, he cracked under her inquisition, and I have been in Coventry ever since. It's not just Karen who has not spoken or written to me, but all my cousins. Even my late parents could not hide their disappointment. Luckily, Philip came along, my second husband, and we had a few happy years.'

'Where does Andy fit in?'

'Andy?'

'The editor of The Chronicle. Didn't you have a fling with him?'

'Oh Andy! When I returned to Hawksmead, I discovered that he'd always held a torch for me. I think we did kiss as teenagers a few times. Fortunately for him, he found Maggie who has proved to be the most wonderful wife and mother.'

'What happened to your child?'

'Sadly, she didn't make it past four months. I miscarried.'

'Oh, I am so sorry.'

'It's no more than I deserved although she most certainly deserved better than me.'

'Utter, utter rubbish. Being in love is not a crime.'

'Giving way to lust is.'

'Really?'

'I ruined everything.'

'Your cousin should not have put all the blame on you.'

'I was responsible.'

Audrey leaned forward. 'Malcolm drove a car, skidded on black ice, and killed a child. If the family of that boy who died on the humpback bridge can forgive Malcolm, your cousin can surely forgive you. Where does she live?'

'Undermere.'

'What?' Audrey was astounded.

'She and Kenneth live on the edge of town. Their girls are all grown up.'

'Get in touch.'

'I can't.'

'Do they know about your tea shop?'

'They've never visited. I saw Karen in town a few years back and followed her home, like a stalker. In my heart, I wanted to see Kenneth. I walked past their house many times hoping that their marriage was over, and I could claim my man, but they're still together, living in a beautiful, double-fronted Georgian house with a semi-circular drive and two entrances guarded by high, black metal electric gates. I may have stolen the limelight at our double wedding, but Karen is definitely the winner.'

'You underestimate yourself. Ron Smith has donated a kidney because he loves you. Everyone in Hawksmead loves you. In fact, I wouldn't be at all surprised if both Kenneth and Karen still love you and would do all they can to help if they knew you were in trouble.'

'I cannot ask. I can't.'

'But I can. And I will.'

Eleanor grabbed Audrey by the wrist. 'No Audrey. Please don't. I'm too ashamed.'

Audrey paused for a moment. 'Karen deserves to be

given a chance to do the right thing. She's your cousin. Your emotional sister.'

Eleanor shook her head. 'Kenneth won't let her. Even if she wanted to, he wouldn't let her take any risks. I know him. He quit acting for her. It was part of the deal to avoid divorce.'

Would she come? Joel sat in his favourite coffee shop around the corner from Harper Dennis the estate agents. Much to his annoyance, that was where Cadence would rush to at lunchtime. Did she really love selling houses that much, did she really need the money, or was something else going on? He'd spotted a young guy who appeared to work at the agency – perhaps she fancied him? He didn't think so, as when school ended for the day, she would hurry back to Hawksmead to work at a beauty salon buffing nails and threading eyebrows, whatever that was. He opened a dogeared copy of *Catcher in the Rye* given to his late father by Alan Bennett, the playwright.

'How come dad knew someone so famous?' he had asked his mother. She smiled. It was the one she adopted whenever Joel asked a question about his father. 'It was in the summer of 1968. Your dad was having breakfast with your grandmother who was reading the personal columns in the Sunday Telegraph. *"Public schoolboys wanted for West End play,"* she announced, suddenly. As soon as your dad heard West End play his ears pricked. Like you, he loved acting. *"Auditions are to be held on Tuesday at Her Majesty's Theatre, Haymarket."* Your father was sixteen and about to go to college to study for his A-levels. *"You should audition,"* his mother said. *"It will be a lovely experience to walk on a West End stage."* Your grandmother had been a professional actress but three children in three and a half years had forced her to seek consolation in amateur theatre. *"I've nothing to wear,"* was your father's first response. To have a chance of being offered a part, he was convinced he had to wear a smart suit.

'If I'd worn a suit when I auditioned for drama school,' chipped in Joel, 'I would've been shown the door before I uttered a word.'

His mother grinned. 'The world has moved on a bit.'

'I presume he got the role?'

'They went to Bromley and bought a suit on the Monday, and he caught a train up to London on the Tuesday. When he arrived at Her Majesty's Theatre, he joined a very long queue of hopefuls. Finally, it was his turn to walk on stage. At the time, the musical *Fiddler on the Roof* was playing. Now it's *Phantom of the Opera*. Anyway, he read a speech and sang a hymn, and went home. The next day, while he was having a bath, the phone rang, and his mother answered. To his horror he heard her say, *"He's meant to be studying for his A-levels. I don't think his father would allow him to miss college if all you want him to do is stand at the back of the stage."* Meanwhile, your father was hastily drying himself, convinced your grandmother was blowing his career. But she wasn't. She arranged for him to have a second audition and your amazing father landed an important role. Two months later, *Forty Years On* opened at the Apollo Theatre, Shaftesbury Avenue, to rave reviews.'

'How do you know all this, mum? And in such detail?'

She smiled. 'Because theatre changed his life, as it will yours.'

Why did his father have to die? How he wished he could remember him. He reached for the coffee cup on the table then realised it wasn't his. He hadn't ordered a drink, preferring to wait for the person who was consuming nearly all his waking thoughts. He remembered watching an old movie with his mother where this woman was obsessed by a man. What was it called? Bridget something? At the time he couldn't understand how anyone could be so affected by another. Now he did. He could understand it all too well. How his heart flipped every time Cadence laughed at another boy's joke or chose someone other than Joel to act a scene in class. There were other pretty girls on the course, but he had to think hard to remember their names. There was one who kept singling him out. He knew she liked him, and she seemed a nice person but nothing she said could deflect his attention. He dreaded the end of term. His mother would expect him to return home but how could he leave Cadence alone in Hawksmead? She'd be a sitting target. He knew his thoughts were all wrong and very patriarchal, but he couldn't help them. He loved her. He loved her with his body and soul.

'Anyone sitting 'ere?' A cup of frothy coffee was placed on the table – some slopped into its saucer.

Joel looked up into a wrinkled face, topped by a mop of dyed hair, white at the roots. Without waiting for a reply, the man who was wearing a grey suit, white shirt, and a dark blue tie, slid onto the bench seat opposite.

'I've not sat down all day. Didn't want to crease me bag of fruit.'

'Bag of fruit?'

'It's Cockney slang for suit. I've been for a job as a pallbearer. They said I tick all the right boxes.' He laughed raucously at his own joke.

'Well, I'm sure you'll get it,' Joel responded. 'You look very smart.'

The man brushed imaginary dust off his jacket sleeve. 'Made it meself in 1972 and it still fits.'

'Very impressive.'

'You might have nimble fingers when using that mobile phone thing, but I've got skills beyond your wildest dreams.'

'You have?'

'I was known as the Sinbad of Savile Row.'

'Sinbad?'

'Sinbad the sailor – tailor. I measured up the greats. *Which way do you dress Sir Lawrence?* Of course, I called him Larry.'

Joel looked incredulous. 'You made a suit for Sir Lawrence Olivier?'

'And for Sir John Gielgud. He was appearing in a play with Sir Ralph Richardson, he referred to him as Rayff, and he needed some new threads. Oh yes, I did all the knights. My mum said she knew I was going to be a tailor when I was born.' He chuckled. 'Do you know why?'

Joel shrugged. 'Your birthday suit was pinstriped?'

'Very good, sir. No, she knew I was gonna be a tailor 'cause I stitched her up on the way out.' He laughed ridiculously and other patrons turned to see who was disturbing their peace. ''cause I stitched her up on the way out.' He laughed again then took a pressed handkerchief out of his top pocket and wiped away his tears of mirth. 'Funny eh? I love that joke. Makes me giggle every day. Of course, if I get the job, I'll be measuring gentlemen for the long box, but they'll still be wearing a suit, I'm sure.'

'Hi.'

Joel had been so distracted by the man sitting opposite he hadn't noticed the door opening and Cadence coming up to the table. He half stood. 'Cadence. I didn't… do you want a coff… an infusion? A health shake?'

The man in the suit held out his hand. 'Sinbad the tailor.' He chuckled. 'At your service madam.'

Cadence briefly shook his fingertips. 'Nice to meet you, Sinbad.' She turned to Joel. 'Let's go to Mere Park. We've got time and it's stopped raining.'

Joel slid along the bench and got to his feet.

The man held out his hand. 'Nice to meet you, sir. And if you need a suit for when you marry this fine young woman, here's my card.' Like a conjuror, a white embossed business card appeared between his fingertips. 'But, don't leave it too long. After all, I am seventy-eight.'

Joel took the card. 'Thank you.' He looked at the name. 'Mr David Garrod.'

'At your service,' the tailor said.

Eleanor stood in the hospital pick up area relieved to be out of Undermere Hospital, relieved to be breathing fresh air without a mask, and relieved not to be wearing a Perspex visor which steamed up every time she breathed out. She was surprised the hospital even allowed her to see darling Ron, but she had tested negative for the virus even though she still felt tired and wretched. She should never have used up so much energy baking cakes for the fayre, but she'd loved being with Ron, working together in the Olde Tea Shoppe kitchen, and seeing all her dear friends after hiding herself away for so long. For a brief time, she even forgot her kidneys were failing.

Where was the taxi?

'Eleanor.'

She looked round and was surprised to see a familiar but drawn, unshaven face. 'Gary! What's happened? You look dreadful.'

'A bit of an accident. Why are you here?'

'I've been with Ron. He's donated his kidney to a young man, or rather transwoman, or woman. I don't know the details. I understand she had a bodged operation in Vietnam and suffered irreversible renal failure. She's only twenty-one. By some miracle Ron is a good blood and tissue match, so she has a chance of leading a normal life.'

'Did they say how long he'll be in hospital? Er Ron, that is, not the trans.'

'Five to seven days. It's really just observation.'

'When do *you* get a new kidney?'

She took a breath. 'Finding a match is proving difficult. I'm starting dialysis this week. Not a happy prospect.'

A minicab came to a halt a few metres away. 'Yours?' Gary asked.

'Yes. Would you like a lift?'

'Thank you, no. I have to see a woman about a dog.'

'Hector?'

Gary nodded. 'Yes, he's a bit of a broken mess.'

She touched his arm. 'I'm sorry. I know how much he means to you.'

'My real concern is Abel. I was driving him here when we crashed. He's pretty bad.'

'What are you saying?'

'He has concussion. It's lucky his skull wasn't fractured.'

'Does Tina know? Audrey told me she's just given birth. She didn't say anything about Abel.'

'Probably didn't want to add to your worries.' Tears filled his eyes. He used the heels of both his hands to wipe them away. 'I don't know why I'm crying.'

'It's shock.'

'I'm an ex-copper. I don't do shock.' He tried to smile. 'I have to go. Hector needs me.'

She watched him hurry away.

The taxi driver tooted his horn and Eleanor hastily opened the rear door.

'Hawksmead, please. The old tea shop on the High Street.'

'It's closed,' the driver said. 'I'll drop you a few doors down at the pub.'

Mere Park was an oasis of green and golden hues that were having a positive effect on Joel's mood.

'I learned, many years ago,' his Great Uncle Ben once told him, 'to mark important moments in my memory. People cannot forget bad events that leave an emotional scar but often forget happy times. From a young age, I made a point of carving moments in my memory to recall almost at will. So, my boy, when something fills you with joy, turn the corner of your memory page so you can easily recover the happy moment long into the future.'

Wise words from a wonderful old man Joel knew he should visit more often. Visit? He didn't even send him a birthday or Christmas card. He would try and set his Great Uncle up on WhatsApp so that they could message each other easily. Putting pieces of card through the slot in an old red post box was not for Joel, or for any of his generation.

So, what were the memories he'd make sure he never forgot? Every single moment spent with Cadence was already crystalised forever. He was desperate to say how he felt as they strolled amongst the trees, occasionally kicking a pile of fallen leaves. He fought the urge to wrap his arms around her, to say how much she meant to him, and to make her untouchable to every other student.

'What's the worst thing that ever happened to you?' She looked him straight in the eye as she asked the question then sat on a wooden bench. He stared, unseeingly, at the confluence of the River Hawk and River Peak.

'Losing my dad, although I don't remember him.' He sat beside her. 'You?'

'Losing my mom.'

Instinctively he took her hand. She didn't resist. 'What about your father?'

'I never knew him. I don't want to know him. I did want to once, but not anymore.'

'Has he tried to reach out to you?'

'No. He'd have a tough time finding me. My mom changed my name when I was two.'

'You mean Cadence Clearwater isn't your real name?'

'It's my real legal name. It's on my passport, my social security, driver's license, but it's not the name my mom first recorded when I was born.'

'What was it?'

She pulled her hand free and stood. 'My father's an actor. Famous. You'd know him.'

Joel got up from the bench. 'He could help with your career.'

Her head snapped round. 'And that's precisely the reason why he'll never know. My mom needed his help when she was pregnant. He told her to abort me. A year later he was born again into some religious cult and contacted her. She told him she'd followed his instruction.'

'He doesn't know you exist?'

Cadence turned to him. 'Come on,' she said. 'We have improv at two. If we're late, we'll have to make up an excuse.'

As the vast plumes of water smashed through the church windows, Cadence instinctively drew in a deep breath, the way she used to when surfing into a big wave wipeout.

HAWKSMEAD CHRONICLE
Autumn Edition

I t was the last glorious day of summer and the good people of Hawksmead celebrated in style. Was it a fête? A fayre? A garden party? It was a joyous coming together of neighbours and friends, desperate to shake off the malaise of recent years and to eat, drink and have fun as we all look forward to better days.

Former Mayor of Hawksmead and regular benefactor, Malcolm Cadwallader, told our reporter that he wanted to lift our collective spirits. 'We are so lucky with the weather,' Mr Cadwallader said. 'Five years ago, Tina Small married former police officer Gary Burton in the newly established Memorial Garden. The weather was glorious, and it is every bit as good, today.'

The garden has become a joyous space for people to visit, to picnic, to ponder life, and to remember loved ones. A memorial stone is the centrepiece, carved with the names of schoolboys whose parents sent them away to the boarding school on the moor in good faith, but who never returned. One of those boys was Audrey's little brother. She came to Hawksmead to discover the circumstances that led to his fatal accident and, in the process, found a new husband in Malcolm Cadwallader.

High resolution photos taken at the fayre can be downloaded *here* but may not be used in a commercial context without express written permission of The Chronicle.

Editor's comment: Christina Cornfield, formerly Tina Burton née Small, has given birth to a baby girl in Undermere General Hospital. On a sad note, her husband, Lord Cornfield, is still in Intensive Care following a car accident. We hope to share better news in the next edition.

CHAPTER TWENTY
Wednesday, 29th September

Audrey parked the Honda and looked up at the sign bolted to a grey pole. It was a one-hour bay. She checked her watch and then looked across the leafy suburban street to a camera attached to a telegraph pole. Should she have the audacity to stay a minute longer than an hour, a traffic warden would be notified by the eager camera operator and she'd be slapped with a heavy fine.

She smoothed the creases in the skirt of her dress, straightened her lightweight raincoat and walked along the pavement coming to a halt at a metal gate. She looked through the vertical rungs down a flagstone path, bordered by neatly tended flowerbeds to a modern, Georgian-style double-fronted, detached house. Her hand hovered over the intercom set into the brick wall to the left of the gate and thought about the conversation she'd had with her husband over breakfast.

'Let me get this straight,' Malcolm had said, as he cut a generous piece of Port Salut and added it to the great mound of marmalade barely spread on his thin corner of buttered toast. 'Your plan is to simply roll up, ring the doorbell and ask if she would kindly donate a kidney to the woman who seduced her husband?'

'They were both away from home on a theatrical tour. It doesn't count.'

Malcolm failed to suppress a giggle as he popped the laden piece of toast in his mouth.

'And,' Audrey continued, 'I think it's a bit sexist to

assume that Eleanor seduced her cousin's husband. He may well have been the Don Juan.'

Malcolm swallowed and took a sip of black coffee. 'I take your point but, guilty as he may be, Don Juan was taken back by his señora and Eleanor cast out as the scarlet woman.

'In a nutshell.'

Malcolm added a slice of cheese to another corner of toast. 'Well, if anyone can convince Eleanor's cousin to bury the hatchet, you can.'

Audrey's fingertip hovered over the button to the intercom. This was crazy. What was she doing? There was a loud clang and the wide metal gate blocking the driveway began its slow slide open. A black SUV hybrid came to an almost silent halt halfway across the dropdown pavement. The window slid down and a woman with brown wavy hair, clearly tinted and recently styled, smiled at Audrey revealing perfect cosmetic dentistry.

'May I help you?' Her voice was refined.

'Er yes. I hope so. My name is Audrey Cadwallader and I'm a friend of your cousin.'

'Which one? I have a few.'

'Eleanor Houghton.' Audrey saw the woman's smile drop. 'She really needs your help.'

The side window slid back up and Audrey was left staring at her own reflection. The car glided into the drive and the gate slid back along its track. Audrey was not sure what to do. She watched the gap between the gate and the brick post narrow and decided to slip through.

'Please go,' the woman said as she slammed her car door. 'The button for the pedestrian gate release is just there.' She pointed to a post with a shrouded button a few paces from the pedestrian gate.

'Would you give me two minutes of your time to explain?'

'No I won't, Miss whatever your name is. Now go. Or I'll call the police.' She pressed her key fob and the car responded by flashing its lights.

Audrey stepped closer to the woman. 'Karen, she's dying.'

'Are we talking about Eleanor?'

'She caught the virus and it has ravaged her body. Her only hope of leading a normal life, any life, is a kidney transplant.'

'And how much do they cost? I presume you're here for a cheque.'

'It's something that money can't buy. Only love.'

'My dear woman, money can buy anything. How much do you want? Ten thousand? Fifty? A hundred? I know she's got nothing but a cake shop.'

Audrey forced a smile. 'She told me what happened. What drove a wedge between you. She deeply regrets it.'

'How deeply?'

Audrey had no answer. The two women stood a few metres apart staring at each other.

'I think we've met before,' Karen stated.

'I'd remember if we had.'

'I know you from somewhere. You look older but your face is familiar.'

Audrey smiled. 'Too many lovely snacks in the Olde Tea Shoppe. You should visit, although not now, not while Eleanor is so unwell.'

'And a kidney transplant will save her?'

'Yes. If it happens soon, before too much damage is done.'

'What can I do?'

'Go to the transplant unit in Undermere General and allow them to test you for compatibility.'

'Compatibility to what?'

'To Eleanor. She needs one of your kidneys.'

Audrey saw Karen's mouth drop open. 'You're kidding? You want me to risk my life by donating a kidney to that harlot?'

'You love her, which is why she hurt you so much. This is a chance for cousins to come together. To be sisters again.'

'Please go,' Karen said. She turned away then looked at Audrey. 'I remember you now. You're the woman who came back from the dead.' She slid her key into the front door. 'Tell Eleanor, she was right. There is a God after all.' She pushed open the front door and closed it firmly behind her.

The Falcon was surprisingly busy for midweek, Cadence thought as she waited for Ted to finish pulling a pint of something brown and frothy and giving change for a tenner. Perhaps the pub's patrons needed sustenance before heading home after a hard day's work, although not many looked to her as regular nine to fivers, or even employed.

'How was school?' Ted asked.

'It's beyond any experience I've ever had.'

'Enjoyably so, I trust?'

She smiled. 'May I ask you a question?'

'I'm all ears.'

'The Ridgeway. You know, out on the moor. I've heard a lot of talk about walking it, but when I ask, nobody ever has, why not?'

'It's because the old duffers know all too well that if something happens such as a heart attack or stroke when tackling some rocky incline, they'll probably die long before they can get to hospital.'

'What about young people?'

'There was a time when the old school on the moor used to make their pupils tackle the Ridgeway. They called it an outward-bound school. I think Murder Academy was more accurate.'

'People died?'

'At this time of year, there'd be three nights camping on the moor and a climb up to the top of the Ridgeway, over two thousand feet above sea level. Crazy without proper footwear, clothing, blankets, First Aid, and a satellite phone.'

'Boys died?'

'Injured, mostly. Falling down rocky scree takes off a lot of skin. It was madness and yet it was compulsory.'

'Okay, you've convinced me.'

'My advice... walk on the fells, admire the lakes, the gullies, the waterfalls, explore caves, have a picnic, but do not risk an accident tackling the rocky edge of the Ridgeway.'

She nodded. 'Sound advice, I'm sure.'

He raised his forefinger. 'Last point. Don't go alone.'

She smiled. 'I know just the person to take with me.'

CHAPTER TWENTY-ONE
Sunday, 3rd October

Joel was in heaven …and in hell. He was with the girl he loved but was hot, tired and a tiny bit scared. He consoled himself by treating the exertion as good, practical research and an excellent way to tone his muscles. He looked up the steep rocky scree at Cadence who was tackling the loose ground with great dexterity. In her left hand was a folded ordnance survey map and, in her right, a climbing pole leant to her by the people in the pub. On her feet were walking boots she'd picked up in a charity shop in Undermere, and on her back a rucksack with an image of a drooping pistol and a slogan: *Only dicks carry guns.*

'What's inside the rucksack?' he'd asked. 'It looks heavy.'

Without slowing her pace, she had said,' A picnic for two, courtesy of Heather from the pub, and water, and safety stuff.'

All Joel had was his trainers, now ragged, T-shirt, and a light, semi-waterproof jacket. He had forgotten to bring a cap and his sunglasses. It was autumn and there was thick, bulbous, threatening cumulous but it was still bright fifteen hundred feet above sea level. He looked up the steep slope to Cadence and for the umpteenth time admired her long limbs, her grace, her confidence… he wanted her to be his above all else, even more than acting.

'Not far now,' she called.

'Can you see the cave?' he shouted back.

'Not yet. Can't be far.' She looked at the map.

'Hold on,' he said. 'My trainers keep sliding.' And on cue, he slipped and fell heavily onto his knees. Sharp stones dug in through his jeans. He wanted to swear but took a deep breath instead.

'You okay down there?'

'I'm fine. You go on. I'll catch up in a minute.' He pushed himself onto his feet, which wasn't difficult. The incline was so steep, gravity helped him.

'Take your time,' Cadence said.

Taking his time, and choosing each foothold with care, he traversed the steep gully, finally joining Cadence at the brow. 'That was not easy,' he gasped.

'Look at the view.' She gestured to a vast, wilderness landscape - a mix of green, brown and light purple hues, crisscrossed with fine lines he knew were drystone walls. 'Over there,' she pointed to a black, oval lake, 'is Drydale Water, a misnomer if ever there was one.'

'Care for a swim?'

'With a wetsuit, sure.'

'Not me. I'm hydrophobic. Water scares me, especially still, dark water.'

'Let's get to the cave then we can sit and have our sandwich.' She turned away and continued up the slope.

Joel stared across the valley to the high Ridgeway several miles away, relieved that Cadence had not suggested they traverse it.

'Coming,' he called as he scrambled over the loose scree, determined to regain his macho pride. He rounded a vast rocky outcrop and stopped in awe. Ahead were trees he recognised but could not name, growing at angles out of the terrain, with clumps of ferns gripping to the side of a jagged cliff rising high above. But his attention lay straight ahead to a shallow cave. 'Not very big,' he said as he fought to control his breathing. 'We've climbed all the way up here to see that?'

'No, but we're close.' She headed off and after a second, Joel followed her. They rounded another rocky outcrop, all sharp edges and pointed corners and then they both came to a halt. Ahead was a vast, cavernous opening, revealing millions of years of rock. The cave stretched back into darkness with the hewn stratum reflected in the still, black water.

'According to Google, the cave is as a result of slate quarrying,' Cadence said.

Fear gripped his gut. 'It looks pretty scary.'

'There is, literally, nothing scary about it at all. It's not like a cave on the beach carved out by the sea. There's no chance of being trapped by a high tide.'

'But anything could be lurking below the surface.'

'Shall we go in?'

'What do you mean, go in?'

She dropped her rucksack on the stony ground and headed towards the mouth of the cave. 'Look,' she called, her voice echoing. 'There are rocks sticking out of the water. Like a path. We can cross.' She bent down and loosened the laces on her boots.

'No,' Joel yelled. 'It's way too dangerous.' He came up to her as she kicked off her boots and removed her socks.

'Would you take my phone, just in case?' She offered him her iPhone.

'Don't, Cadence, please. It's too dangerous.'

She slotted her phone in his jacket pocket. 'If I fall in, I know you'll rescue me. But take your jacket off first.'

He looked into her blue pools. 'Please don't fall in. I'm begging you.'

She laughed and kissed him on the cheek. It was the brush of an angel. He reached for her wrist. 'I love you!' It was blurted out before he could shut his mouth.

'That's good to know if I lose my balance.' Her long legs took her to the edge of the dark, silent water. The cave stretched ahead, disappearing into the deep recesses of the excavated rock. Joel reluctantly followed her. She looked at him and smiled. 'Don't worry, I'll be back.'

He watched her jump with grace onto the first rock.

'Wow,' she said. 'It feels real smooth. Must be 'cause of all the water dripping down.'

Before he could respond, she leapt onto the almost flat top of the next rock. And again. And again, until the contrast of daylight with the gloom of the cave, meant she was lost from view.

'Cadence!' he yelled, his voice repeating back.

'Joel,' he heard her call. 'I wish I had my phone. I swear the rocks are sparkling. It's like Aladdin's Cave.'

'Okay,' he replied. 'I'll bring it to you.'

'Stay there. I'll come and get it.'

He took a breath and walked to the edge of the water.

'I'm on my way,' he called as he examined the first rock. He jumped and landed easily in his trainers. The next rock looked a bit trickier, and the surrounding water seemed very dark and very deep. Drips of water dropped from the roof onto his head. He eyed his landing point and leapt across the divide onto the next rock. And on to the next and the next. He smiled. He could do this. Then his trainer slipped, his balance went, the cave tipped, he screamed, and he was enveloped in the grip of bitterly cold water.

He couldn't touch the bottom. Water surged into his lungs. His eyes were open, but he couldn't see. He felt something grab him. A claw, sharp, terrifying. He fought its grip, but it wouldn't let go. It was pulling him down, pulling him up. His head broke the surface, but his vision was blurred. The pain in his lungs was beyond anything he'd ever experienced. A hand slapped his numb cheek. He was dragged onto the flat rock and a fist drove into his diaphragm. Water shot like a geyser from his mouth. He coughed, he vomited, he groaned. Hot blood dripped into his eye.

'Sorry,' he croaked.

'Lie still.' He felt her gently wipe the blood away. 'In a minute, Joel, we'll both get in the water, and we'll go from rock to rock until we're out of here.'

'I'm cold.'

'I'll get you warm.'

'Your phone. It's in my pocket.'

'I have travel insurance.' She eased into the water and Joel willingly entered her embrace. She kept his chin above the surface as her long limbs paddled to the next rock, and to the next, until his feet felt the stony floor.

Dripping wet, and shivering, they emerged from the giant mouth into the early afternoon light. Choosing a spot behind a boulder, and shielded from the light wind, they eased down to the rough ground.

Her face moved close to his and despite being chilled to the bone, all he wanted to do was kiss her.

'You have a bit of a gash.'

He smiled. 'You saved my life.'

'It's going to need more than a band aid. I'll call for help.'

'How? Our phones went in the water.'

'Wait here.' She got up and hurried to where she'd left the rucksack and carried it back to Joel. She lifted the flap and rummaged inside.

'You know, those guys at The Falcon are great. Heather insisted on packing food for us both, and Ted gave me the map and a satellite phone. Fully charged, I hope. He said it was left in his pub and nobody came to collect it.'

'I've never used a satellite phone.'

'Nor I.' She pressed a red button and extended the antenna. 'That's good. It's charged. Ted entered their numbers just in case. As it's international he said I can't call the emergency services, direct.' She smiled at Joel who couldn't control his shivering. 'It's ringing. We'll soon get you warm.'

He felt himself sliding, her smile lost to black sheets flapping. The last sound he heard was a discordant voice.

Cadence did all she could to keep Joel warm, but the bright, cloudy day had turned wintry. Mercifully, the rain held off. She had given their coordinates as noted on the ordnance survey map to Ted who contacted the emergency services. He'd rung back to confirm Mountain Rescue was on its way, but would it be soon enough for Joel? She'd covered his wound with a gauze pad held with sticky tape, but the blood still oozed.

'Holy Mother of God, I love this boy. Do not take him from me.' She hugged his unconscious body to her. Why had she come to this godforsaken place? Why had she encouraged Joel to climb the gorge to what was nothing more than a man-made cave? It wasn't even a natural phenomenon. She was scared. She bit down on Heather's cheese and pickle sandwich without enthusiasm but was surprised by how good it tasted. There were sandwiches for Joel, but only medical attention in hospital could save him. She shivered. Was it cold or fear? Their clothes were wet and were unlikely to dry anytime soon.

The satellite phone rang and she immediately pressed the green button.

'Hello.'

'This is the rescue helicopter. Is there a flat place to land near you?'

'I, I don't think so. It's full of large rocks, steep slopes, and a few trees. My friend needs help, real bad.'

'Are you out in the open so we can find you?'

'Yes. I'm by a big boulder not far from the crystal cave.'

'Hang on. I'll be down.'

A few seconds later, she felt the air change and then heard the chop-chop of an enormous orange and white helicopter. Within seconds, a man wearing a white helmet was hanging from a winch and lowered to the ground about fifty metres away. He unclipped his harness, gestured to the helicopter, and ran towards her, removing his backpack as he squatted down.

'Are you hurt?' he gasped.

'No, it's my friend. He fell in the cave and hit his head.'

'Any other injuries you know of?'

'He didn't complain of any before he fell unconscious. I think he's got hypothermia. Perhaps concussion.'

The medic opened his backpack and fitted a neck brace to Joel. 'I'm going to do a few checks then my colleague and I will strap him to a stretcher, and we'll get you both to hospital.'

'I'm fine. I can walk back.'

'I know you can, but I'm not leaving you out here alone. It'll be dark before long.'

CHAPTER TWENTY-TWO
Two weeks later - Sunday, 17th October

People said they had never experienced a wetter autumn. The rain came in torrents, with drops seemingly the size of saucers. Out on the moor, the boggy valleys could no longer absorb the continual deluge, sucked up from the warm Caribbean Sea. Streams turned into rapids, gullies into lakes, and the River Hawk into a mass of churning, reddish brown that pounded the high arches of the humpback bridge at the northern end of Hawksmead.

In the early hours of that Sunday morning, the black sky was lit by jagged lines of blue flashing light to be followed by deafening crashes of thunder that disturbed even the heaviest of sleepers. Forked lightning struck a mighty oak on the bank of the River Hawk. The surge of incalculable electrical power boiled the sap deep within its trunk forcing it to split with a night-rending crack as though cleaved by a giant axe. The vast weight of ancient timber hung precariously above the raging river.

Cadence was surprised to see quite so many people within the plain church, but it was a special Sunday for a certain couple. She reached for a woven kneepad hanging from a brass hook and knelt to pray and, as always, asked the Good Lord to protect her Aunt Angela, back home in Southern California, who had done so much to help her recover since the terrible day that cost the life of her mother. She whispered a prayer for her best friend Diana who had seen her through the trauma. She also prayed for the man she'd helped rescue from the car and hoped he was on the road to full recovery. And she prayed for the brave dog.

She asked the Almighty to give her the strength to be a better, kinder, and more open person, although she knew in her heart, she could never be entirely open, entirely honest, entirely the person God and her late mother had meant her to be. She gave thanks for sparing Joel and felt terrible guilt for the scar he would carry for the rest of his life. Mercifully, he had recovered well and was back to his old self. In fact, the experience seemed to have given him confidence. Instead of hiding at the back of the class he would volunteer to recite pieces for Miss Maynard; he would happily fight with sword and dagger for Mr Plant; and dance with the sex appeal of Ryan Gosling in Ms Dearlove's movement classes. Cadence smiled and recognised an inconvenient truth that resided within her heart. Lastly, she prayed for the couple who were marrying today; both damaged souls but two very special people.

By mid-morning on that autumnal Sunday, there were decent breaks between downpours. The cloudy sky kept in some of the warmth, so at thirteen Celsius it was not too cold for the bride's bare shoulders. Magdalena had wanted to wear sackcloth and a studded cinch belt around her thigh as punishment for her sexual wickedness. She had also wanted to marry in the Roman Catholic church in Undermere, but the process of getting an annulment agreed with the Pope, and her husband, from whom she was legally divorced, would have taken too long, and so she decided to speak to Reverend Longden.

'I have only one question,' the Reverend said as they sat together in the vestry of the Victorian, red-brick pile.

She waited for the wise old man to continue. After a few seconds she said, 'What is question?'

The Reverend smiled. 'It's the one you've been asking yourself - why do you wish to marry Mr Harper?'

'He's nice man. Simple reason.'

'There are many nice men in this world.'

'Ha!' Magdalena rocked back on her chair. 'There are many men in world but most I would not call nice.'

'Tell me about your first husband.'

Magdalena stared unblinkingly at the old man whose brain seemed as sharp as ever.

'What was he like?' the Reverend asked.

'He lied – too often.'

'In what way did he lie?'

'He lied with woman, many womans.'

The Reverend leaned closer to her. 'You mean, slept with?'

'Not much sleeping!'

The Reverend smiled. 'I understand. And Mr Harper, you are confident he will honour his marriage vows?'

She shrugged. 'I have hope.'

The Reverend stood. 'Well, my dear Magdalena. Thank you for coming. Perhaps you would ask your intended to pay me a visit?'

She stood. 'Why? You want talk him out of marriage?'

'Most definitely not.' He touched her hand with the tips of his forefingers. 'I want to be absolutely sure that he is worthy of you, worthy of your love, your commitment. Worthy of such a wonderful person.'

She smiled. 'Don't worry. I make sure.'

'In that case, our regular service begins at ten

o'clock. At ten thirty, approximately, the children will leave with their parents. At ten forty-five the groom and your guests arrive for the marriage service and as the bell in St Michael's Church chimes the eleventh hour, you, my dear Magdalena, make your grand entrance, supported by your Matron of Honour.'

'Dear Reverend, why your church not ring bell?'

'Our only bell was cracked. We had it removed for repair but in the interim, it was stolen and no doubt sold for scrap.'

'Travellers. They take everything not nailed down. They would take Christ off cross if they could.'

The Reverend smiled. 'Whoever took it has saved the church a repair bill. And we can hear the bells pealing from St Michael's belfry perfectly well.'

Wearing faded hospital pyjamas, Abel looked up from his new iPhone as the door to his semi-private room swung open and Doctor Manson entered. He'd grown fond of the young woman who worked long hours.

'How are you feeling today?' she asked.

'Never better. Even the headache has reduced to a dull almost infinitesimal thump.'

She picked up a clipboard hooked to his bed and looked at the latest entries on the chart. He was encouraged by her beaming smile.

'Well, Lord Abel, I am pleased to say, it's time we saw the back of you.'

He pushed himself into a sitting position. 'As much as I have enjoyed my fortnight's holiday in this fine hostelry, I have yet to change Rowena's nappy and, truth be told, I can't wait.'

'Nappy changing is highly recommended but no driving until you feel one hundred per cent. And please come back, or see your own physician, if the headaches persist, or you suffer dizziness, blurred vision, memory loss, brain fog, nausea, or feel like sleeping all the time.'

'I have done enough sleeping to last a lifetime.' He swung his legs out of bed and planted his feet on the cold floor.

The doctor hooked the chart over the end of the bed. 'I'll be back to see you before you leave.'

'I'm leaving now. I have to get to Hawksmead Methodist Church.'

'Then you'll be needing these.' She picked up a set of clothes wrapped in protective plastic which was draped over a comfy chair by the window and placed it on his bed. 'I hope you've got shoes.'

'My Churchill brogues appear to have gone walkabout, but your dear Professor Bisterzo is lending me his handmade Bontoni's.' He opened the door to his bedside cabinet and lifted out a pair of shoes, protected by a soft cloth bag.

'It's fortunate you have the same size feet,' she said.

'I offered to buy them, but the dear Professor refused to sell. His only request was that I return them unscuffed.'

She laughed. 'Italian men, what would we do without them?'

Magdalena, wearing a Versace off the shoulder floral dress and blush suede-leather heels, stepped from a hired Daimler, carefully avoiding a large puddle, and smiled as she listened to the bells ringing joyously, cutting through the heavy morning air.

Christina followed her out of the luxury car. Blessed with the glow of new-mum hormones, she wore an Air Force blue Christian Dior blazer and cream pleated skirt, with a matching camisole top, sheer tights, and cream leather heels. On her left wrist was the Patek Philippe watch Abel had given her before they married, and on her right was a gold charm bracelet with a matching locket engraved with the letter R. She handed Magdalena a simple bouquet of white freesias tied with a lace bow, and kept for herself a bouquet of pink, apricot, white, and yellow gerbera.

'Nice manicure,' Magdalena said, examining the nails of Christina's left hand.

'Your lovely new assistant. She gave me the Matron of Honour special.' Christina smiled and looked deeply into her friend's eyes. 'Ready?'

'Butterflies creating havoc.'

Christina touched her arm. 'You do love him, Mags?'

'What you think?'

'I think he's a very lucky man.'

Magdalena smiled. 'And I lucky woman.' She slipped her hand through Christina's arm. 'Let's go. Can't keep God waiting.'

Ron Smith was enjoying the organ music. Of course, in large part because it was played by the woman he loved. He still felt weak and a little sore even though the incision was not big. Laparoscopic kidney removal was a surprisingly simple procedure. Well, as long as you knew what you were doing, and the surgeon most certainly did. Ron spent three nights in hospital then returned to his Airbnb. And thanks to the miracle of antibiotics, he'd suffered no post-operative infection. His big problem was the itchiness he felt and the temptation to scratch as the wound healed. He was told not to do any heavy lifting for at least six weeks but lifting a pint in The Falcon he felt was worth the risk. All in all, he decided, donating a kidney was no big deal. Well, he laughed to himself, no big deal for

Ron Smith who was in love with a gorgeous woman, but certainly out of the question for his previous incarnation, Frank Cottee. And as Frank Cottee he was checking the church's exit points. It was something criminals naturally did. Also, he had spotted Gary Burton amongst the congregation and feared that the former police officer who had defiled his only child, his beloved Stacy, would try to arrest him.

Whilst listening to the ebb and flow of organ music he considered his options. At the main entrance, were two sets of doors. The inner pair were part oak with heavy brass pull handles and coloured leaded glass panels. The outer doors were also oak but solid, no glass, and thick enough to stop an army. To the rear of the church, he'd seen a sign for toilets and had decided to take a leak. There were no exit doors and no convenient windows.

At the front of the church, to the left of the pulpit, was a single oak door which Ron assumed led to a vestry and other rooms, and to an exterior door that opened to the graveyard, which he'd spotted when walking around the church. To the right of the pulpit was the organ. Although Eleanor's back was to the congregation there was an angled mirror above her in which she would glance and make eye contact with him. Her little gesture meant a great deal. To the far right of the organ, were double fire doors, made of steel, that opened out into the cemetery. No doubt some health and safety jobsworth had made the church put them in. *Waste of bloody good money.*

Joel was late. The bus from the cottage took longer than scheduled as it had to keep slowing down for the many deep pools of water that flooded the narrow strip of tarmac as it traversed the marshy moor. He could have gone with Malcolm and Audrey in their car, but it meant getting up an hour earlier. Since his accident, he found mornings really difficult. Perhaps the medication for his headaches was tiring him out. Every morning, he examined his scar. It was nearer his hairline than Harry Potter's and, for the most part, hidden from view by his floppy hair. Would it stop him playing leading roles? Although it still looked red and raw, the nurse had assured him when she removed his sutures that the cut hadn't affected his good looks. Maybe not. Thankfully, it was quite a while before he graduated from drama school and would need photos. By then the scar should've faded.

The bus rattled to a halt near the Olde Tea Shoppe. He could have asked the driver to stop by the Methodist Church, but he fancied having a short walk before joining Cadence for the wedding service. She had saved his life. He knew it to be true and couldn't imagine loving her any more than he did now. She consumed his every waking thought, even when his head throbbed.

Sunday dog walkers out on the moor, a couple of miles away from Hawksmead as the crow flies, heard a staccato crack carried on the breeze that caused their retrievers to stop chasing rabbits and to cock their heads. Nobody was close enough to the River Hawk to witness an enormous section of severed oak break free from the dying trunk and crash into the rapid mass of red water causing a giant wave to wash over its banks.

A Ford Galaxy was approaching the humpback bridge when the cleaved trunk crashed into its supporting arches, driving a wall of water high above the parapet and into the path of the car. The log jammed fast against the ancient stone and organic debris piled into the growing dam. The angry river breached its southern bank and coursed a lava-like stream through trees and shrubs.

Malcolm eased his lean frame up from the wooden bench in the Memorial Garden and took a firm grip of a baby carriage. 'My licence may have been revoked, but I can still drive a perambulator.'

Audrey sidled up to him, and they both looked at the sleeping angel. 'She is beautiful.'

'She is …and so are you.' He put his arm around her shoulder, and she kissed him on the cheek.

'Better put your foot down, Mr Cadwallader. A young couple are about to get married.'

'I think Magdalena and her beau will forgive us for taking an extra turn around the garden. It's not every day one gets to handle a Silver Cross Balmoral. Look at the suspension, the upholstery. Classic.'

Audrey squeezed his arm. 'And to think, we had a hand in bringing Rowena's wonderful parents together.'

'We did.' He took a deep breath. 'It feels so good to be here.'

They both surveyed the walled oasis of lush green.

'The warm, wet autumn,' Malcolm continued, 'has been a boon for plant life.'

'Can you hear that?' Audrey asked.

'Hear what?'

'Water. I can hear rushing water.'

More branches, flotsam and assorted river debris added to the humpback bridge logjam, forcing the raging torrent to entirely alter its course.

Cadence got off her knees and sat back on her pew as the organ music swelled then fell to an echoing silence. There was a moment's anticipation before Nocturne in E Flat Major by Frédéric François Chopin filled the cavernous church. The congregation rose as one and turned to welcome the beautiful Polish bride and her Matron of Honour. They made their way down one of the two side aisles to the front of the Victorian church where Trevor Harper and his elderly father stood, all beaming smiles and tear-filled eyes.

Rowena bounced under her tucked-in covers. Fortunately, the sides to the pram were so high there was little risk of her flying out. Malcolm was running as fast as his old muscles could move his long limbs. His only hope of saving Christina's baby lay just ahead. He didn't dare look back at Audrey. Even a quick glance would slow him down and he couldn't save them both. The change in air pressure and the terrifying sound of rushing water told him he had seconds at most. The end of the horseshoe-shaped brick wall lay ahead. He pushed the perambulator behind the bricks as water rushed past, sucking at his ankles. The wall, for now, gave them sanctuary. He gasped for breath as he looked at Rowena in the pram. She stared up at him and gurgled, her blue eyes shining brightly. But Audrey... where was she?

There was only one other time in his life that Malcolm had felt such helpless fear. He was a young man when he drove onto the humpback bridge and slid uncontrollably on black ice. That day he killed a schoolboy. Fifty-six years on, his decisive reaction he hoped would save the life of this baby girl. The rapidly expanding lake was contained, for now, by the brick wall, but rushing water was all around them, cutting off any hope of escape. Without warning, a large central section of wall gave under the mighty weight of water and Malcolm watched in horror as a tidal wave swept across the graveyard towards the Methodist Church.

Reverend Longden in his long black robe hitched it up as he climbed the wooden steps to the carved pulpit and looked down at the congregation. Cadence felt almost overwhelming affection for this grandfather figure as he opened his arms in welcome. But before he could utter a word, the air was filled with a cacophonous roar as windows to one side imploded and vast plumes of solid water shot across the church.

Trevor was the first to act. He grabbed Christina then Magdalena and shoved them towards the pulpit's steps, but the returning wave was too quick, and they were pushed and pulled in the growing swell. More and more water poured through the shattered windows as waves bounced back and forth off walls, swilling around as if in a giant bowl.

Ron's first instinct was to duck down below his pew and wait for the force of water to subside. He knew exactly what had happened. His second instinct was to try and make his way to the organ and rescue his beloved. Between each, great, sloshing wave, he grabbed a breath. Many in the congregation climbed up onto pews but the water was so powerful they were easily swept off.

Eleanor was no longer seated by the organ and Ron looked frantically amongst the bedraggled bobbing heads for sight of her. Panic was everywhere. The force of incoming water he knew was far greater than any possible drainage through the floor vents or inwardly opening doors. There was only one solution to save the woman he loved but it could cost him his life. He had already sacrificed a kidney. Was he prepared to pay the ultimate price? Frank Cottee, career criminal, certainly wouldn't. His daughter had drowned in the River Hawk. Was he going to let the only other person he loved also drown? The internal lake continued to fill. Many attending the wedding would succumb unless he did something. He admired the Reverend who, despite his great age, was helping to pull people from the water up into his crowded pulpit.

Malcolm lost his grip on the pram's handle and it was immediately snatched away. He watched it bob and spin in the swirling, frothy mass and then capsize. He crouched down on his knees, hugging the precious bundle to his chest as water roared around both sides of the section of wall that gave him and Rowena some protection. He was not sure how long they had before the entire wall collapsed so he decided to make a phone call.

'Emergency, which service do you require?'

'All of them, I fear,' Malcolm shouted above the roar of water.

'What is your name?'

'My name is Malcolm Cadwallader and I am calling from Hawksmead.' Rowena's cry cut through the enveloping mass of sound.

'What is wrong with the baby?'

'The baby? The baby's fine, for now.'

'Malcolm, it's important that you take the baby away from danger.'

'I can't. I'm trapped by rushing water. The river is pouring through the town of Hawksmead. It's a disaster. Many people will be hurt if not drowned.' Rowena cried again.

'You're doing very well, Malcolm. Other calls are coming in. Could you please confirm the baby's name?'

'Rowena Audrey Cornfield.'

'Malcolm, help is on the way but in the meantime, please do what you can to seek a safe place.'

The wall behind Malcolm shifted and streams of water shot through cracks above his head.

Joel could not believe what was happening. He had his arms wrapped around a lamppost as river water rushed past, pulling at his clothes, a greedy torrent as it tore down Hawksmead High Street, crashing cars into bow-fronted shops and cottages. He had been scared of the still, black water in the cave, but this raging force took his fear to a whole new level.

Ron peeled off his jacket but left his shoes on as he doggy paddled past bobbing heads towards the emergency exit. Water swamped his face, and his lungs heaved as he breathed it in but, he knew, he had to keep going. Seconds counted. He reached the double fire doors which opened outwards but were still securely closed despite the water pressure. Coughing and spluttering, he groped for the emergency release bar on the right-hand door, pushed it but it wouldn't budge. The weight of water was too much for him to release the locking bolts. He tried to kick the bar but all he did was shove himself away from the door. He needed some sort of leverage.

'Frank! Push against me.'

Ron turned and looked into the exhausted face of his nemesis. He was too breathless to speak but just gave Gary a small nod. Feeling the pressure of the former police officer behind him he was able to stamp on the release bar. Both doors burst open, and he and

Gary shot out on a shaft of water, adding to the lake already swirling amongst the headstones. A wooden fence that separated the graveyard from the first of many rear gardens, was flattened by the wave.

Abel felt a pounding in his head. His whole world was upside down. What had happened? The last thing he remembered was sitting in the back of the taxi, driving across the moor. He couldn't think straight. He was partly in freezing water hanging by his seatbelt. He reached out with his hand and held it against the roof of the Ford Galaxy then pressed the release button. He fell into a crumpled heap.

'Driver.' His voice came out strained and croaky. He shook the upside-down man by his shoulder. No response. He crawled awkwardly across the roof to the other rear passenger door and pulled the catch. Water was halfway up the window but going down. What was happening to the river? At first the door wouldn't budge but after a lot of pushing it opened a bit and he scrambled out onto the stony bed. He stood ankle deep in the draining river and looked towards the humpback bridge, now more a dam. Vast streams of water, like firefighters' hoses, were squirting through gaps in the stones. He could only imagine the weight of water pressing on the aged structure. More cracks appeared and a great fountain of water pounded the upturned car. He reached for the driver's door handle and tried to tug it open, but it was jammed. He banged on the door aware that within seconds the bridge would collapse, and they'd be swept down river. He knelt on the riverbed and felt around with his hands. His fingers gripped a jagged rock. He shattered the side window, pushed aside the safety glass, and eased through the gap to reach the driver's seatbelt release above him. As soon as he pressed it, the heavy man fell trapping Abel within a cushion of deflating airbags. He wished he'd taken a deep breath as the river was now deepening and filling the cab. He fought to free himself of the tangled arms and with the water and airbags taking some of the man's weight, extricated himself back out of the window. He leaned in and took a firm grip of the man's jacket collar and pulled the driver free of the car. When he was out and his head safely above the increasing flow, Abel stole a quick glance at the bridge where enormous plumes were blasting through great cracks in the ancient structure. Not knowing for sure whether the driver was actually alive, Abel staggered as he dragged the man through the flowing water to the riverbank, which was too high for him to climb out. Making sure the driver's head stayed above the surface he continued to drag him downstream towards the converted textile mill, where a section of river had been diverted long ago to drive the mill's giant water wheel. He shouted for help, hoping someone would hear, but he knew his voice was drowned out. He was confident he could haul himself from the river but to do that he would have to let go of the driver, who was still unconscious, or dead. Unsure what to do, the decision was made for him. The bridge gave and the sweep of the enormous wave was truly terrifying. Giant stones and great hunks of solid oak were driven downstream by the force. Abel renewed his grip on the man's coat collar and waded as fast as he could to the section of river divided by the wall that led to the waterwheel. Within seconds he was lifted and engulfed by the rushing river. He lost grip of the driver as he was hurled onto the grassy riverbank, rolling and tumbling until he slammed into the side of the former textile mill.

Joel was soaked. Fortunately, the force of water had considerably diminished and was now draining away. The High Street looked like a war zone. Vehicles had been tossed and were smashed together in piles of bent metal and shattered glass. Shop front windows were broken, and organic river debris was everywhere. When the flow was at its fiercest, he had screwed his eyes shut and imagined the lamppost he was hugging was Cadence. He had to make sure she was okay.

Tentatively, he unlocked his hands and eased away. 'Thank you,' he said as he patted the green metal pole. He walked up the High Street, lifting each foot above the dwindling stream with every step. His black leather shoes his mother had said he should wear on smart occasions were now ruined.

He splashed as he walked down the path towards the Methodist Church, where great pools of water surrounded the red-brick building. Headstones, those still standing, stood at precarious angles. But what truly horrified him, was the sight of an upended coffin, its lid swept away and its occupant nowhere to be seen.

'Help.' The voice was faint above the roar of rushing water. Abel pushed himself up and staggered towards the fearsome torrent, washing over the riverbank. He looked upstream. A whole section of the humpback bridge had given away and the remainder looked ready to capitulate.

'Help,' came the cry again, louder this time. He turned and looked towards the historic waterwheel and saw the taxi driver clinging onto the aged wooden paddles.

There had been times when a giant rogue had taken Cadence, and she'd rolled within a carpet of water for what seemed like minutes. It was a few years since those joyous days surfing on the Pacific but her instinct to take a swift, deep breath had never left. Even protected by the wooden pew, she was still surprised by the force of water that had rushed past, pulling at her clothes. She'd tried to keep hold of her rucksack, but the surges kept coming and it was as much as she could do not to panic. The moment came when she had to take a breath, but she was trapped, blocked in. And then miracle upon miracle, the water subsided, and she could lift her head and gasp for air. Once her panting had eased, she ran her fingertips over her abdomen and was shocked by their discovery.

Where was her rucksack?

She tried to move but was hemmed in by a mass of sodden kneeling pads and hymn books. At least she was okay. She prayed everybody else was too, although she doubted it.

The double wooden doors to the main entrance were closed. Joel turned the old iron ring on the right-hand door and pushed it open. Water, several centimetres deep, immediately drained out. He stepped into the vestibule and looked through the broken panes of the interior doors. The sound of moaning and crying made him want to run away, but he had to find Cadence. He pushed open one of the doors and stared at the carnage. The high windows to the left were completely smashed and he could see a helicopter silhouetted against the white clouds. He walked with measured care down the side aisle to a chorus of wails and moans. Limbs twisted to unnatural angles turned his stomach as others, shocked and bedraggled, struggled to recover. The tall figure of the Reverend moved amongst the injured and Joel hoped that Cadence was not one of them.

'Help is on the way,' spoke a refined voice from the back of the church.

'Is it over,' the Reverend responded. 'Or can we expect more?'

The man took care as he walked around injured people, past Joel and on towards the Reverend. 'The bridge was dammed,' he said, 'but it's down now, and the river is back within its banks. Have you seen Christina?'

The Reverend paused for a second. 'I... I have not located her as of yet. Nor her friend who was to be married this morning.'

'And our baby? Is Rowena safe?'

The wail of a siren cut through the wails of people in pain and relief flooded through her. If she could just get out from under the pew and find her rucksack, all would be fine. If not, she would have to hurry back to the privacy of The Falcon.

'Cadence. Are you hurt?'

The voice was all too familiar and belonged to the one person she didn't want to see in her exposed state.

'Hang on,' Joel said. 'I've just got to get rid of this stuff.' The blockage of kneepads and hymn books was tossed aside, and a face appeared under the pew. 'Hello.'

She smiled. 'Hi Joel. I see you've been swimming too.'

'Incredible. I expect it'll be on the news.'

'Then I'd better get to hair and make-up.' She wriggled out from under the pew.

'Wait!' Joel commanded. 'You're injured. Don't move.'

'I'm not injured.'

'Cadence, listen to me. You have a puncture wound in your abdomen.'

Instinctively, she covered the wound with her hand. 'I'm fine. Get me out.'

Joel helped Cadence up and she adjusted her top. 'Have you seen my rucksack?' She looked about her. 'I need it. It's got all my stuff.'

Joel looked at the mess that surrounded them. 'It may take a while to find it. Sit here, cover your wound and wait for medical help.'

'I can't wait. I'm going back to The Falcon. If you find my rucksack, can you bring it there?'

'Of course.'

She sidled down the pew, stepping over kneeling pads and assorted handbags and hats. 'And don't look inside. Okay?'

'How will I know it's yours?'

'You'll know, it's the one with the badge.' She reached the aisle and with her hand pressed to her side, carefully eased her way around hurt and bedraggled parishioners, lying on the wet tiled floor.

Abel climbed into the pulpit and scanned the mess of half-drowned parishioners. 'Christina!' he shouted. 'Has anyone seen my wife?' No reaction. He slumped to his knees overwhelmed with despair and loss. A hand rested on his shoulder.

'Lord Cornfield.'

Abel cleared his throat. 'My apologies.' He got to his feet and looked at the man whose suit jacket was ripped at the shoulder and his shirt had brown blood stains.

'My name's Trevor. Let's find them.'

Abel nodded.

He followed Trevor down the pulpit steps. 'Where were you when the flood happened?' he asked.

'I was standing about where we are now. We were lucky to miss the full force, but Magdalena and Tina were washed out when the fire doors burst open. I managed to grab hold of my dad, but I couldn't do anything about the girls.'

Abel looked towards the emergency exit.

An authoritative voice spoke from the rear of the church. 'Please listen.' They turned and saw a uniformed police officer. 'The first ambulance has arrived. More are on their way. Please allow the paramedics to treat those with life-threatening conditions first.'

Abel turned to Trevor. 'Let's go.'

The two men splashed out of the emergency exit into bright midday cloud. The undulating graveyard was awash with water which came up to their knees in places. Partly submerged tombstones were at sharp angles.

'Look,' Abel said as he pointed. 'The water's flowing through those rear gardens.'

'I don't know about you,' Trevor shivered, 'but I'm really feeling the cold. I'm worried they'll suffer hypothermia.'

'Then we'd better find them.' Abel stomped through pools of water and climbed the slight incline to where two sections of fence were flattened. He looked into the rear gardens of several cottages and saw tables, chairs and plant pots strewn, and border fences with neighbouring properties smashed down.

Trevor stood beside him. 'What a mess.'

Abel nodded. 'It looks as though the bulk of water flooded through the gardens and continued to lower ground towards the south of town.' He stepped off the small bank and waded through water into the rear garden of the first cottage.

'I think we must prepare for the worst,' Trevor called, before following him.

Abel ignored the doom-laden words and pressed on, doing his best to avoid hazards lying under water. French windows to the first cottage were shattered with the doors hanging off their hinges.

'Should we go in?' Trevor asked.

Abel shook his head. 'The force of water would've carried them much further.'

They trudged on through the rear gardens. Every cottage had smashed windows and broken doors. Finally, they came to a brick wall.

'The water hit this wall,' Abel said, 'then some crashed through into the cottage, but it looks as though most flowed down the slope to the rear of the garden.' Abel pointed to where a broken fence led to woodland and they both hurried over to it. Side by side, they looked down the wooded incline, where much vegetation had been uprooted.

'Where does it lead?' Abel asked.

'To the railway at the southern end of town. There's a tunnel under the track where rainwater is funnelled. I expect the track is flooded.'

'Let's go.'

'You think they're down there, in the woods, amongst the trees?' Trevor asked.

'Coming?'

Trevor grabbed Abel's arm. 'Wait. We don't have a phone. If we find them and they're injured, we need to call for help.'

Without answering, Abel sloshed towards the rear of the cottage and stepped through the shattered doors into the sitting room. 'Any phone left in here would be ruined,' Abel said as Trevor joined him.

'*Help.*' The cry was faint.

'Did you hear that?' Abel walked back to the broken doorway and called out. 'Hello! Anyone there?'

'Yes, I'm here.'

Abel turned back to the room and saw a tall man, bent over a walking stick. 'Why are you in my house?' His voice was a mix of Irish and what Abel thought he recognised as the local accent.

'Have you a phone?' Trevor asked.

'The telegraph pole was felled. The line is dead.'

'Do you have an iPhone?' Abel interjected.

'Do I look like a man with an iPhone?'

'Any mobile phone?' Abel pressed.

'*Help.*' The cry cut through from outside and both Abel and Trevor raced for the door.

'What about me?' The crooked man fell to his knees. 'My home is ruined.'

The two men splashed through the waterlogged garden.

'*Help.*'

'I know the voice,' Abel said as they looked down into the scrubland.

'If you're looking for a woman, she's upstairs,' shouted the man from the cottage.

Abel and Trevor turned and hurried back. 'What woman?' Abel asked.

'Come and see for yourself.'

They followed the bent man as he trudged across his sodden carpet into his hallway.

'She's up there.'

Abel was the first to make a move and he hurried up the stairs. At the top he turned left and pushed open a door. There was a double bed, cottage size, but no woman.

They left the room and crossed the landing to the second bedroom and pushed open a door. The room was small, with drawn, sill-height chintz curtains and an unmade single bed. A small pile of clothes lay on the carpet.

Abel picked up a sodden dress. 'Medium height, slim build.'

'Definitely not Magdalena's,' Trevor said.

'Nor Christina's,' Abel responded as he dropped the wet dress back on the carpet.

'Can you hear that?' Trevor asked. 'It's water. Whoever the dress belongs to, is taking a shower.'

'Let's go.' Abel followed Trevor down the stairs. They entered the cottage's back room and saw the man slumped in an armchair.

'Is she the person you seek?' the Irishman asked.

'Sadly not, but we wish her well,' Abel said. 'She's taking a shower.'

'It'll be cold. The power's off.'

The two men stepped out of the cottage and saw a man on his hands and knees at the end of the garden.

'Gary,' Abel called.

'You know him?' Trevor asked.

'He's Christina's first husband.'

'Of course.'

Both men went to Gary's aid and lifted him onto his feet.

'I'm never going on a water slide ever again.' Bedraggled, Gary looked at Abel. 'Tina and Magdalena are down there.'

It was a relief for Joel to see the Methodist Church filling up with first responders. Firefighters were sweeping out excess water; police officers were taking names, phone numbers and addresses; and paramedics were tending to the injured. Hovering above, he could hear the chop-chop of the search and rescue helicopter.

Reverend Longden was going amongst his flock giving what comfort he could. Joel decided to take on the job of collecting personal possessions and placing them on the front pew. There were many handbags, umbrellas, the occasional walking stick, and numerous ruined women's hats. He picked up one and tried to reshape it.

'Sarah McAlister is in for a lot of business.'

He looked at a tall woman who appeared to have escaped the onslaught.

'Sarah's our local bespoke milliner,' she said.

'Aunt Eleanor!'

'Hello Joel. It's lovely to see you.'

'I thought you were isolating?'

'I was. I'm on the transplant list but cannot just sit at home. As my friend Magdalena was getting married today, I thought it was worth the risk of catching an infection. I didn't factor in flooding. I'm looking for the man who donated a kidney on my behalf.'

'I'm sure he'll be fine.'

'Where were you when the water hit?'

'On my way here. A lamppost saved me.'

'You must let your mother know you're okay.'

'My new phone's ruined.'

'My phone survived. Follow me.' She led Joel towards the organ with its three rows of keys, numerous ivory stops, and alloy pipes leading to the roof of the church. 'I fear the organ will need a little work.' She went behind the grand instrument and opened a narrow door. 'When the water smashed through the windows, I slipped through here into the vestry. I felt bad just saving myself.'

Joel followed her into a darkened room. 'You did the right thing.'

She half shrugged. 'I managed to slam the door shut before the worst of the flood. Water squirted through the keyhole and seeped around the edges, but the Victorians knew how to build churches.' She picked up a leather handbag and took out her phone. 'We have a signal.'

The earth was incredibly slippery. They did their best to avoid the stream of water that still poured through the tangled roots, but Professor Bisterzo's handmade leather shoes were no match for the mud. Trevor was also shod inappropriately for the sodden terrain, full of trip hazards, and often clung to Abel when his smooth leather soles slipped.

'I'm not surprised Gary couldn't get them out,' Trevor said. 'This is treacherous.'

'I think the dense undergrowth,' Abel gasped, 'although a nightmare to walk through, probably saved their lives.'

'But they'll be scratched to buggery,' Trevor added.

Joel and Eleanor stepped through the little door by the organ, back into the church. 'Come home with me and dry off. I might be able to rustle up some food. Hopefully, the power is still on, and my friend Ron might be waiting there.'

'I would love to, but I need to find a rucksack.'

'It may have washed out when the doors were opened.'

Joel nodded.

'Does it belong to the young lady Audrey told me about?'

'Yes, she's gone back to The Falcon. I'm a bit worried about her. She said she was all right, but I could see a hole in her abdomen. A puncture wound.'

'Go to her.' She looked at the sad row of bags sitting on the wooden pew. 'You've done sterling work collecting all these possessions. The Reverend will make sure they're returned to their owners.' She pushed a couple of handbags aside and sat on the pew. 'I don't feel all that good.'

'Take my arm, Aunt Eleanor. I'll see you home.'

She smiled and got to her feet. 'For a young man you're very mature.' She took his arm and they walked together, treading carefully around people who were slumped on the floor awaiting medical attention.

'How is life with Audrey and Malcolm?'

'They're wonderful people. So old and yet so young. I think I love them.'

'You'll not be the first. I'm sure they love having young blood in their home.'

The main entrance doors were open. They sidled past police officers and paramedics and entered a world of devastation. Most shocking for Joel, was the sight of a Honda Jazz rolled on its side by a hedge.

'That's Malcolm's car,' Joel blurted. 'I forgot. Oh my God.' He ran to the car.

'Keep away!' The force of the command stopped Joel in his tracks.

'It belongs to a friend,' he said to the firefighter. 'They may be trapped inside.'

The uniformed man approached him. 'It's empty. We're just about to right it, to stop it being a danger.'

'Do you know where the people are?'

'I'm sure they're fine,' said the firefighter.

Eleanor gripped Joel's arm. 'They're tough old birds. We'll find them soon enough.' She led Joel away from the upturned Honda and they headed towards the High Street. The water had drained away leaving cars tossed on top of each other, plant pots and troughs shattered across the road, and windows to the bow-fronted cottages and shops smashed as far as they could see.

'Oh dear,' Eleanor said.

Trevor grabbed a Juniper shrub that was clinging to the side of the hill and shouted, 'Magdalena'.

'Here,' cried a voice.

'We're coming to get you,' Abel gasped.

'Tina needs hospital,' Magdalena called back. 'As soon as possible.'

Both men slipped and fell, and cursed, until they arrived at an oak tree. It was vast, and old, with a hollowed-out trunk, within which sat Magdalena with her arm around Christina.

'She's bleeding from bun. Lost much blood.'

'How did you survive?' Trevor asked.

'We can discuss the miracle later,' Abel said.

Magdalena looked up at Trevor. 'We survive thanks to tree catching us. We float in our own little pool until water go away.'

'Has Christina any external injuries?' Abel asked.

'A thousand scratches, as do I. The pain will come later. But she is bleeding.'

Trevor looked up the hill. 'How are we going to do this? She's too heavy to carry over such difficult terrain.'

Abel looked at him. 'What about if we follow the stream down? Won't that be easier?'

'I have solution.'

Both men looked at Magdalena.

'I carry her on my shoulder, and you support me from each side. We go quick. Downhill, not good. Who knows what is by railway.'

It was a plan and the only one with a realistic chance of success. Magdalena eased her way from under Christina, and Trevor helped her stand. She flexed and stretched her muscles. 'Wedding dress fit for bin,' she said.

Abel got into the hollow tree and lifted Christina's shoulders.

Trevor gripped her ankles. 'She is surprisingly heavy,' he said, 'despite no longer carrying the baby.' Together, they eased her out from the womb of the tree. Trevor reached for Magdalena. 'I think she's too heavy for you, Mags.'

'First, I Polish,' she said. 'Second, we have no choice. This is only way.' She peeled off her skirt revealing torn tights and scratched and scraped legs. 'Don't look, my darling,' she said to Trevor.

'Where are your shoes?' Abel asked.

Magdalena shrugged. 'Bare feet is better.'

Both men undid their laces and threw their shoes into the hollow of the oak tree.

'We make this quick,' Magdalena said. She knelt down on one knee and Abel and Trevor lifted Christina onto her shoulder. She wrapped her arm around Christina's legs and clamped her hands together. 'Grip my elbows,' she said, assertively.

The men did as she instructed.

'Whatever happens, we don't give up,' she said. 'You are my wingmen. Now lift me.' Abel and Trevor helped Magdalena get to her feet. 'I will choose best route. You keep me balanced.'

And so the six-legged beast began the treacherous climb up the drying stream. Bare foot, each one would yelp when they trod on a sharp stone or hidden tree root. Slipping, falling, determined, they tramped over bedraggled shrubs, sliding, slipping, skidding until, more than exhausted, they made the final heave, stepping on bits of broken fencing and falling to their knees in a jumbled heap onto sodden lawn.

Abel and Trevor eased Christina's inert body off Magdalena's shoulder and laid her down on the waterlogged grass.

Magdalena bent over and wept with exhaustion as Abel nursed Christina's head in the crook of his arm.

'All the phones are out,' said a woman's voice. 'How is she?'

Abel looked up and saw Audrey standing in an old, oversized bathrobe.

'Not good,' he said.

'Gary has gone to find a car that still works.'

'Where's Rowena?' Abel asked.

Audrey paused. 'Malcolm and I were walking with Rowena in the Memorial Garden when the water came.'

'What are you saying?'

'He ran ahead of me...'

'He ran?'

'He will keep Rowena safe of that you can be sure.'

'But you weren't safe,' Abel said. 'The water caught you.'

'Malcolm ran faster.'

Gary stepped from the cottage into the garden. 'I have a car.'

'Could you help me lift her?' Abel asked.

Together, ex-husband and current husband lifted Christina until Abel could cradle her in his arms. He looked towards Magdalena and Trevor. 'Come with us.'

She shook her head. 'I cannot move. Go. Please go.'

Helped by Gary and Audrey, Abel carried his wife through the damp cottage into the hall. The tall man with the crooked back opened the front door.

The only way out of the narrow entrance was to traverse sideways. Once Abel was standing on the pavement, he took a moment to admire a classic teal blue, two-door Mercedes 220 SE.

'Where did you find that?' Abel panted. 'It has to be mid-1960s.'

'It belonged to Tina's father,' Gary replied. 'It was in the garage at the house.' He opened the passenger door. 'We'll strap Tina in the front seat.'

While Abel and Gary eased Christina into the car, Audrey turned to the man with the bent back. 'Mr O'Brien, thank you.'

'You know my name?'

'We met many years ago when I first arrived in Hawksmead.'

'I remember. I warned you about the Russian property developers.'

'You did.' She smiled. 'Thank you for saving me again.'

He shook his stick. 'I'm glad we could help.'

She kissed him on the cheek, much to his evident pleasure.

Gary called from the car. 'Audrey, are you coming with us?'

'I'm going to look for Malcolm and Rowena.'

'How can I contact you?' Abel called.

'I'll bring your baby to the hospital.'

Joel stood in the Olde Tea Shoppe and looked at the mess caused by the flooding.

'Go find your friend,' his godmother said.

'I'll help you clear up first.'

'I think I'll take a few photos with my phone, for the insurers, then I'm going to have a lie down.'

'You should see a doctor.'

'I'm just a bit tired.'

'When will you get a new kidney?'

'Hopefully, soon.'

'You can have one of mine.'

Eleanor gave Joel a hug. 'I love you.' She pulled away. 'My friend Ron has already done the honours, so I should get one soon.'.

'Was he in church?' Joel asked.

'Yes.'

'I'll go look for him.'

'No. He's a survivor. He'll be okay, I'm sure. Now go get your girl.'

'She'll probably send me packing. She's very strong-willed.'

Eleanor smiled. 'And if she weren't, you wouldn't be interested.'

'I think I'm in love.' He half laughed. 'Real love, I mean.'

'And real love hurts,' she said.

He nodded. 'I just want to protect her.'

Eleanor gripped his shoulders. 'Your young lady has travelled halfway across the world, on her own, to attend drama school. Does that sound like a person who needs your protection?'

He shrugged.

'If I were her,' Eleanor went on to say, 'I would want your friendship, your respect for her talent as a performer, but not your protection. Of course, if a bunch of guys attacked her, she'd appreciate your help fighting them off.'

'I'd kill anyone who hurt her.'

'Be her friend – don't stress her out by coming on too strong, too early.'

'I'll try not to, but I can't promise.'

Eleanor kissed her godson on the cheek. 'Of course, if it really is true love, move heaven and earth to make her yours.'

He burst out laughing. 'You are brilliant, Aunt Eleanor.'

Swamped by the towelling bathrobe and wearing a couple of pairs of Mr O'Brien's socks within his oversized slippers, Audrey trudged up the devastated High Street. She knew she'd been lucky. She'd clung to a branch that got jammed by a no parking sign, and O'Brien with his crooked back and gnarled walking stick had helped her to the safety of his cottage. She was recovering in his rear room when a vast wave of water smashed through his French windows.

Audrey did not find it easy walking in the slippers, stepping around detritus, avoiding upturned cars, and past many shattered bow-fronted windows.

An ambulance was just leaving and another just arriving when she opened the lychgate and headed for the Methodist Church. The sun was low in the sky and the interior looked dark and dismal. As she stepped through the vestibule, she saw the familiar, tall, albeit stooped figure of her dear friend.

'How's it going, Reverend?'

'Audrey!' He looked admiringly at her bathrobe. 'You always dress so well for church.'

'I caught the new fashion wave.'

'I'm sorry to hear that. It's been frightening for us all. Many injuries but so far, no one has died. Pray God it remains that way. And how is your dear old man?'

Audrey paused. Her face serious. 'I was hoping you could tell me.'

Joel entered The Falcon's gloomy interior.

'Sorry, we're closed. No power,' Ted called.

'You escaped the flood, then?' Joel said, looking around the dry interior.

'Hello Joel. Yes, our entrance is pointing the right way. Have you heard from Eleanor?'

'She had a lucky escape. I've just left her.'

'That is good news,' Ted said. 'I will go and lend a hand up at the church, but I thought I'd let the paramedics do their work first.'

'It is pretty shocking.'

Ted placed a brandy glass on the bar counter and pulled the stopper out of a bottle of Courvoisier. 'You look a little chill. This'll help.'

'I don't drink spirits.'

'No, my boy, this isn't a spirit, this is Dutch courage.'

'I don't understand.'

'Drink this, then go through that door.' Ted pointed across the bar. 'Go up the stairs, down the corridor and knock on the second door on the left.'

'Do you think that's a good idea?'

Ted pushed the glass towards him. 'I do,' he said. 'And if you drink this, you will too.'

Joel picked up the glass and sniffed the amber liquid. 'It actually smells good.'

'It should. A bottle of this costs more than your

student loan.'

Joel admired the brandy. 'Here goes.' He emptied the glass. 'Wow!' he said as his eyes almost popped out of his head. 'Amazing.'

'Upstairs is an amazing young woman, although you don't need me to tell you that.'

'Thank you,' Joel said. 'And thank you for the satellite phone. I think we'd still be up there without it.'

'How's the head?'

'A bit tender.' He touched his fresh scar. 'She saved my life.'

'Go, or you'll make an old man cry.'

In the fading autumn light, Audrey found it increasingly hard to suppress her anxiety. There were still a lot of comings and goings from the flooded church. She approached a uniformed police officer who seemed to be in charge.

'I would like to report a missing person. Two, actually.'

'If you go online, there's a dedicated page on our website where you can register a missing person. It's Undermere police dot com, forward slash, Hawksmeadflood.'

'If I had a phone I would do it now. Although, I don't think the baby will survive such bureaucracy.'

'Baby?' The police officer was now fully focused on Audrey. He took out his notebook. 'How old?'

'Fourteen days. We were walking in the Memorial Garden behind that broken wall when the river flooded. I was swept down the High Street and have not seen my husband or the baby since.'

'Baby's name?'

'Rowena Cornfield. My husband is Malcolm

Cadwallader.'

The police officer turned his head towards his radio attached to the front of his bright yellow vest. Audrey gripped his wrist.

'Madam, let go.'

'I just heard something. A baby, I think. Please tell everyone to be quiet.'

The officer looked into Audrey's stressed face and pulled a steel whistle attached to a chain from a pocket. 'This is a museum piece. Not standard issue these days but it comes in useful every now and then. Block your ears.'

Audrey did as she was ordered but still heard the shrill blast. It was effective. All activity came to a halt.

The police officer spoke. 'A baby is missing. We think we heard a cry. Please give us a few moments of absolute quiet.'

A strange form of silence descended and added weight to the sombre mood.

Aaaahhhh.

The cry of an infant cut through to everyone listening. People turned their heads in all directions as they tried to locate the source.

Aaaahhhh.

Audrey pointed. 'It's coming from near the broken wall.'

'Okay, everyone, thank you,' said the police officer.

Nobody moved. Nobody spoke.

He turned to a female colleague. 'Come with me.' To Audrey he said, 'Madam, wait here.'

Audrey ignored the police officer and followed him in her bathrobe and slippers across the sodden, waterlogged graveyard, with its toppling headstones, towards a pile of bricks.

Aaaahhhh.

'I think the baby's under there,' Audrey said as she rushed ahead of the two police officers. The three of them slid and skidded as they traversed the slippery ground towards an igloo-shaped structure.

The senior officer gripped Audrey's arm. 'We must do this very carefully. I don't want it to suddenly collapse. I'll reach for a brick and hand it to you. You give it to my colleague.'

She nodded. He took care as he removed the first Victorian brick and passed it to Audrey. She handed it to the female officer who cast it aside.

Another brick. And another. Again and again, each brick carefully removed.

Aaaahhhh. Louder this time.

'Do hurry,' Audrey beseeched.

The officer pressed on, carefully removing brick after brick, after brick.

'I can see a coat,' he said. 'I think it's a man's.'

Audrey's heart soared. 'Is he breathing?'

More bricks were handed to her. Desperate, she grabbed bricks herself and flung them aside. 'Malcolm!' She could see him on his knees, with his elbows bent in an L-shape, his head pressed against the ground.

'Madam,' the officer said. 'He's created a human bridge to protect the baby. Let's not undo his heroic work by rushing.'

Audrey held back and the officer carefully removed more bricks which he handed to her.

'I can see the baby,' the officer said. He handed Audrey another brick then reached into the cavern created by Malcolm and pulled out a little, wrapped bundle. Almost losing his balance, he handed the baby to Audrey.

'We must get her to hospital,' Audrey said. 'She's hypothermic.'

The officer spoke to his colleague. 'Get paramedics here, now.'

Audrey was torn. She wanted to be with her husband, but the little bundle could die in her arms without swift medical attention. She didn't wait for the paramedics to arrive but strode through the sodden graveyard in her slippers and bathrobe towards one of the attending ambulances, tears streaming down her cheeks.

'This baby needs to be warmed immediately.' She handed Rowena to a surprised paramedic and climbed up the step into the ambulance.

'Madam, what are you doing?'

Audrey looked at the overweight paramedic in her tight green uniform. 'I'm making sure this baby lives. Her mother is fighting for her life in Undermere General. Today has been shocking, terrible. I'm not going to let it end in tragedy.'

'We don't have an incubator.'

'Then we wrap her in a warm blanket, and I hold her against my body.'

'For safety, she must travel in a child stretcher.'

'She needs my body warmth. Let's go.'

'We can take another patient.'

'If this baby was a full-sized adult, you would go now. But, because she's a baby, you are prepared to put her life at risk by waiting to fill your ambulance.'

'Sit there,' the paramedic pointed to a flip down seat with a restraining belt.

Audrey gave her the baby to hold. Sat down, strapped herself in and reached up for Rowena.

'Room for one more?' a paramedic asked. Audrey looked to the rear of the ambulance and saw her unconscious husband strapped to a lightweight evacuation stretcher.

Heart pounding, Joel crossed the dark landing. He took a breath and tapped on the heavy wooden door.

'Hang on,' he heard, and he hung on. His heart was now beating in overdrive. The door opened and Cadence stared at him. She was wearing a pale blue, towelling pyjama suit. 'Joel! What are you doing here?'

'I wanted to check you're okay.'

She smiled. 'As you can see, I'm fine.'

'But you're not, are you? You're wounded.'

Their eyes locked. This was a moment that would be carved in his memory forever. She stepped aside.

'Come in.'

He entered. 'Nice room. A bit gloomy.'

'The power's off.'

'Surprisingly tidy.'

'Why surprisingly?' She closed the door behind him.

'I expected to see clothes everywhere, knickknacks, make-up. You know... mess.'

'That's a cliché. I'm not a cliché.'

He smiled. 'You most definitely are not. But you need to get medical attention for your wound.'

'You mean for this?' She lifted up her top to reveal her flat abdomen. To one side was a bag, clamped to the hole Joel had seen in the church.'

He had no words.

'My mother was killed, and I was wounded. My bowel got infected. They cut some of it out to save my life. This stoma is a small price to pay, but now you understand why you and I can't date.'

'Do you think because you have a colostomy, I

wouldn't want to be with you?'

She shrugged. 'Well, would you?'

'Oh my God, yes. You may have to give me some guidance, but...' He looked into her beautiful face, free of all make-up. 'I love you. I love all of you.'

She turned away from him and he saw her wipe a cheek. 'We can be friends. Good friends. But nothing more.'

He reached for her.

'No, Joel. Think about it. Understand why.'

'You are everything to me, Cadence. Please don't push me away.'

She turned and he saw her tears. 'I'm not!' She lifted up her top. 'This is. This stinking bag.'

'We all stink,' Joel said. 'Sometimes I have bad breath. Body odour. Smelly farts.'

'We're nineteen, Joel. Even without my ostomy we're too young to be in love.'

'Today I nearly died for a second time,' he said. 'As I hugged a lamppost with the water trying to tear me away, my only thought was of you. How I'd never kissed you, told you how much I love you, seen the sunrise with you in my arms. I clung onto that lamppost and made a promise.'

'What promise?'

'That if I lived, I wouldn't waste another precious moment. That as important as theatre is in my life, it is nothing compared to my feelings for you.'

Her fingertips touched her golden crucifix, and he closed his eyes, and prayed. He waited. Not daring to breathe until he felt the warmth of her hand on his cheek. He opened his eyes.

'Dear Romeo.'

He took her hand in his and kissed her palm, and

said, 'Arise, fair sun, and kill the envious moon, Who is already sick and pale with grief, That thou her maid art far more fair than she: Be not her maid, since she is envious; Her vestal livery is but sick and green and none but fools do wear it; cast it off. You are my lady, You are my love – always and forever.'

Cadence leant forward and for the first time, Joel felt her lips on his. Their tongues met and their bodies came together. He wrapped his arms around her and knew he would love her to the end of his days.

She whispered in his ear. 'My bounty is as boundless as the sea. My love as deep; the more love I give to thee, the more love I have, for it is infinite, my precious, precious Joel.' And they kissed and kissed. Finally, she took his hand and led him to her bed.

'I have never done this,' he said.

'Nor have I.'

'What about contraception?'

'Protection is always a good idea, but as we are both virgins and I am about to get my period, the chances of you and me making a baby are very low.'

'And if we do?'

'We'll Christen the baby Romeo or Juliet.'

Joel laughed. 'Promise me you will never call our baby Romeo.'

She pulled back the duvet on the bed. 'What do you suggest?'

'I remove my damp clothes and take a shower.'

'Be my guest but the water's cold.'

'The river most certainly was.' Joel went into the bathroom and stripped off. He stepped into the shower cubicle and turned on the water. It was freezing and he yelped.

He heard her laughing from the bedroom. 'Come

here, Romeo,' she called. 'Juliet will warm you up.'

Audrey, dressed in hospital scrubs, hat and slip-ons, and a mask, stood in the neonatal unit. Baby Rowena lay in an incubator with a drip delivering fluids into a vein in her scalp. A feeding tube from a bottle containing formula milk ran up her nose and into her stomach.

'She looks content,' Audrey said to the nursing sister standing by her.

'Your granddaughter?'

Audrey smiled. 'Almost.' She turned to the nurse. 'Is she going to be okay?'

The nurse smiled. 'She's already okay.'

'Thank you.' Audrey stepped out of the unit and a few minutes later arrived at the double doors to Intensive Care. She pressed a button on the intercom. Whilst waiting for a reply, squirted cleansing gel into her palm from a wall-mounted bottle and rubbed her hands together.

Following a short stand-off, via the intercom, she heard the door buzz and pushed it open.

'Mrs Cadwallader, not again!'

Standing by reception was her favourite Italian doctor, dressed in blue scrubs. 'Mr Bisterzo, how lovely to see you.'

'I must congratulate you, Mrs Cadwallader. You and I first met after you nearly drowned. Then you were caught in a fire; then you drove through a storm to deliver four injured people; and today, an entire church's congregation.'

'Thank you,' she said and smiled. 'I try to keep you busy.'

'Let me take you to your dear husband.'

Someone was shaking her shoulder.

'Christina. Wake up.'

She wanted to be left in her warm, cosy, world.

'Christina. Open your eyes.' It was a woman's voice, kind but commanding. She ran her fingers down her abdomen and felt a plastic tube. Not good.

Her shoulder was shaken again.

'Wake up Christina.' A man's voice. English. Refined. She forced her eyes open and blinked. What time was it? What day was it? Where was she? What had happened?

'Christina.' She stared at the man. His hair was dishevelled, he had greying stubble on his chin, and his clothes were creased and dirty. A bag of blood dripped into a tube which was taped to her arm.

It hit her. Giving birth. Her baby. Abel unconscious. Getting ready for the wedding. The rush of water. Terror. Nothing. 'Abel?' she asked.

'Yes, it's me, darling.'

'We've had a baby girl.'

'Yes, my sweet.'

She pushed herself up and looked around the unit. 'Where is she? Where is our baby?'

Abel took her hand. 'Our baby is fine. They want you to feed her.'

She felt her damp gown over a swollen breast. 'I want my baby.'

'We'll bring Rowena to you,' said the young doctor.

She slumped back onto the pillows and looked at her husband. 'I love you.'

'And I love you.'

The old man's eyes were closed. His skin looked wafer thin and pale with light brown age spots. His head was part-bandaged and his visible hair, always his crowning glory, looked faded, dull.

He coughed and opened his eyes. For a moment he seemed shocked by his surroundings.

'Malcolm.'

It was as though a charge of electricity shot through his nerves. 'Audrey! You're alive!' He tried to push himself up. 'You're alive.'

'And so are you, my darling.'

His face immediately clouded.

She gripped his hand. 'And so is Rowena. You saved her life.'

He tried to sit up again.

'Let me,' she said, and pressed the control to adjust the tilt of the bed.

'Thank you.' He took her hand in both of his. 'Is she really okay?'

'She is going to be absolutely fine. You are my hero.'

'I chose the baby over you. I am so sorry.'

'Hawksmead certainly delivers surprises,' Audrey said. 'I clung to a branch, and it protected me when I crashed into an upturned car. Dear old Mr O'Brien, you know, the Irish property developer, dragged me into his cottage. Thankfully I was wearing my best quality pantsuit, so my legs didn't suffer too much.'

'Show me.'

She stood and lifted the oversized hospital scrubs to reveal scraped and scratched shins and knees. 'No worse than when I crashed my bicycle going down Garth Road in Sevenoaks.'

'You're way too brave,' he said, and gripped her hand as she sat down. 'I did my best to protect the baby. I thought we were goners when the wall gave.'

She kissed his wrinkled forehead. 'You are so clever

my darling. She was perfectly protected.'

'No injuries at all?'

She shook her head. 'Hypothermia and very hungry, but she's going to be all right.'

'I presume the church was flooded out?'

'Yes. But it could've been so much worse. Eleanor's friend acted quickly and opened the emergency doors. Unfortunately, Tina and Magdalena were washed out and ended up in the woods towards the railway line.'

'Good God.'

'They're alive, but Tina's not well. She suffered a postpartum haemorrhage and has lost a lot of blood. They're topping her up, now.'

Malcolm thought for a moment. 'Something must've blocked the bridge.'

'I heard it was an oak tree that was struck by lightning. Fortunately, the bridge collapsed, and the river is flowing normally again.'

'I'm going to campaign for a new bridge wide enough for two cars to pass.'

'Hawksmead Historic Society might object to that.'

'I'm sure they will.' He smiled and she spotted the old, familiar glint in his faded blue eyes.

CHAPTER TWENTY-THREE
Monday, 18th October

Magdalena had no idea how long she'd been asleep. She felt ragged, wretched, sore. She threw back the duvet and looked at her legs. They were coated in a thick cream with sections bandaged.

Her abdomen was also covered in cream. She examined her boobs. How did they survive? She felt her face. Cream. What must she look like?

'Hungry?'

Silhouetted by the morning light was a familiar shape.

'Not for sex!'

He laughed. 'Maybe after you've eaten.'

'Ha!' She swung her legs out of bed. 'Thank you for taking care of me.'

'You were truly heroic.'

'I don't think so.'

'You were. You saved Tina's life.'

'How is she?'

'I don't know. Landlines are down and our mobiles are ruined. I'll ask the landlord in The Falcon if we can borrow his phone.'

'I must get up.'

'Stay in bed. You've been through the mill.'

'I have customer.'

She stood and examined her naked form in a full-length mirror. 'Good creaming,' she said. 'But I scare customer. Must take shower.'

'No Mags. Let the antiseptic do its job.'

'I have to prepare salon.'

She reached in her wardrobe for a pair of joggers and a sweatshirt.'

'Wait. I've something to tell you. It's the salon.'

She stared at him for a second then brushed past, grabbed a dressing gown hanging on the back of her bedroom door, and hurried down the stairs. Before she reached the final step, horror set in. At the front of the salon, her bow windows were smashed, and the chevron-patterned tiled floor was wet with pools of water and covered in beauty products, swept off once immaculate white shelves and flattened workstations.

She slumped on the stairs as tears poured down her cheeks. After all she'd been through, her wrecked salon hurt her more.

Trevor sat beside her and put his arm around her shoulder.

'We'll make it right. I promise.'

'How? What money?'

'I'm going to sell Harper Dennis. It's not worth much as a going concern, but we can make your business work.'

She turned and looked at him. 'You would do that for me?'

'On one condition.' He kissed her lips. 'We go back to church and ask the Reverend to marry us.'

'I think church is worse than salon.'

'It doesn't matter.'

She touched his cheek. 'Okay,' she said. 'Invite your children this time.'

'I promise. If Olivia will let me.' He kissed her fulsome mouth. 'Do we have a deal?'

She held out her hand. 'We have deal.'

'You're a match,' spoke the voice on her mobile.

Eleanor's heart soared. 'You have a kidney for me?'

'Yes, we do.'

She sighed. 'But someone has to die.'

'Not this time. It's a swap. A man's wife is donating her kidney to you and he is receiving a kidney from an altruistic donor who matches him.'

'When do I come in?'

'Wednesday.'

'Will there be tests that include needles?'

'There'll be a blood test to determine your general health, so keep clear of fellow human beings.'

'Nothing else?'

'We've already matched tissue type and tested for antibodies and any signs of cancer. On Thursday we will undertake an ultrasound of your blood vessels to determine which side to position your new kidney. Nothing to worry about.'

'And that doesn't involve a needle?'

'Just a lot of lubrication.'

'Lovely. Anything else?'

'This is your time, Eleanor. Your friend, Mr Smith, has given you a priceless gift.'

HAWKSMEAD CHRONICLE
The Great Flood

Where was Noah when we needed his ark? A bolt of lightning severs a mighty oak still heavy with autumnal leaves. A bough breaks and falls into the swollen River Hawk and creates a dam when it strikes the humpback bridge, the northern gateway to Hawksmead. Originally, the town was located above the river, but mill owner, Sir Richard Arkwright, changed its course in the eighteenth century to generate a faster flow to drive the waterwheel that powered his invention: the spinning frame with fluted rollers for mass production of yarn. When the tree turned the old bridge into a dam, the river burst its southern bank and poured through woodland until it came to the walled Memorial Garden, lovingly created by Malcolm Cadwallader. The horseshoe-shaped wall held the water back until a vast lake was formed. The weight eventually breached the wall and water coursed through the Methodist graveyard and smashed through windows into the church where the congregation was celebrating the marriage of local resident and owner of Wax Polish, Magdalena Jablonski, to Trevor Harper, proprietor of Undermere estate agency, Harper Dennis.

A quick-thinking parishioner opened the emergency exit doors and although there were many bruises, broken bones, and shattered nerves, nobody died within the church. However, Ronald Smith who saved the day has been reported as missing by church organist and owner of the Olde Tea Shoppe, Eleanor

Houghton.

Hawksmead High Street also suffered much devastation. Many parked cars belonging to parishioners attending services in the Methodist and Saint Michael's churches were damaged beyond repair. Windows in eighteenth century bow-fronted cottages and shops were smashed, destroying antique rugs, furniture, porcelain knickknacks, and much-loved photos and mementoes.

The day was saved by a miracle. The old stone bridge, an oft-feared landmark for drivers, collapsed, allowing the river to return to its usual course within its banks.

Autumn has been particularly warm and the rainfall especially heavy. Even climate-change deniers must accept that our world is warming and that extreme weather patterns are becoming more and more frequent.

On a brighter note, a recovery fund has been instigated by Lord Cornfield, husband of former local resident Christina Burton, now Lady Cornfield, with a generous donation that should do much to repair the damage. If you would like to donate, please visit our GoFundMe page. For immediate financial help, please email Hawksmead Chronicle or drop a note through our door. Lord Cornfield understands the need for swift action and has tasked our editor with the job of distributing grants.

CHAPTER TWENTY-FOUR
Saturday, 30th October

'All packed?' Gary asked the question from the doorway to Christina's bedroom in Rise House.

She paused the process of stuffing toiletries into her suitcase and looked at him. 'Very smart.'

'I'm going to church. I've a wedding to attend.'

'Of course. I'd love to be there, too, but Abel is desperate for me to bring home his little girl.'

'Sam and Luke are going to miss their niece,' he said. 'So am I. Rowena's the most beautiful baby I have ever seen.'

'We've plenty of room for visitors.'

'What about ex-husbands?'

'You're always welcome. You know that.'

'And Hector?'

She pushed down the lid of the suitcase and pulled the zip around.

'Let me get that for you,' he said.

She stepped back. 'Thank you.'

He hauled the case off the bed and placed it on the carpet. He looked at her. 'Abel's a good guy.'

She leant forward and kissed him on the cheek. 'Don't be a stranger.'

'I won't, but Abel has given me a big job.'

'Everything with Abel is big,' she said.

He laughed and picked up her case and carried it downstairs into the hall where there was a large collection of baby paraphernalia.

Christina followed him down as the doorbell rang. Gary pulled it open and was confronted by a liveried chauffeur.

'Sebastian. Perfect timing,' Christina said.

'You're not going by chopper?' Gary asked.

'A bit noisy for Rowena. The Bentley under Sebastian's control will glide us back to Mayfair.

'Hopefully, Lady Cornfield,' Sebastian said, 'there won't be any hold-ups. By the way, the baby seat is fitted behind me.'

'Perfect. Thank you.'

Sam came into the hallway carrying Rowena who was wearing a baby grow. Tears trickled down his cheeks. 'I'm going to miss her so much.'

Luke joined him from the sitting room. 'I am too. More than I thought possible.

'All the more reason why you both must visit. We have a lovely guest suite.'

Gary kissed the baby's forehead. 'Bye bye my angel.'

'I've just changed her,' Sam said to his sister. 'So, she's all set to go.' Christina relieved him of the baby.

She spoke to her daughter. 'Uncle Sam and Uncle Luke will see you again soon.'

'Everything for the boot, Lady Cornfield?' Sebastian asked.

'Everything apart from these two.' She pointed to a baby's changing bag and a cool bag. 'I'll have them in the back with me.'

Sebastian picked up the suitcase and lifted it over the threshold and onto the front path. Sam and Luke grabbed the other items and followed him.

Christina looked at Gary. 'Give everyone my love at the wedding, especially Audrey and Malcolm.'

'What about Eleanor?' Gary asked.

'I doubt she'll be there so soon after her transplant. I'll write to her.'

'The Reverend told me she was determined to play for the bride and groom.'

'I hope it works out for her.'

'I'm hoping Frank Cottee, alias Ron Smith will be there. We've still got unfinished business.'

'He saved our lives.'

'That'll work for him when it comes to sentencing.'

'He donated a kidney.'

'That too.'

'Gary, don't.' She touched his arm.

'Are you going to say goodbye to Hector?'

'Say goodbye for me.' She kissed him on the cheek. 'He knows I love him. He is the bravest of the brave.'

The bride entered the church with her aunt and waited in the vestibule. Through the open inner doors, she watched the bowed figure of Reverend Longden climb the steps to the raised pulpit. Candlelight was augmented by sunrays streaming through gaps in the boarded-up windows above the stained and peeling walls. In her hands was a beautiful bouquet of autumnal blooms and berries that perfectly complemented her simple, sheer dress. Her aunt had tried to persuade her to wear a veil.

'I've hidden my true self for too long,' she countered, but she did concede to her aunt buying a crystal and pearl silver vine that was clipped to the back of her head to hold her pleated locks in place.

Eleanor felt almost well for the first time since she'd received her new kidney. Following the operation, her wound was very sore and had needed strong painkillers but, fortunately, the intravenous drip that had delivered fluids into her arm was fitted whilst she was still unconscious in the operating theatre.

All in all, she'd begun to feel better quite quickly and very soon her donated kidney was functioning well, thanks to the immunosuppression tablets she took every day. Another reason for her speedy recovery may have been the flowers she'd received just before the operation. They were a beautiful bouquet of blue forget-me-nots with a card that read: *To my darling Eleanor, I feel privileged to have fallen in love with you. Yours forever, Ron.*

It was the first she'd heard from him since the flood and even when she was wheeled to the operating theatre, the smile never left her. And now she could see him, all smartly dressed and sitting in the front pew, nearest the upright piano that had been lent to the church until the organ could be repaired.

Gary was seated in the second row, determined to apprehend the criminal mastermind who'd kept him prisoner for two years. He didn't hate Frank Cottee, also known as Ron Smith, but he did want justice.

He had persuaded his former colleagues at Undermere Police Station to don suits and attend the wedding. When he gave the signal, they would come forward and arrest the former Essex-based gangster.

The bride heard the music change to one of her favourite songs of all time. In her head, Ed Sheeran sang it for her, and she knew she would never look more perfect than she did today. She took her aunt's hand and saw the man she would love forever, standing alone at the end of the aisle waiting for her.

The congregation stood and all bar one turned to look at the bride and her aunt, but Gary kept his eyes fixed on his target. When the bride came level with the groom, Eleanor brought the romantic melody to a gentle close.

'Please be seated,' Reverend Longden said from the pulpit.

The congregation sat back down on the hard pews and the bride's Aunt Angela joined the groom's mother.

Gary remained standing. He looked to the rear of the church and nodded. Four men in suits hurried down the two side aisles closing off all means of escape. Gary turned back to grab hold of Frank, but he was gone. Where was he? Puzzled faces stared up at him.

'Please be seated,' repeated the Reverend, his voice firm. The police officers looked at each other and, a little sheepishly, slipped into available pews. Reluctantly, Gary also sat down.

Reverend Longden smiled. 'Good morning and welcome to a very special occasion. Today, two young people are committing to a lifetime of love.'

'Reverend.' Gary stood. 'I must pause you there.'

A ripple of whispers spread through the congregation.

Reverend Longden looked pointedly at Gary as the ex-policeman shuffled down his pew and strode to the front of the church.

'Mr Burton,' the Reverend said. 'There will come a time when I ask if anyone here present can show just cause why this man and this woman may not lawfully be joined together, but now is not that moment.'

'My apologies Reverend, but a criminal is hiding in this church, and I request a pause in the proceedings to enable the police to apprehend him.' He turned to the pianist. 'Eleanor. Where is he?'

'I don't know the criminal of whom you speak.'

'Where is the man who was sitting right here at the front?'

Eleanor stood. 'The man who was sitting on that front pew is the same man who donated a kidney allowing me to live; and when the church was flooded, had the wit and courage to release the water through the emergency doors.'

Joel clapped his hands. And again. And again. At the rear of the church students from Undermere School of Dramatic Art stood and joined in. Other members of the congregation got to their feet and joined the slow, rhythmic handclap. More and more added to the staccato cacophony, filling the church with a pulsing boom, boom, boom.

Gary went up to Joel, gave him a brief nod and headed down the side aisle to the rear of the church, followed by the police officers. The clapping stopped. Silence descended, and the Reverend looked at the upturned faces of the bride and groom.

Through the small door behind the organ appeared a man in a smart suit. He kissed Eleanor and took his place in the front pew.

The Reverend gestured for the congregation to be seated. He stepped down from the pulpit and stood in front of the young couple.

Bells could be heard coming from the belfry of St Michael's as Cadence and Joel stepped out of the plain and battered Methodist Church. The pealing bells were swiftly drowned out by cheers and clapping from their fellow drama students as confetti and rice rained down on the beautiful, smiling couple. Amongst her new friends, Cadence spotted a very special person.

Joel leant towards his bride and gestured to a group of men and women wearing various items of green tartan. Within the throng was the Irish traveller, Dermot O'Hanlon, who stepped forward and handed Cadence a gift-wrapped box with a white silk bow. 'For you, my darlin' from Madam Petralee. If you're ever confronted with a conundrum, the tarot will always provide the answer. Not necessarily the one you want, but the one that will lead you along a better path.'

Eleanor, released from piano duties and with her arm through Ron's, joined her friends, Audrey and Malcolm who were standing with Magdalena and Trevor.

'Dear Reverend Longden,' Eleanor said to Audrey. 'What a wonderful sermon. How will we ever cope without him?'

'He's survived pestilence and flood,' Malcolm interjected. 'I don't think he has any plans to meet his maker just yet.'

'One, two, three!' shouted the drama students and all watched as the bridal bouquet took flight, arced through the air, and was caught by the bride's best friend, Diana.

Everyone whooped, cheered, and clapped.

As the cacophony abated, Joel made an announcement. 'Refreshments await your presence, my friends. To The Falcon, make haste.'

'I would give all my fame for a pot of ale,' Malcolm called back.

Joel laughed and pointed. 'Henry the fifth, Act three, Scene two.'

Cadence gripped his arm. 'Husband, let not onions nor garlic pass our lips, for we are to utter sweet breath until the third cock doth crow.' And they laughed and kissed to much cheering.

Aunt Angela leaned towards Joel's mother. 'Her

mom would be so proud.'

'As would his dad.' And they hugged and wept happy tears.

Thank you so so much for reading my novel. I hope you enjoyed it. If you did and have a moment, would you please leave a review or star rating on Amazon? It helps others discover my book and it encourages me to continue writing. Romola xx

ABOUT THE AUTHOR

Romola Farr first trod the boards on the West End stage aged sixteen and continued to work for the next eighteen years in theatre, TV and film - and as a photographic model. A trip to Hollywood led to the sale of her first screenplay and a successful change of direction as a screenwriter and playwright. Bridge To Eternity was her debut novel, and Breaking through the Shadows and Where the Water Flows are standalone sequels.

Romola Farr is a nom de plume.

romolafarr@gmail.com

@RomolaFarr

Amazon Author Page

BOOKS BY THIS AUTHOR

Bridge To Eternity

'Lose yourself in this wonderful story.' SUSIE FOSTER
'An outstanding debut novel and a hugely satisfying read.' ALLIE REYNOLDS
'A stunning debut by an author I will actively seek out in the future.' AUDREY DAVIS

'What separates this book from others are the subtle yet powerful emotions which trip from the first page through to the last. This novel left its mark on me long after I finished it.' LEE-ANNE TOP 1000 AMAZON REVIEWER

'Absolutely loved this debut novel. Fantastic characterisations, intriguing and clever plot which took twists and turns. I genuinely could not put it down.' Elizabeth Estaugh, Amazon.co.uk

'The different strands of the story in this book were beautifully woven together. I found it really exciting and couldn't wait to find out what happened.' Sarah McAlister, Amazon.co.uk

'I absolutely loved Bridge to Eternity so much, I read it within a day. I look forward to reading more from Farr as this was such a wonderful debut.' Jojo Welsh girl, Amazon.co.uk

'The icy bleakness of the landscape is expertly reflected in the lives of many of the central characters. Deeply buried emotions are intermingled amongst present and past events. It is both atmospheric and unnerving in equal measure as characters struggle with their own personal demons. This is a really intriguing and powerful debut novel.' S J Mantle

'A brilliant read ...a real page-turner with finely-drawn characters that the reader cares for.' Sue from Wimbledon, Amazon.co.uk

'A gripping novel ...a thrilling read. I read it in two sittings.' KJA, Amazon.co.uk

Breaking Through The Shadows

'Another must-have novel from Romola Farr.' HELGA HOPKINS
'Absolutely gripping, I could not put this book down!' ELIZABETH ESTAUGH
'An absolute gem of a story.' SUSIE FOSTER

5-stars WHAT AN EXCITING READ!
'It's a page-turner for sure. The book follows Tina's story and she's a great character; really ballsy in spite of everything that life has thrown at her. The many strands of the story are skillfully interlocked and come to a very satisfying conclusion.' Sarah McAlister, Amazon.co.uk

5-stars ANOTHER EXCELLENT READ
'It was captivating from the start, I was hooked. There were so many twists and turns throughout that I had to force myself to put it down to get on with some work. It truly was an excellent read.' Jojo Welsh girl, Amazon.co.uk

5-stars A GRIPPING TALE
'Breaking Through The Shadows is a gripping stand-alone exciting story. A real page-turner, with well-defined characters. Televisual in nature, full of movement and pace. It kept me guessing right up to the thrilling denouement. More please Ms Farr!' Sue from Wimbledon, Amazon.co.uk

5-stars STUNNING SEQUEL to 'Bridge to Eternity'
'Absolutely loved this sequel! The dramatic events encountered by the characters, including Tina, Audrey and Malcolm, took unexpected twists and turns. Absolutely gripping, could not put this

book down!' Elizabeth Estaugh, Amazon.co.uk

5-stars ANOTHER MUST-HAVE NOVEL from Romola Farr
'Superb thriller romance which hooked me right from the start! I loved Romola Farr's first novel, and the author has absolutely nailed it again with another page turner that I simply couldn't put down. The descriptions of people and places completely immerse one in the plot, and the roller coaster ride of suspense and romance, is such that the reader is captivated right to the final page.' H. Hopkins, Amazon.co.uk

TO LOVE AND TO BE LOVED
IS THE GREATEST GIFT

For Benita, Harry and Ollie, whose love and wisdom I cherish more than they will ever know.

For my sister, Rowena, who inspired my lead character, Audrey; and her husband, Chris, who is so much more than my brother-in-law. For my paternal grandmother, Audrey, whose name I took for my protagonist and whose grit comes through in many of the actions she takes. For my father, Guy and his wife Julie, who are shining examples of what making the best of every situation can achieve. For my brother, Ashley, who is my brother in every way and at all times. For my paternal grandfather, The Reverend William Longden Oakes, for playing an integral role in my life and this story. For my Aunt Margot, whose love and intelligence turned the course of my family's history.

For my dear mother, Jean, whose love, support and talent imbues and inspires me every day.

For all my aunts and uncles, cousins, nieces and nephews, Goddaughters and close friends who may not realise how much they mean to me.

Made in United States
Troutdale, OR
12/27/2023

16469565R00202